W9-DJI-765

EXECUTIVE PRIVILEGE

By Geoffrey Perrett

DAYS OF SADNESS, YEARS OF TRIUMPH

EXECUTIVE PRIVILEGE

EXECUTIVE PRIVILEGE

Geoffrey Perrett

Coward, McCann & Geoghegan, Inc.

New York

Copyright © 1974 by GEOFFREY PERRETT

All rights reserved. This book, or parts thereof, may not be reproduced in any form without permission in writing from the publisher. Published on the same day in Canada by Longman Canada Limited, Toronto.

SBN: 698-10579-6
Library of Congress Catalog Card Number: 73-88541

Printed in the United States of America

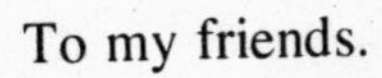

To my friends.

EXECUTIVE PRIVILEGE

Chapter One

"Funny how we make our own inevitabilities," Specci said almost mockingly.

I stared at my plate and pushed my fork to one side.

"Well," he went on, "you must admit, it's all your own doing. And considering that's the case, you can probably still do something about it. Although I really can't see why things are all that bad. What it amounts to, as far as I can tell, is that you've got an interesting job and a loving wife and you're still not satisfied."

"You wouldn't think the job was so great if you had it. You don't know what he's like."

He looked at me closely, then sighed heavily as he poured himself the last of the wine.

"The solution's elegantly simple—give it up. I don't imagine there's any great shortage of people willing to manage the Vice President. But"—he spread his hands helplessly—"if being a big fish in a small pond doesn't suit you, try a bigger pond. That's an old Italian proverb."

"Which you just made up."

"Look," he said patiently, "your trouble has always been that you've got a temperament that runs naturally to extremes. That's why you weren't really cut out for practicing law. You took it either too seriously or not seriously enough."

"That's why you took me on."

He genially waved a finger under my nose. "Don't misunderstand. That sort of thing was ideal for you—it was a crusade. No, what I'm talking about is the more prosaic stuff, the daily grind that goes with practicing law, without any of the heroics or the martyrdom. That's obviously why you moved into politics: It was more dramatic." He started to laugh. "You remember that guy in Chicago, the one who came in saying 'Mister, mister, I didn't do it. I swear I didn't do it. You gotta help me 'cause I'm innocent.' And with a completely straight face you said to him, 'Innocence of the law is no excuse.' "

We both laughed.

"Sure it's funny," said Specci. "But that poor bastard didn't know if you were serious or not. You scared the hell out of him."

"I defended him. Saved his ass, as I recall."

"But you couldn't resist shaking him up, could you?"

I ignored the question, signaling the waiter for coffee and the check. Specci swallowed his wine appreciatively and put the glass down with a slight thump.

"Not bad, that."

"It's a good thing your secret isn't better known," I said. "You've got to be the only Supreme Court Justice in history who could be had for the price of a good dinner and a bottle of wine."

"True," he said, pretending to be troubled by the suggestion. Then he brightened. "Let's just be glad there's not a restaurant or a house in town with a chef who's really up to it."

The coffee arrived, and I looked over the check.

"Mind you," he murmured, "I enjoyed the lunch."

Then, without warning, the gentle sparring was over. He looked at me intently. "Anybody would say you've had a pretty good deal in life. Don't go screwing it all up because you've got a routine case of middle-age sweats. It happens to everybody. Even me."

That drew me up short. Specci was the last man I expected to reveal a confidence like that, even to me, and he knew it.

"It's perfectly true. A few years ago, when I got to roughly the age you are now, I felt almost exactly the same way."

"Oh, come off it, Frank," I scoffed. "You'd just been appointed to the Court."

He grinned, embarrassed. "That's why it was such a bitch. In maybe three months I went from being on top of the world to feeling the whole thing was utterly pointless. Futile."

"Futile?" It was hard to believe that someone appointed out of the blue at the age of forty to be an Associate Justice could feel useless. Anything but.

"Don't ask me why, but all of a sudden everything I did seemed a complete waste of time. I got very depressed, for the first time in my life. My whole life, in fact. . . ." He shrugged. "Oh, in my mind I *knew* it was a great honor. I knew that even if I couldn't do a lot of good, I could at least help stop a lot of bad. The problem was I didn't *feel* it anymore. I just couldn't care, about anything. The only things that mattered were in the past. I found myself reliving things I'd done, saying to myself, 'That was good,' or 'You were smart there,' things like that. Hell, I even started going to the library to read old *newspaper* stories about myself."

"That's incredible," I said.

He smiled wryly. "We've all seen it happen. It just takes different forms. A guy gets to that age, and after a lifetime of being responsible and reasonable, he suddenly starts chasing the twenty-year-old secretaries in his office or drinking too much, or he buys a sports car that's faster than his reflexes, and so it goes. Anyway"—his voice dropped to a whisper"—"we—that is, Joan and I—even we thought of splitting up for a while."

"I never realized. . . ."

"No." He cut me off. "You weren't supposed to. And now that I've told you I expect you to forget it fast. All you need to remember is that you've got a wife in a million."

He finished his coffee, took a look at the check and started counting out a tip.

"It's not so much my marriage, Frank," I said, pretending

to be slightly obtuse. "It's the job. If I got that sorted out, I think everything else would fall into place."

"So?" He raised his shoulders and made an imploring gesture with his hands. "Sort it out."

After I'd paid the check, we walked to the door in silence. His car was already waiting at the curb halfway down the block. He motioned to the driver to stay where he was and turned to look me full in the face.

"Have you tried to get a transfer?"

I shook my head. "That's not in the cards. If he knew I wanted out, I'd be finished with him. And I couldn't get across the street now if my life depended on it; they've got every job within five miles of the President locked up and nailed down."

"You never know," he said blandly, "something might turn up."

"That's what I used to tell myself. But not anymore. Let's face it—I'm up a dead end. And that's not a matter of temperament. It's a fact."

He looked at me, evidently unconvinced or unimpressed. I started ticking off the alternatives on my fingers.

"If I quit, the only thing I'm qualified to do is practice law, and you said yourself I'm not really cut out for that. Or I could always get some sort of overpaid PR job, in which case I'd be no better off than I am now, massaging a lot of self-important egos. Or I could stick with this guy and go where he's going—which is absolutely nowhere." I stopped counting. "Because apolitical as you're supposed to be, Frank, even you've got to admit he has nowhere to go but into early retirement. At a guess I'd say the odds against his being on the ticket again are astronomical. Next time around he'd be a liability."

Specci looked down at his shoes and coughed. "Don't you think you're being a bit disloyal?" he asked softly.

"Okay. Maybe I am. But I'm not in the position of a guy like George Reedy. He took one look at Lyndon Johnson and said, 'This man's going to the White House. I'm going with him.' A lot of people told him it wasn't so. But Reedy was convinced, and that kept him going for a long, long time."

Specci signaled for his car. The driver started easing the limousine into the traffic.

"It galls you, I guess, to see what the President's doing and still be so close and yet so far away, doesn't it?"

On almost any other day I might have denied it. But not on this one.

"I think he's the greatest President since Roosevelt," I said flatly. "And you're right. The better he looks, the worse he makes the Vice President seem."

The limousine pulled up smoothly, and Specci put his hand on the door.

"He is pretty impressive," he conceded. "But you shouldn't be so down on your boss. He's no genius, but he's not a bad guy." Specci started to get into the limousine. "Anyway, I'm sorry I couldn't be more help. . . ."

"No need to be sorry. Just talking things over with an old friend always helps."

"Can I drop you anywhere?"

I thought for a moment. "No, thanks, Frank. I think I'll take a walk."

"Ah, yes." He laughed, sounding faintly like W. C. Fields. "A little postprandial perambulation to aid the digestion."

The sight of Specci, so short, swarthy and obviously Italianate, offering that piece of advice, in that particular voice, momentarily shook me out of my mood. I laughed aloud.

"That's better," he said. "I suppose I'll see you at Andrews tonight?"

"I wouldn't miss it," I said. "The whole country ought to be out there to thank him for what he's done."

"Comes the hour," he said cheerily as I closed the door, "comes the man."

When the time came to leave, there was a sharp nip in the air. It promised a welcome and early end to the muggy leftovers of a quasi-tropical summer. A bright earnest of crisp fall days soon. As the big official limousine rolled its shiny black bulk over the Douglass Bridge and onto Suitland Parkway, I could make out the faintest hint of mist starting to straggle up from the muddy banks of the Anacostia. Half turning in the back seat, I looked back at the District in that softening, flattering light where late afternoon imperceptibly shades into early evening.

When I turned back in my seat, a murmur of contentment escaped me, and for once the others let it pass without question or comment. Incredible to recall that the man we were going to meet was the same one who less than three years before had squeaked (some said sneaked) into the White House with barely a third of the vote in what must have been the nastiest four-way fight since the Allies met at Versailles.

Yet he was coming back now to a country suddenly light-headed with hope and gratitude. Certainly he was returning to a happier land than he or anyone else, including the last few Presidents, had seen for a long time. I think most people felt we were on the road back at last. We'd traveled a long, agonizing detour, with dead dreams, dead careers and even deader men for milestones. But we'd stuck it out for a lot longer than anybody would have ever thought possible. How we did it I don't know; I don't think anyone does, for all the second-guessing. The important thing had to be that we'd done it for just long enough—long enough, that is, to be saved.

There was no doubt in my mind that the President deserved most of the credit. From the afternoon of inauguration day, he'd steadily grown in the job. Starting as pretty much an unknown quantity, he'd come up with one success after another, both at home and abroad, so that we'd almost recaptured that combination of self-respect and optimism most people thought had gone forever. Of course, it helped that people generally responded as they did. Maybe some of us responded too much. We were almost embarrassingly eager for a leadership that managed to be honest, effective, courageous and compassionate. But on that afternoon one thing seemed obvious: He was coming back with a triumph. A negative triumph, maybe, but what a positive response!

For an instant he appeared in my imagination as some latter-day Caesar, coming home with the shades of a war, a miserable, futile, potentially endless war in the Persian Gulf, chained to the wheels of his chariot. Or, I corrected myself, lashed to the undercarriage of Air Force One, and I laughed quietly to myself at the absurdity of the image. We had all said no to more Vietnams, to more Arab-Israeli face-offs. But where oil was concerned there was still a sinking feeling we might not have the luxury of choice. That he hadn't only kept us out of a war involving half a dozen small countries with more money, guns and pride than they could sensibly manage was a brilliant achievement, but to go on from there and get the shooting stopped was amazing.

There were the inevitable ugly rumors about some sort of "sellout" of the country's interests, but I doubt any reasonable person believed them. My own supposition was that he'd somehow convinced the Chinese to stop arming the Arabs to the teeth; that despite the new hard-line regime in Moscow no amount of renewed trouble in the Gulf would bring the United States and the Soviet Union back into direct confrontation; and that they, the Chinese, would therefore have to find some other way of easing Soviet pressure on themselves. Backed up with enough carrots and sticks, including a cut in our support of Teheran, it might just work. And if that wasn't the deal exactly, I was fairly sure it was something very much like it.

The arrangement was bound to be fragile, of course. But as far as anyone could tell at the time it looked reasonable enough to have a fifty-fifty chance. And now you could virtually reach out and touch the feeling in the air in Washington, it was so electric. It was a feeling of a brand-new start. What impressed me most, though, was how it was accompanied by a sense not so much of striking out on a new road but of having found our way back to an old one. One that we somehow knew, trusted and were confident would take us where we wanted to go.

Was it nostalgia? Something fundamentally conservative in our character? Or merely social dregs—a habit? I don't know. But it was unmistakable. And I could tell that this feeling of renewal was radiating out from the capital clear across the country. A great nation's overflowing closetful of ghosts and demons was to be exorcised at last.

By the time we reached the Andrews west gate it was starting to grow dark. Off to one side I could see a circling knot of protesters. It looked like a score of politicals and the usual handful of crazies. Someone in the car started grumbling.

"Christ on a crutch, will you look at that? What in hell do they want—jam on it?"

I studied the protesters. I thought they looked pretty dispirited, merely going through the motions of dissent if only to remind us they were still there and always would be. But they didn't seem to have enough energy to be a real nuisance, let alone a threat. They almost made the Fort Bragg paratroopers strung out along the perimeter look irrelevant, to say nothing of the marksmen up on the taller roofs waiting for the darkness to thicken and make their infrared scopes tell.

An immaculately tailored Air Force lieutenant pointed to our near-side windows and made a brisk lowering motion.

"Identification and passes, please, gentlemen."

ID's and passes went out in a bundle, were fanned out, matched up with faces and handed back.

"All you gentlemen on the Vice President's staff?"

"That's right, Lieutenant. We're the second team."

It was a private joke. But the lieutenant didn't laugh. He only saluted.

"You'll find him in the reception area," he said, and waved us on. But as the car pulled away, I noticed him smile, evidently amused by a private joke of his own.

We found the Vice President already in the Presidential lounge, trying his best to appear at once self-possessed and vaguely distant. In a word, Presidential. Typically, he was betraying himself by stamping his feet slightly as if they were cold. Why, I muttered to myself, did he always have to be so jumpy? Milling about him, busily swapping the usual small change of high-level gossip, were various Cabinet members, generals, admirals and Presidential assistants. He immediately pulled the four of us—the only people there who owed him anything—off to one side. He was like a girl on her first date.

"This is the best damned thing he's ever done. The best damned thing! Didn't I tell you we had a winner, eh? Didn't I? We make a great team. We surely do,'' he gloated, wallowing in another man's triumph. ''A winning team.''

I could feel us all silently bracing ourselves for ''Life's a lot like football.''

''Life's a lot like football,'' he announced. ''It really is. Especially when you're in politics.''

And to him life did indeed seem to consist almost exclusively of politics and football. He had few deep passions, and they had only those two outlets. However much he could be faulted in the one, there could be no doubt of his love of the other. He was not so much a fan, more a fanatic. In football he really did see, crammed into the limits of four fifteen-minute quarters and a rulebook, all the struggle and variety of life. There was color; there was noise; there was fervor. On a neatly ruled plot of grass (or plastic) a quintessential symbol of combat unfolded in which the strong, the skilled and the brave would go forth to meet—and usually defeat—those not quite as strong or as skilled or as brave. Yet always there was chance, fate, luck, with its inevitable but unpredictable injustices. How much more true to life could it be?

He carried the message everywhere. Once, running for the governorship, he floored a women's-something-or-other club in Santa Barbara by agreeing to offer up thanks over half a rubber chicken, bowing his head, then rhythmically and noisily chanting, ''Rub-a-dub-dub/Thanks for the grub/Gooooooooo-oh, God!''

An Air Force major interrupted my reverie, saluting artistically. ''Sir, the President's plane is landing.''

The Vice President noisily cleared his throat, nodded stiffly and turned in the direction of the double doors. Coach was set to lead the team out for the Big Game. Homecoming, I presumed.

The Cabinet fell into line behind him. Then came the Joint Chiefs, followed by those top Presidential aides who'd been left behind. Then came the four of us. High and low alike, we walked out briskly, a trifle self-conscious, I thought, about having to tread the fifty yards of red carpet snaking out onto the runway. About halfway along we stopped, with the bulletproof lectern in front of us and another red carpet behind, this one still folded up, ready to be rolled out to a White House helicopter.

Along both sides of the lounge there was a system of ropes and portable posts, its effectiveness magnified by scores of air police. Hedged in by ropes, posts and police, the crowd seemed well under control. Secret Service agents in short hair and raincoats moved discreetly around the fringes. Yet for all the security precautions the atmosphere was happy. You might even say festive. It was a warmly welcoming crowd. The President should like it.

No sooner were the Vice President, the Cabinet and the Chiefs sorted out and properly posed than the landing lights of Air Force One glowed dully in the haze. The roar of engines wedged uncomfortably in our ears. Television lights flicked on, tearing a hole in the darkness in front. Into the hole rolled the modified B-1 bomber; then gravely it swung its nose around toward us.

The crowd noise went up in a crescendo, following some inner geometry of its own, as the engine noise slackened. Cheering mingled confusedly with chanted slogans, the slogans of three years before. Hollow as they sounded then, they were, like all forecasts come true, triumphant now.

Suddenly the cheering lost its full-throated quality. Something was being kept in reserve. The television lights focused on the doorway high up on the plane, making that part of it shimmer as the shiny white surface bounced back the light. Without warning the door quickly slid away, and with a measured hydraulic dignity the ramp came out and down. At the instant its aluminum lip brushed the concrete apron he materialized out of the glare.

Invisible strings high in the darkness pulled his arms straight up to the sky. The hands waggled wildly, briefly clutched each other, then waggled again. His tall, slender body rocked back, curving out from the heels, arching out toward us, almost offering himself. The face—tanned and handsome in an understated way—that famous, much-loved face, was lit by a grin of pure delight.

He quickly loped down the ramp, the twenty-year-old youth

in a grown man of fifty. All the way he was grinning and waving into a sea of light and sound that now broke over him with all its power. At the bottom he paused, looking back over his shoulder as if intending to say something to his wife. But she was barely halfway down. To mixed laughter and applause he bounded energetically back up the ramp and nearly carried her bodily the rest of the way.

The Vice President started by reading the short speech of welcome I'd written for him, but he couldn't resist a few extemporaneous remarks. He seemed to suggest that he'd kept the Republic together and was now handing it back in as good a condition as he'd found it, maybe better. I gritted my teeth.

The President's reply was gracious and short. He took no particular credit for the dramatic cease-fire in the Persian Gulf. He spoke sincerely about the efforts made by other people, particularly in Moscow, Peking, Teheran and Kuwait. He admitted that if he'd done anything at all to help the peace of the world, he was glad. Not just because it was right, but because that's what the people who'd voted for him wanted—he knew that was true because he knew them all personally.

When the laughter died down, he said he also thought he was a lucky man, lucky to have a job where he couldn't go wrong. If what he was doing was right, his wife and children let him know. If it wasn't, everybody else did. More laughter

On a more serious note he thought, and hoped, that the country would take advantage of the great opportunity it now had. Only the day before he had been talking to an idealistic young Chinese, an interpreter, who had spent several years in the United States perfecting his English. What, the President had asked him, did you think of my country? Your country is very rich, was the reply, but your people are poor. I want to be able to send that young man a message, said the President. I want to be able to say to him: Come back to America, as my guest. Come back and see a different America, a better America. Come back, and see what a rich people we really are.

Then he swiftly turned around, shook a few hands, grasped

his wife's arm and, yielding to the best of political impulses, plunged through the Secret Service carapace and bore down on the crowd. Thunderous applause turned into ecstatic cries of delight. A thousand hands in front shot out while still more went up behind. He was advancing on an enormous, noisy, human porcupine with hands waving and flapping from the tips of its myriad quills. The already eerie quality was heightened as television camera crews scurried for position, creating a shifting kaleidoscope of stroboscopic light. I was still not fully aware of what was happening when I saw that something was rising steadily into the air.

At once it seemed all conscious centers of thought and action froze. For an eternity of seconds I searched for comprehension, trying to get them to work. Then I knew what it was. Of course! It was only some futile, stupid attempt by somebody crammed back in there trying to get his attention. Merely a show of affection—something soft, harmlessly thrown. Once it was handkerchiefs and flowers. Now it's crumpled Dixie cups and wadded tissues.

But as it tumbled and wobbled through the air, its shape becoming definite as it fell back into the upper reaches of the cone of light, I understood.

A Secret Service agent who was half a second ahead of me was already reaching out, lunging for the President. Out of the corners of my eyes I could tell that other agents were also in motion. And the Vice President, thinking what, imagining himself on what Saturday afternoon gridiron, I still don't know, leaped up to catch it. In the shifting tides of light and shadow he completely misjudged it. He succeeded only in knocking it down. It landed with a dull metallic thud and rolled to a stop at the First Lady's feet.

The President, instinct and love more powerful than judgment or office, spun around toward her, reached out to her—up when he should have been down, facing that way when he should have been this. The M-4d fragmentation grenade, a tangerine-sized fruit with the power of a small howitzer shell, pinnacle of five centuries of hand bombs, launched into the air on twenty years of bitterness and anger, tore him apart.

Chapter Two

"Here, here and here"—the pointer waved at several dark pools in a streaky gray sea—"you can see the extravasated blood. There"—it swung upward a few inches—"are the missile tracks, or permanent cavities. And along through this region are the temporary cavities; many times the size of the missile, of course, but already starting to close up." The tip of the pointer went around in ellipses. "Extensive pulsation and collapsing tissues all through this region. And this"—the pointer jabbed savagely —"is where you can see how some of the neck muscles were torn apart under the strain, splitting pretty much along their axes. But this is the most worrying aspect to all of us, I'm sure." The pointer rested on the ghostly white blob of a head, the film cryptically marked up to make sense to the initiated, of what otherwise looked like a mess. "You can see signs of breakdown here . . . and here . . . of the rigid cranial walls. Even if only to a slight degree the skull bones have been forced apart along suture lines. Bear in mind, too, that many of the large blood vessels leading to the head have probably been stretched out of shape, which will retard the circulation of blood throughout this critical area." Down came the pointer.

At least a minute passed without anyone choosing to break the gloomy silence. The explanation was clear enough. But what did it mean? Each of us was wrestling with that question when a voice in the front row asked, "How long will it take for these injuries to heal sufficiently for him to function more or less normally, Doctor?"

"The Vice President is a strong man, in good physical condition until this happened, Mr. Farb," the doctor said briskly. Then he paused. "But he might not be able to function . . . shall we say, effectively . . . for several months. Certainly not for some weeks. And remote as the possibility might be, I think it only right to point out that a genuinely complete recovery could take years."

Perhaps weeks, perhaps months; maybe now, maybe never. To have a murdered President and First Lady was bad enough. But a Vice President who was, to all intents and purposes, neither dead nor alive made even that ghastly situation worse. For the third time in its history the United States was like some primitive tribe: It was acephalous—it had no head. First when Cleveland disappeared for three days to have a cancer operation performed on a yacht in New York Harbor. Then when Wilson had his stroke. Now this. Perhaps things could have been worse, I thought. The Secret Service agents hadn't been able to save the President or Vice President, but at least they'd covered up most of the Cabinet, and somebody was quick enough to get Farb and Morrissey down behind the armored lectern. There was that much to be thankful for if nothing else. And now I strained to get a better view of Farb, the Secretary of State.

All I could see clearly though was his profile, the full features accentuated and made repellent by the ghostly glow from the banks of fluorescent light in front of him. Fluent in four languages (and fluent with Farb meant fluent), he was also rich, funny in a sarcastic way and clever. He was unquestionably the most self-assured man I'd ever known, and in his heart I had no doubt that he believed he deserved to be the first Jewish President. No one questioned the universal, at times exaggerated, respect he enjoyed. Yet he was always a hard man to like, as everyone who knew him admitted. And now, for once, he had almost nothing to say. His face was a study in concentration as he stared at the films of disaster.

It occurred to me that he was probably relapsing into silence because it wasn't really his place to speak. For now that we had had the nature and scope of the Vice President's wounds explained, attention in that room was already shifting, silently but unmistakably, away from the traumatized body of the Vice President and the mortal remains of the late President onto the tall, grave personage of the Senate Majority Leader, Holden Van Riebouw.

The line of succession had been changed twice in less than twenty years—each time to deal with an earlier loss of nerve. First, after Tom Dodd came unglued when the early word from Dallas was that both Kennedy and Johnson had been shot. So it was shifted from President pro tempore of the Senate to Speaker of the House. But then came the Agnew mess, and Carl Albert was so obviously frightened of being catapulted into the White House that the succession was changed again. An elderly, unprepared, little-known Speaker did not seem such a good idea after all. It was better to put the mantle on a man who stood on three legs—elected by the people of a whole state, elected by the majority party in the Senate and in all likelihood the most powerful man in Congress. And there were recent precedents enough: Both Alben Barkley and Lyndon Johnson went from being Senate majority leaders to being Vice Presidents, while no one could remember the last Speaker of the House who'd done the same. So Van Riebouw was next in line, and in him we had more than a man—we had a statesman. He had made his entire career out of being above and beyond the narrow call of party. He was the very man the country could rally around in this abysmal hour. And the idea occurred to me that if he also had nothing to say, then the government of the United States was about to collapse in a total vacuum wherein was neither sound nor action.

But Van Riebouw finally exhaled a drawn-out, unhappy sigh. "This is terrible news." He made a vague, despairing gesture.

"Terrible. I don't know how the country is going to take it at all." He hesitated as if overwhelmed, but still no one else spoke. He drew himself up. "But we've got to act . . . and soon. It's up to us."

Farb bowed his head, apparently in grief-stricken agreement. Yet I noticed one eyebrow rise expressively beneath his cupped hand, and in that instant it was clear that the Secretary had also long since seen right through the Great Reconciler, the Great Compromiser, the Great Whitewasher. Like me, he had plumbed Van Riebouw looking for depths and had struck only shallows. If there ever had been a solid core to the Senate Majority Leader, and his early reputation suggested there had, it had evidently fractured somewhere along the way to statesmanship. Perhaps there was some scandal, some sad private vice, maybe only self-disgust, lurking behind that handsome mask. Real power, real responsibility might bring whatever it was into the light of day. Better to be a statesman. And as long as the people of Pennsylvania kept reelecting him, he could go on being a statesman. But I never saw a man who wanted so much to be loved for the wrong reasons.

"What do you suggest, Van?"

This time I couldn't see the face, but I recognized the voice. And the face it conjured up was unforgettable, distinguished as it was by cauliflower ears, a badly reset nose and sizable patches of scar tissue—the result of countless amateur pummelings and twenty-six professional fights. Still, the people of Seattle were less interested in looks than ability. They kept sending Big Dave Czecky back to Congress with such monotonous regularity that he was able to become a legendary parliamentarian and a first-rate Speaker. Czecky, as someone pointed out, was one of those men who looked too much like a villain to be one. If anything, he'd proved to be one of the most honest men ever to come to this town. So far as anyone knew, he never lied and he never broke a promise. According to Georgetown dinner party wits, he loved the Constitution so much that he slept with it under his pillow. And why not? Czecky believed every word of it.

As Speaker he was currently in line after the Senate Majority

Leader for accession to the Presidency. And he must know, I thought, that Van Riebouw's simply not up to it. But I also realized that Czecky wouldn't elbow him aside.

"Whatever you want, Van," he said, "you can count on me."

"Well, Dave," said Van Riebouw thoughtfully, "I was thinking of maybe you and me kind of setting ourselves up as a sort of temporary committee."

Someone let out a gasp of surprise. I was startled myself. A committee? To run the United States? He couldn't be serious, even if it was only a two-man committee. Farb was looking at him coldly. John Morrissey, the Secretary of Defense, drummed his fingers irritably on his knee. He was nervous and no longer cared who knew it. I saw him glance at the wall clock, and everyone in the room must have known what he was thinking. The time was a little after 10 P.M. The country was going into its fourth hour without anyone who could give an unchallengable order to use its nuclear weapons. The ambiguous statements that were going out would become counterproductive if they were used for much longer; simply repeating them would tell the world what it wanted to know. The Senate Majority Leader, Julian ("Call me Bud") Carter, nervously shuffled his feet under his chair.

"What kind of committee were you thinking about, Van?"

"You see," said Van Riebouw in a tone that expressed relief that someone was interested, "Dave and I could share the responsibilities between us. That way no one could say either of us was trying to push the Vice President into a corner, and there'd be no question about whether we'd step down the very minute he was ready to take over." He paused for a moment, then continued in a more emphatic vein. "We have to carry this thing through in such a way that when we assume the powers of the Presidency, everybody knows we're in business. At the same time it has to be just as clear that we don't have any ambitions for ourselves. I think joint responsibility—sharing the power—is the best way to do both those things. And we could get Congress to set up a joint committee to keep an eye on us and at the same time see how the Vice President's coming along. When they say he's okay—which Congress is supposed to do anyway in case of Presidential disability—we'll hand it over to him and step down."

"But you're supposed to take over on your own, Senator," said Farb. "It's spelled out pretty clearly in the disability statutes."

"I'm not at all sure that the legislation you refer to had quite this situation in mind, Mr. Secretary. My God"—Van Riebouw's voice quavered—"another President's dead. The Vice President . . . lying downstairs in God knows what condition. Nobody knowing how long it will last or what sort of shape he's going to be in ever again. And you think the Congress expected this sort of situation and provided for it years ago? With all due respect, Mr. Secretary, I've been in the Congress a long time, long enough to know that if you pass a law one year to take care of something that might or might not happen in the future, when it does happen the law hardly ever fits all the facts. So you end up using the parts that fit, and you change the parts that don't. And because we've got a constitutional system you go back to the Congress to change the parts that don't. You tell them what you need. And what we need here is a joint setup." He sat down, wetly blowing his nose.

There was another long silence. The doctors stared intently at the X rays as if they'd just discovered something new in them.

"You don't want to go it alone, do you, Van?" Czecky gently asked. Van Riebouw raised his hand as if to protest. But Czecky quickly reached over and touched the Senator on the shoulder. "That's all right. If that's what you want. It doesn't matter how you read the statutes. At a time like this I guess our job is to support you however we can."

"I disagree," said the Secretary of Defense. Now someone thought to ask the doctors to leave, and their exit gave everyone else a chance to catch his breath.

"You disagree, John," encouraged Farb.

"Yes, I do. Please understand, Senator." He turned to Van

Riebouw. ''I think it would be fine if we could do it the way you suggest. If this were 1920 or 1930, it would be almost ideal, under the circumstances.'' I could sense Van Riebouw bristle, but Morrissey plunged straight ahead. ''Only now, I think it would jeopardize the security of the nation.''

He gave them a moment to study his ace. ''With one hand on the button everybody knows where he is. Make it two hands, and all bets are off. You might as well make it fifty or a hundred.''

''The Secretary of Defense is right, Senator,'' said Farb softly, and looked over at Czecky. ''Don't you agree, Mr. Speaker?''

Though it was obviously painful for him to say so, Czecky said, ''Yes.''

Van Riebouw started to flounder, but Farb took him firmly in hand.

''How about this, Senator? You take over as Acting President, just as the statute provides. Congress sets up a joint committee to examine the Vice President. Also provided for by law. And if in a few weeks, maybe a couple of months, it looks like he'll never recover sufficiently, then—and only then—we consider some new sort of arrangement outside the current statutes?''

Van Riebouw had enough sense to see at once that Farb was on firmer ground than he was.

''All right,'' he said. ''If that's what everybody wants.''

Carter nodded agreement. So did Czecky. Farb and Morrissey stood up.

''I think you can count on the Cabinet's support, Senator,'' said Farb. ''If there's anything I can do personally, I hope you won't hesitate to ask.''

Morrissey shook Van Riebouw's hand and wished him luck. They began to arrange for the formal assumption by Van Riebouw of the President's powers. I was asked if, as the senior member of the Vice President's staff, I would help the late President's press secretary draw up a statement on the Vice President's condition. Van Riebouw's principal aide would help draft an announcement that the country now had an Acting President.

I spent almost the whole of the following week at Walter Reed. It was one of the strangest weeks of my life. Most of the time I felt trapped in a smoothly running, superaseptic limbo. On the one hand were the staff people like myself. We couldn't decide anything, plan anything or do anything that seemed either real or important. Everything came out "if." The late President's staff kept themselves busy showing Van Riebouw the ropes. But we could only wait. In contrast, the hospital staff went on with their work calmly and effectively, and we were utterly dependent on them. Before the week was out you could feel it becoming a world of Us and Them, and They were clearly on top. We felt helpless and useless, hanging on the words of nurses and interns.

Yet no matter how inverted and unreal life in the hospital seemed to us, no one assumed things were much better outside. Not since Edith Wilson ran the country from the antechamber to Woodrow's sickroom had Washington been so up in the air. For the first couple of days there was a lot of worry about what the Russians and Chinese might do. But they didn't suddenly make up their differences in the fashion of Hitler and Stalin and start to pick us clean. If anything most of the top Communist leadership in Moscow and Peking seemed sympathetic. Perhaps the President had worked his spell on them too. More likely they were worried themselves: Who knew what the inscrutable Americans might do in this new grief and alarm? Wiser to keep a low profile until something like normality returns. Still, many people were surprised, myself included, that the cease-fire in the Gulf held up.

Throughout that week I never, for all the unreality, felt isolated there in the hospital. I always had a good sense of what the mood was in the country at large. I knew it not just because I too was jittery and depressed but because the general mood seemed to seep in through the cracks in doors and windows, or to be brought in on visitors' clothes, to be shaken off inside like rain or snow. And I did go out twice. Once to the White House for several hours to discuss integrating the various staffs in case the Vice President recovered sufficiently and was allowed to take the oath. The second occasion was the President and First Lady's double funeral.

I don't know why it should be so, but the only time we seem able to match the Europeans at mounting a quietly moving ceremony is when we have to bury a President. Especially if he's been assassinated. We somehow rise to the tragedy of swift, enormous loss as if to the manner born.

We watched the burial at Arlington, hardly hearing the words. Then we mingled with the crowd, many people still sobbing, as it drifted clumsily back across the river and into downtown. I collected my car, and on the way back up Sixteenth to Walter Reed, my wife, who hadn't spoken a word since the funeral, said, "Do you have to get back right away?"

"A few minutes more won't make any difference. Why?"

"If we can, I'd like to stop off at Rock Creek Cemetery on the way."

Even at a time like this, I marveled, she could think of just the right thing. Arlington had been too huge, too public, for essentially private people to assuage their grief.

When we arrived, there were already about a dozen people there, gathered around the Saint-Gaudens statue. Most stood. A few sat. Still others kneeled on the damp earth. Puffy cumulus clouds drifted through a pastel blue sky, while the trees shook down brilliant autumn leaves. How very appropriate, I thought. Here we are, mourning still another murdered American President at a suicide's grave. Mrs. Henry Adams, why did you do it?

On the way back up North Capitol I wondered about the crowd at Arlington, the somber people at the cemetery and the tens of millions more who at this moment were also plunged in grief. Together we as a people had cause enough to mourn. It seemed that every time we were about to pull ourselves together something else happened. But how long could we go on like this before some irredeemable calamity brought the whole edifice of our national life crashing down on us? Surely everyone must see by now that the country couldn't carry on as if disaster were a commonplace. Had killing Presidents and routinely replacing them become a tolerable part of the Consitution, just another aspect of politics?

Well, why not? When the Vice President recovers sufficiently . . . I stiffened involuntarily.

"Are you all right?"

"I'm fine. I just remembered something I had to do, that's all."

She looked at me, expectant, half-hoping, I thought, to be asked to do something.

"But it's not very important. I can take care of it later."

No. Having him as President was obviously out of the question, even *if* he recovered. And then I realized that I had been trying to arrange his swearing in partly to numb my feelings and partly out of habit. But I never expected it to happen. The contempt that had been slowly accumulating over the past few years suddenly turned to anger.

The President and Vice President made a winning ticket, a reporter once said, because one of them appealed to the best side of America and the other to the worst: They divided the political spectrum between them. In my heart I'd known that he was right. Still, it was tolerable so long as the best half was in the White House. But now?

I'd been vaguely assuming that if I knew how unequipped he was to be President, then Congress and the Cabinet must also know. He hadn't wielded any real power, but he'd hardly been a recluse. He'd embarrassed the President time and again with his heavy-handed attempts to draw attention to himself. He was a laughingstock among people in the media. Surely they must see. . . . And they probably did. They had a perfect excuse to stop him: brain damage, no matter how slight. But that didn't mean they were going to. It dawned on me that so far no one had made a single move to block him. They were actually going to go through with it—with bated breath, no doubt, and crossed fingers—but not one of them would try to bar his way.

By the time I pulled into Walter Reed's VIP parking lot I was torn between rage and disgust. I kissed my wife good-bye and for the dozenth time asked her if she still wanted a divorce.

"Not now," she said huskily and stared at the steering wheel.

"What do you mean 'Not now'? Not now, you don't want to discuss it, or not now, you've changed your mind?"

"Both," she said, squeezing my hand, then drove off.

Later that afternoon I was able to say that the Vice President was much improved in that most of the vital signs were stronger, but he was not yet fully conscious. No, he had not been told of the President's funeral. Yes, his wife had seen him for a few minutes but had not been able to talk to him. No, I had not yet been in to see him.

I kept myself occupied for most of the evening by returning telephone calls, trying to sort out the people with serious business from those who were only using their expressions of sympathy to angle for something they wanted in case he recovered. The night wore on, and the list of calls to be made shrank to a handful of names. I found myself considering the various alternatives I could suggest, from my resignation to his. And at some point I felt suddenly lighthearted. I was close to something really historic. What was that if not power? It was certainly the stuff power is made of. I laughed aloud for a moment.

It was ironic. Just as I'd grown used to thinking of myself being permanently sidelined I had finally made it! The natural competitor in me thought briefly of the Presidental staffers, and I gloated that all they really had now was a dead President while, bloody and battered though he was, mine was a live Vice President.

The sense of triumph was short-lived, however, for though everything I'd set out to achieve in politics was now possibly within my grasp, it had come in such a way that there was little true joy in it. The man I had wanted to serve had been buried that day. The man I could go with to the White House was a fool. The joke was on me.

Shortly after dawn a white-coated young doctor stepped softly into my room.

"The Vice President's conscious now, if you'd like to go in."

I planned to talk no more than ten minutes and, as gently as possible, break the news of the President's death. His family had been called and would see him after me.

Two wan-looking Secret Service men let me quietly into his room. He was a comic strip version of the ultimate accident victim, his head swathed in bandages. One of his eyes was completely covered. His left arm was flung out, taped to a board. I stared down at him with a strange pity he had never inspired in me before. He looked completely helpless.

"I hear you're feeling better."

He moved his head slightly and rolled up his undamaged eye. When he spoke, I was startled by his voice. It was soft, no longer the booming, hearty country club voice I could imitate perfectly in my mind.

"So they tell me."

We stared blankly at each other. The destiny of a great nation, possibly of the world, was involved in this room. But we were as tongue-tied and awkward as any routine patient and visitor on a normal visiting day.

"Is there anything I can . . . anything I can get you?"

"No," he whispered. "How's the President? I hope he's okay. I tried. . . ." He faltered. "I tried to. . . ." He broke off. His one good eye searched my face and a slight burning sensation started up in my cheeks. I shook my head.

"Oh, my God!" he moaned. "Not him. What have we done?" A tear welled up in the corner of his eye, trembled, then slid across his cheek to disappear behind an ear.

I stared out the window, listening to the hum of the electric clock. A full minute or more passed before I sensed I should speak.

"Try not to worry." Stupid thing to say. I started again. "The whole country's praying for you now. All you have to do is rest. Get your strength back." He stirred as he tried to give shape to the questions already rising in his mind.

"It's all right. Van Riebouw is acting as President and a Congressional committee's been set up to check on how you're coming along. They'll manage until you're"—I choked momentarily on the words—"until you're ready to be sworn in."

"Yes," he whispered fiercely. "Sworn in. Got to be sworn in. Defend the Constitution. Enemies. Foreign and domestic. Defend the Constitution. Uphold. Must uphold. No doubt. Continuity. Must have continuity. No break."

Quickly I pressed the buzzer beside the bed. In a few seconds two doctors were in the room. "He's raving," I whispered. They nodded and pointed to the door for me to leave.

Chapter Three

Slowly, of course, he mended. More and more of his faculties returned. The physical damage to the brain proved to be gratifyingly small. But his eyesight looked likely to be permanently, if slightly, impaired. And his speech was slurred, reminiscent of a stroke victim's or a drunk's. As his strength returned, his mind fixed increasingly on a single event—taking the oath. By the time he was released from Walter Reed it was becoming an obsession. The oath had become the be-all and end-all of his recovery. He could see nothing beyond it.

I kept hoping to the last that someone, almost anyone, would at least try to make him look realistically at what he was undertaking. Yet the days dragged by, and nobody did. Not one person, so far as I could tell, ever made a serious effort to raise the subject with him. When it got to the day he was scheduled to be released, I felt there could be no more putting it off. I found myself now looking for an opportunity. And after lunch he began musing aloud about how pleased his parents would have been to see him sworn in as President. In the most offhand way I could, I said, "You're absolutely certain that you're doing the right thing then, Governor?"

He jerked around sharply in his wheelchair and glared at me. "What?"

Evidently I'd touched a nerve. I tried to sound casual. "Taking the oath."

"Why shouldn't I take the oath?"

Before I could reply, he was boiling over. "It's this wheelchair." He pounded the top rim of a rubberized wheel with the palm of his hand. "You think I can't run the country from a wheelchair! Goddammit. Franklin Roosevelt ran the New Deal from a wheelchair. He ran the biggest war in history from a wheelchair. Anyway, I'm not permanently chained to this thing. Roosevelt was. I'm getting out of it one of these days. Roosevelt couldn't do that."

He paused for breath. Perhaps it was only his pride I'd stung. After a lifetime of being proud of his robust good health and stocky physique, being an invalid was itself an affront.

"Eisenhower. Look at Eisenhower. He had a bad heart. My heart's all right; nothing wrong there. That," he said as if he should be congratulated, "that's what pulled me through. And there's something else you seem to be forgetting. I have a duty, under the Constitution."

When, I sourly wondered, had he last read the Constitution? But there was no point in trying to talk to him when he was like this.

"Anyway, you know what I always say."

I knew.

"When the going gets tough, the tough get going."

Several times during the next week I began to wonder if perhaps I'd been wrong. Daily he grew stronger and more clear-headed. And once you became accustomed to the slightly slurred vowels they were no more noticeable than a clock's ticking. What impressed me most, however, was that he seemed more confident, more secure. That was the last thing I'd expected, and I wasn't the only one to be struck by it. There were a number of inspired news stories wondering out loud if perhaps the imminent responsibilities of the Presidency had purged his frivolous side—a side that sprang from deep insecurity.

Certainly his approach to the swearing in seemed sensible.

Despite all his hot desire for it he was coolly level-headed. No need to rush, he said. Let the Congressional committee decide if he was fit. Once they'd cleared him, he wanted only a simple ceremony on the South Portico, but with maximum television coverage so that people would be able to vouch for his recovery themselves.

The Disability Committee consulted with the doctors for several days. They talked with him for almost an entire day about major defense, foreign policy and domestic matters, straining to keep it nonpartisan. They asked him if he remembered this and that and finished by shaking his hand. It all seemed properly done, but I had an uneasy sense that while almost none of them would have ever voted for him to be President, they wanted even less to declare him unfit, for whatever reason. They obviously didn't care for the responsibility they bore. I thought they were principally intent on getting it over and done with as quickly as possible. Wanting him to be well, they found him so.

The day before the swearing in I went into the Oval Office. He was looking out over the South Lawn, watching the camera crews setting up. He gestured toward them.

"Seems like we finally made it."

"Yes, Governor, you've made it."

"Hell of a way to get here, though," he said with evident feeling.

I nodded in mute agreement, feeling profoundly depressed.

"Anyway, it's just for a year. I'll do the best I can for a year; then they can have anybody they want. I want you to put that in my speech."

I stared at him in disbelief. Was he seriously saying he wouldn't seek the office in his own right? It might make sense from several points of view. It might even be creditable. But to begin like that was, given the way he was already regarded, suicidal. There was also the fact that government had been almost paralyzed this past month while people waited to see what was going to happen. He was back to his old form: blundering his way toward chaos. He could be a lame duck if he wanted. But there was no point in publicly cutting himself off at the knees. Yet here he was, blithely throwing away his one chance of being taken seriously.

"I know what you're thinking. But aren't you the fellow who was wondering if I should even be President at all?" He chuckled to himself. "Still, you were the only one who was honest enough to lay it on the line. I respect that, you know. But I've thought about this thing a lot, and my mind's made up."

I started to protest, pointing out that even if his decision was unshakable, there was no need to announce it. He cut me short.

"I want to do what's right by everybody. And the best way I can make up for not being completely one hundred percent, the way I was before this"—he hesitated—"trouble . . . is not to want anything for myself, not even the nomination. I want to be able to promise to do my very best for everybody; then"—he made a saluting motion—"it's good-bye to Washington, D.C."

I was stunned. He was utterly sincere. He looked at me.

"You want out?"

I managed to say, "No. Not as long as you think I can be of any use to you here."

"I'd sure hate to lose you. Christ, I *trust* you. You're just about the only one around here I can trust."

I smiled tentatively, wondering what to say, embarrassed by such a direct compliment. He twitched his face in what was meant to be a reciprocal smile, but the damaged nerves and muscles produced a grimace instead. Then, without warning, he began to jerk spasmodically and thrash about wildly in his wheelchair.

"But those others," he snarled. "They laugh at me. I can see it. Even now. Even when I'm going to be President, they still laugh at me. Football freak. That's what they call me. I know that. All those wise-ass journalists. And the Congress. . . "

For ten minutes or more he raved, following some inner spiral of mounting hate and anger, recalling old grievances, old snubs, often enough imagining insults where no slight was ever intended.

His speech became increasingly slurred, his movements more erratic. Before he finished, he was completely incoherent. But the burden of his outburst was unmistakable: It was all venom and revenge. He took honest criticism for contempt—and returned it. Indifference for spite—and promised to double it. Everywhere he looked he saw enemies.

And this, I thought as I watched him, disgusted and ashamed, was to be the next President. I tried desperately to imagine what the results would be. I succeeded only in conjuring up a fuzzy picture of chaos—in the White House, in Congress, in the courts, in the great federal agencies, in the party organization, in the press, eventually in the streets, which were turbulent and dangerous enough.

Then he began to run down. In the space of less than a minute he went from a ranting, hate-filled fanatic to being simply a middle-aged man in a wheelchair. Slightly weak, perhaps, but in full possession of himself. I expected him to apologize, to say something that would indicate that he knew how wild he'd been. I expected embarrassment, contrition, no matter how slight or easily passed over. Instead, he seemed merely like a man waking from a trance, with no memory of what had passed.

I went cold with the realization that I had just seen the emergence of a new personality, one capable of going in seconds from humility to murderous paranoia. A doctor might have understood it. I found it incomprehensible. Yet he'd been given a dozen psychiatric and memory tests and had passed them all. Had the doctors, like the committee, believed what they wanted to believe? There were too many times when that seemed to be becoming a national characteristic. Maybe there never was a time when we would have been more morally courageous, but it was hard to believe. At any event, a man who'd been simply a hearty bungler with a talent for doing the wrong thing at the wrong time had definitely changed. At least before, he'd been neither humble nor paranoid. Now, suddenly, he was both. I reflected wryly that there might be a rough kind of justice in having him—the product of haste and violence—as President. But I found my taste for irony had fallen flat.

My immediate inclination was to tell somebody, almost anybody, what I'd seen. The swearing in must be called off. We would have to reconvene the Disability Committee. We? I stopped. Whom could I tell? More precisely, whom could I convince? I saw myself dragging hundreds of Congressmen into the Oval Office in twos and threes. When they were packed in wall to wall, I pointed excitedly at him, saying, "Now if you observe closely, you'll see him go crazy." I also saw myself watching the swearing in from the psychiatric ward at D.C. General.

In the next few months enough people would, of course, see him come unhinged. Enough, that is, for Congress to declare him incapable and remove him from office. *If* they were the right people, and they probably would be, there could be no doubt of that. Van Riebouw would simply have to "bite the bullet," in Lyndon Johnson's phrase.

But what might happen to the country in the meantime? What might happen if he chose to make a fight of it? What might happen if. . . . I could no longer think straight. Depressed and confused, I made some excuse and got away from him.

It was the first time I'd had a secret I had never sought and did not want. My only desire was somehow to get rid of it or at least to share the burden of it. But if I broke it to too many people or told it in the wrong way, there could be no foretelling the consequences. In the country's present state it might lead to almost anything, or so I feared. The more I thought about it, though, the more it seemed to me there were at least two other people who ought to know. Or rather, there were three others, but I would only trust something this explosive to two of them. I called Farb first.

"Look," he grumbled, "it's almost eleven."

"I know that, Mr. Secretary, and I apologize for calling you at home so late, but I'm afraid this can't wait."

"I'm sure it's as important as you say it is," he said, his voice heavy with forbearance, "but I find it hard to believe that this matter, however critical, can be settled by just you and me in the middle of the night."

"I'm not so sure of that, sir. And it's not only you and me. It involves the Speaker . . . and others."

Farb grasped the point at once. "It's the . . . swearing in?"

"Yes, sir."

"You anticipate some sort of problem, I take it."

"Possibly a very serious one."

He hummed and hawed for a few moments in a show of making up his mind. But he appreciated as well as anyone that he didn't have a great deal of choice.

"All right," he said sharply. "I'll expect you in about half an hour. And you'd better be right that this won't wait."

I called Czecky and went through almost exactly the same exchange, except that he didn't catch on quite as quickly as Farb.

"What do you mean it might be too late in the morning?" he demanded.

"Exactly what I say, Mr. Speaker."

There was a pause of several seconds. "Damn it," he said, exasperated, "are you calling me up and asking me to meet you in Georgetown at this hour just because you've run into some hitch with the swearing in?"

"It isn't the ceremony as such," I spoke as evenly as I could, through slightly clenched teeth. It seemed to work.

"Well, if it isn't the ceremony"—Czecky began briskly; then he slowed down as his mind raced ahead—"then it must be. . . ." He stopped short.

"I'm afraid so."

"Okay. I'll be there."

Before I left my office, I checked to see if the Vice President had gone to bed. In case he called for me I left word with the switchboard where I'd be and hinted that it was a matter of checking a few routine appointments that the secretary hadn't been able to get around to before. I hoped that would satisfy him. What I really hoped was that he was fast asleep and would stay that way.

I drove my own car up Pennsylvania Avenue, along M and then north on Wisconsin. I found Farb's house in a lovely little side street near Dumbarton Oaks Park. I waited almost ten minutes until Czecky's car pulled into the street. He greeted me a little stiffly, I thought, and led the way across to Farb's front door.

Farb himself was polite, but nothing more. By the time we were seated I was feeling uncomfortable and started to wonder if perhaps I'd made a mistake.

"You have our complete attention," said Farb, as if to say that was all I had.

I didn't bother with the polite preliminaries. I tried to recall everything the Vice President had said when he went out of control. I wanted to convey to them something of his wildness, his irrationality. It seemed important to impress on them how consumed he had been by unreasoning hatred. Most of all, I wanted them to grasp how suddenly and totally he'd changed, veering from one extreme to the other without any apparent reason.

But somehow it didn't come out right. Everything I said was true, but it seemed to fall flat in the telling. I kept having to backtrack, take up loose ends, grope for the right words. Silently I kicked myself black and blue for not rehearsing it in my mind before I came out. That was to prove a mistake I would not make again. But now, as I pressed on, I felt increasingly hapless. And I felt trapped, too, because once I had begun, there was no way back. I told it to the bitter end, concluding lamely, "That's why I felt I had to call you."

The words were hardly out of my mouth before Farb snapped, "Is that all?"

"Isn't that enough?" It was meant to sound defiant, but it didn't come off.

"Why didn't you call the Acting President?" asked Czecky.

"Because I didn't want to go to him alone. I wanted you to go with me—if I go. He'll listen to you. You'd be the first people he'd turn to anyway." It was circular, but it seemed to satisfy them.

"What do you think, Dave?"

Czecky shrugged his muscular shoulders. "There might be something to it. He's known the Vice President longer than either of us."

"I grant that," said Farb, "but do you actually think there might be something serious that the committee or the doctors could have overlooked?"

"No," he said firmly. "Nothing that serious. Let's say for the moment that what we've heard is true—and I don't doubt that it is—I think it could be interpreted in a completely different way from what we've heard suggested."

From the way they were talking I might as well not have been there.

"How would you account for it?" Farb asked.

"We all know the Vice President's tendency to be impulsive," said Czecky blandly. "At a guess, I'd say he probably had a case of last-minute jitters. He simply let it all come out in front of somebody close to him."

"If you ask me," said Farb, "it's likely to be all to the good. The media's been down on him for as long as anybody can remember. And a lot of us have said some pretty harsh things about him in the past. He's bound to be a little defensive, wondering if people are going to give him a fair chance. Better to let him get it off his chest now, I'd have thought."

"But you're missing the point," I objected. "So far I'm the only person who's seen him 'getting it off his chest,' as you call it. And I can tell you, there was nothing healthy, nothing normal about it. What are you going to do when he blows up like that at a press conference? Or a Cabinet meeting? Or starts groveling in front of the Soviet ambassador?"

Dryly Farb said, "We can jump off all those bridges when we get to them."

"Listen," I pleaded, "this is no joke. I'm telling you that we're about to swear in a man who's mentally unstable to be President of the United States. I don't care what those psychiatric tests say, I've known him closely for almost ten years, and he's *not* the same person anymore. I've seen the change for myself. And now that I've told you, you can do what you like. Do nothing, if you want. But at least I've told you."

I sounded petulant, which was exactly the way I felt.

"Don't try to play at Pontius Pilate with me," Farb murmured quietly, "because it won't work."

I tapped my chest melodramatically with my thumb. "I'm only a special assistant. There's not much more I *can* do."

Czecky exhaled loudly, then said, "I'd like to think about this."

Farb poured out coffee, then fiddled with his stereo for a few minutes until Czecky said, "Sorry, son, but I'm afraid it's no sale." He paused and lighted a cigarette. "What it comes down to is this: If you can't convince *us,* we can't convince somebody else for you."

"And not just somebody," Farb interrupted. "Everybody."

"That's right. We wouldn't only have to persuade the committee they were wrong, tough enough in itself; we'd also have to make two hundred and twenty million other people go along with it." He paused a moment to let it sink in, then went on, "But there's no need to think your effort's been wasted. If you're right—*if,* mind you—it'll come out. Now that you've told us what you saw we'll be more on the alert than ever."

No doubt he meant well, but it sounded patronizing. And by now I felt too miserable to say another word. I wanted only to get away and forget this meeting.

"If you ask me," said Farb, intending to be kind, "I personally think that what you've said is essentially true. I simply can't accept your interpretation of it, that's all. It's possible you let yourself dwell on it until it got all out of proportion. Let's face it," he said, in a tone that was friendly-conspiratorial, "tomorrow's an important day for all of us, but for you more than most. It wouldn't be surprising if you felt a bit of pressure."

Doubtless he meant well, too, but it seemed to me that in his last remark there was a hint that I was out of my depth; that being assistant to a cowboy governor was the limit of my abilities. It was small thanks for what I'd tried to do—when convincing them would have meant the end of my career. I'd done as much as I could do. They, in return, had made me feel small and stupid.

I went back to the Executive Office Building. The Vice President was still sound asleep. Then I went home and spent a restless, almost sleepless night.

The lack of sleep made me feel groggy in the morning, and my mind kept going back to the conversation at Farb's. I tried to keep busy, even to the point of meddling in details that were the responsibility of other people. I felt tired and irritable, and I didn't care who knew it. I realized that to some of the others it probably seemed my sudden elevation had gone to my head. But it no longer seemed to matter. In my current don't-give-a-damn mood nothing did.

I managed to avoid the Vice President for most of the morning, and when I did see him, I was tempted to tell him I was quitting and spell out the reasons why. But I didn't. I merely went over his speech with him, complete with suicide clause, and after that I had to watch the swearing in, if only out of curiosity. Standing there on the South Lawn on that gray fall day watching him take the oath, a single thought insinuated itself into my mind as he droned:

"I do solemnly swear [better me than him] that I will faithfully execute the office of President of the United States [me than him] and will to the best of my ability preserve, protect and defend [me, not him] the Constitution of the United States." (Me.)

Chapter Four

By getting out of the cab on Euclid, I could walk slowly down toward W and try to get the full benefit of the thirteen waterfalls and pools. I wanted to let the Florentine charm of falling water and grassy slopes within a formal design relax me. The day was perfect for it, one of those days that confound the forecasters and come like a bonus to the human race. But I had only a stolen half hour of it to spend in Meridian Hill Park, and I needed to make the most of the chance.

I began by acknowledging to myself that the idea was outrageous. It wasn't even a genuine idea, merely one of those wild notions that occur to everybody at some time or other, like rape, or murder, or suicide. Yet these past few days I hadn't been able to shake it. If anything, the more I tried to escape, the more it clung to me, like one of those straw finger grippers that holds on only tighter when you try to pull it off.

So I forced myself to consider the prospects as coolly as possible. Let's say that I had the will, the determination, to see this thing through, where were the means to bring it to fruition? As yet, I couldn't see any.

It was also obvious to me that if somebody else tried to interfere with the continuity of Presidential government, I would have done anything I could to stop them. Yet I simply couldn't feel hypocritical about attempting it myself. There was something in the air these days, something like the taste of defeat and pointlessness, that made it seem somehow inevitable. If it weren't me, it would be somebody else. If it weren't now, it wouldn't be long. So I couldn't feel guilty, not as I would have done before—although I wouldn't have even considered it before.

As I stared at the water rushing up from one of the fountains I thought, *You've come a long, long way*. It was a feeling that came to me frequently, and secretly, when I was younger, with each step up the ladder of conventional success. I suppose anybody who thinks he's getting ahead is seduced by that particular thought at some time. But there was an odd twist to it now. Trying to seize the government certainly was a novel way to finish up a career. Any career.

I thought of the mediocre bedroom suburb where I had grown up—less a place than a convenience. Men went there only to sleep, to play with their kids, to fix the porch, to cut the grass, to fight with their wives. All the important things they did twenty miles away. It was a place with no past—no history—and even less future. I called it Ground Zero, to the mixed bafflement and anger of my parents, who took it as a personal rebuke, an accusation of failure. Anyway, I got out as soon as I could, a year short of my high school diploma.

My wife used to joke that where once upon a time a young man who couldn't find his niche in life would run away to sea, nowadays he'd go into public relations. Yet in the years between once upon a time and nowadays there was the Army, and I both hated it and needed it. I needed it to provide me with the security of food and shelter while I learned about the stupidities of grown-up existence. I learned enough of brutality and violence not to fall into the mistake of romanticizing them. I acquired a schooling in the ways of large organizations. But above all, it gave me time—time to read and time to think. What the Army needed me for I never did figure out. Vietnam was looming on the horizon just as my three years came to an end, and I checked out. I was glad to be able to leave the Army while it still had its self-respect.

During the next few years I parked cars, tended bar, played the gigolo, gave dancing lessons, sold things and generally hustled my way across two continents. Most of the time I was neither happy nor sad. I just kept moving. But it came to an end on a beach in the Azores. I'd teamed up with a girl whose absorbing interest turned out to be not me but herself. After listening to more than a hundred hours of her do-it-yourself psycoanalysis, *I* started to have nightmares. For some reason, each night every bum, hobo, down-and-out drifter, hustler, failure, huckster and phony I'd ever met or seen paraded through my dreamworld. Every morning I woke up more scared than I'd been the day before. I got out before I started psychoanalyzing myself.

Two weeks later I took an entrance examination to get into junior college in California. My scores convinced them to overlook the matter of the high school diploma. Five years after that I was in my second year at Harvard Law School. That summer I got a job with Frank Specci. After becoming absolutely convinced I would never be any good working for or with somebody else, Specci came as a revelation. Working for him was more exciting, more demanding and more satisfying than anything I'd ever done before. For someone with a temperament like mine, it was ideal. Frank gave you problems that were supposed to be a shade too tough for you. If you failed, he'd politely say goodbye, but if you somehow succeeded, there were no limits to his praise and encouragement.

But he wouldn't take me on full time until I had more experience. So I clerked for a district judge for a year, then I joined Specci's Lawyers' Circuit and learned to smile graciously at the predictable half-witted pun on the name. For three years I followed his lead, working myself into bone-weary exhaustion fighting loan companies, ward heelers, crooked and brutal cops, petty hoods and all the other scummy predators who batten on the weak and ignorant. They were the happiest three years of my life. Whatever Frank Specci asked me to do, I did. Whatever he told me, I believed. Whatever questions he asked, I answered.

After an experience like that it was impossible to settle down to a routine law practice. But I couldn't go on being the boy crusader forever. That was when I got interested in politics. I found a bright, ambitious history professor and got him into the State Assembly. It was more interesting than writing briefs, and we were both doing nicely until he decided he wanted to skip a step and go straight from there into the U.S. Senate. I almost won it for him, but he had to spoil it by getting drawn into a losing debate over religion, of all things. After that, he had nowhere to go but home, back to Santa Monica.

It was about then, just as I was halfheartedly looking for a nice political law practice, that the Congressman (as he then was) called me. We'd met each other only in passing, and I didn't think he amounted to much, but he liked the campaign I'd just run. Would I like to work for him if he ran for the governorship? I told him I'd think about it, but I didn't give it much time though till it became obvious the people of California were going to be faced with a choice between an honest mediocrity and a crooked one. I called the honest one up and said yes.

But having learned from my last experience, I insisted on running a tight operation. He agreed to that, and he stuck to it. On my side, I know how to run a statewide campaign; on his, he was photogenic. He never said anything controversial, and he was so damned friendly that hardly anybody cared. He won in a landslide. I intended to see him through one—just one—four-year term, then find another job.

Two years later he was asked onto the national ticket. From the moment I heard the invitation was coming his way, I knew right down to my toes that he wasn't cut out for it. And if the top of the ticket had been anybody else, I would have signed off right then and there. But instead of having to choose between two men, one of whom was barely acceptable, it was four men, only one of whom was a serious Presidential possibility. I reasoned that since he was a man I would have voted for twice, I could at least do him some good by keeping his Vice Presidential nominee under control. And until a year or two before this afternoon in Meridian Hill Park, I believed I'd made the right decision—right for the President, right for the Vice President and right for myself.

But the longer the two of us moped around the Executive Office Building staring at the walls, the less I *could* manage him. When the President first said he wanted an activist Vice President, I think he meant it. Then he took a closer look at the package under the flossy wrapping and began to have second thoughts. The Vice President, nothing deterred, turned himself into an activist, and there was nothing the President or I could do to discourage him. Meanwhile, any chance I might have had of switching over to the White House during the second term went straight down the pipe. And now *he* was in the White House, after all. Incredible!

So if I resolved to try to ease him out of there on my own initiative, how was I going to do it? One thing at least was certain: There was absolutely no one I could turn to for help. I thought of the other members of the staff, and though I'd okayed them all myself, there wasn't one to whom I could confide something like this. It would scare the hell out of them. I've also made a point of never forgetting Huey's Rule: In politics if you tell somebody a secret, then three people will know it—you, the person you told it to and the one other person he just happens to know who can be trusted. In short, if you can't control the third man, you can't control the secret.

That meant no allies. There was also the not inconsiderable fact that I was virtually anonymous. Anonymous, that is, as far as the majority of people were concerned. Not one person in a hundred knew my name. Back then, I doubt that one in ten thousand recognized my face. True, it was familiar to a lot of people in the party, like county chairmen and national committee people. I also had quite a few friends among the press. If there was anybody worth knowing in California politics, I knew him to some degree. But to all these people I was merely an instrument. I could be used (or they could *try* to use me) when there was a favor needed. The favors were often squalid or petty or simply stupid, but there was always something going on that was important and required my attention. Yet there was never any doubt that I had no political base of my own and no independent ambitions. I worked almost entirely behind the scenes. In my wife's phrase, I was Mr. Fix-it. And that was all I ever wanted to be. Before.

Supposing you succeeded, I asked myself, *could you make it stick?* That brought me back to the Army. Of the four services it was the only one that seemed relevant. It could make or break any effort to overthrow the Constitution. At the moment, the latter looked a lot more likely than the former. But the Army these days was like everything else, in a state of flux. Most of the time it looked like a force made up wholly of embittered generals at the top and sullen, half-trained volunteers from the ghettos at the bottom. Nobody I knew of seriously expected the Army to defend anything. Maybe a war in the Gulf would have made it shape up. But its principal value at the moment seemed to be in dying as noisily as possible so the rest of us would know that a war had begun. And like all armies that have ceased to be capable of large-scale combat against a genuine foe, it had turned in on itself. In time there was the chance of its becoming unreliable and starting to intervene openly in politics. That wasn't much use to me yet, I realized, but those were the facts—important ones and worth keeping in mind.

Overall, my prospects were sufficiently daunting that common sense alone dictated I should do as my wife had been urging—either resign or devote myself to the job I was supposed to do. But I still couldn't suppress a powerful feeling that I had to make the attempt—that it was somehow *right*—that the time was right. And if that last judgment was correct, then even if I could not yet see a way to succeed, the opportunity must be there somewhere.

For someone without mystical or religious inclinations it was unsettling to feel as I did now, that some force outside myself was steeling me to an act that only one other person had even attempted, and that in the very early days of the Republic. If I failed, my name and memory would be cursed for generations. Yet the very contemplation of so enormous an undertaking seemed to carry a reassurance of its own. As if in the daring was the seed of success.

This was no plan. It was not even an idea around which a plan might be developed. All I had was a resolve to seek out the opportunity and follow it through. Yet if my intuition was right, surely that opportunity would present itself. And I should be able to recognize it when it came. With an insider's position I was at least already in the arena.

I laughed under my breath. Here I was making out a résumé of sorts: age, neither young nor old; honors degrees from Berkeley and Harvard; elegant, intelligent wife; no surviving children; ten years experience in politics; a little law practice, mainly litigation; member Phi Beta Kappa and the Union Club in San Francisco; likes classical music, twelve bar blues, sports cars and paintings; works hard; moderate drinker, nonsmoker. References available. Sincere replies only. I was in an optimistic mood by the time I reached W.

I hailed a cab and realized, as I sat back in the seat, that the walking and thinking had relaxed me. It was clear now that it was me or it was chaos. Van Riebouw was not a reasonable alternative to our current incumbent. The Senator was terrified of the responsibility. There was altogether too much about him that reminded me of Tom Marshall, Wilson's Vice President—so frightened of being thrust into the White House over a sick man's body that he left town the day after Wilson had his stroke. Power fell by default into Edith Wilson's hands.

Once again executive power was slipping around from hand to hand, ready for the grabbing. I was confident I could use it as fairly and effectively as anyone, if not more so. That entitled me, in the current climate, to seize it if I could. My main worry was that I might not be able to get a strong enough grip on it before the whole country was thrown into the unholy fight that would erupt once the President's true condition became public knowledge. At most, I assumed, it was a matter of weeks.

Chapter Five

"Do you want to be on this commission to investigate the . . . you know?" he asked. It was the second day after the swearing in.

The commission was something we had to go through with. If he hadn't recovered so quickly, Congress would have set up an investigation of its own. The press was already insisting it was overdue. But what were they going to find that the FBI hadn't already uncovered? I assumed he was aking me if I was interested chiefly to be polite.

"Not particularly," I replied.

"Sh-it," he said, thickly slurring the first syllable. "Nobody wants to be on the goddamned thing. But we've got to set it up. It's been in abeyance too long as it is. Well, I thought you might be interested."

I shook my head.

"Anyway"—he tried to smile—"I need you more here."

"Fine," I said.

It was hard to see why anybody would want to be on a commission to investigate the assassination, not after what the last one had had to put up with. Nobody came out of that experience with any cause to be grateful, least of all the commission members.

"The Chief Justice already called me. Said he wasn't going

to be another Warren.'' He saw the expression on my face and before I could speak brought up his hand. ''I know. I know.''

Then he picked up a typewritten list of names, set fluttering gently by his trembling hand. ''What do you think of these?''

I looked over the list. There were about ten names, all fairly well known, almost evenly divided between Congress, Wall Street and the academic community. Standard stuff for a Presidential commission on anything. We talked for a few minutes about some of the most likely possibilities, and I asked him, ''Don't you think you ought to have somebody from the Court, even if you can't get the Chief Justice?''

He must have known, but he asked nonetheless. ''Who do you have in mind?''

''I think Frank Specci would be a good choice. I'm pretty sure he'd accept, if you asked him.''

He looked at me for a moment. ''Specci,'' he snorted, tripping heavily on the double *c*.

''If you do have a Justice or some other leading federal judge, I don't honestly think you're going to be able to find anyone better.''

''Specci,'' he repeated. But he thought for a moment. ''I know he's a friend of yours,'' he said, sounding apologetic, ''but I don't like him all that much. He thinks he knows it all.''

It was a hopelessly wrong judgment; but he'd picked up that idea somehow, and I wasn't going to be able to change it.

''Maybe so,'' I said. ''But that's not relevant in this case, is it, Mr. President? The only thing that matters is that we get this commission going, get it to write its report and make it look good. You said yourself that nobody would think you were doing him a favor.''

In the light of later events, I ought to point out that at this time I was merely doing my job. I was trying to form a commission that would look impressive and act conscientiously. At the time that was my only interest in it.

By the end of the week we had almost the whole commission set down on paper. Specci, with the Chief Justice's blessing, agreed to serve, So did Carter, the Senate Minority Leader, although he didn't seem at all happy about it. Someone, I don't recall who, suggested the former all-American flanker and current president of Stanford, Eberle Dalgleish, and the President liked the idea if only because of the California connection. But the pick of the bunch had to be Malcolm Hutchison, the relentlessly courteous President of the Rockefeller Foundation.

Hutchison was the most distinguished man we could find who wasn't already involved in government; even then, he wasn't all that far outside. Some of his poetry still holds up. But he was better known for having been a professor of Oriental languages at Yale, onetime ambassador to Peking and a good friend of the late President. Like him, Hutchison was a self-made millionaire who, for all his aristocratic tastes, never lost the common touch. Tough, unsentimental and shrewd, he was the kind of person who is invariably made chairman—if he's available.

Going over these four names and the names of the various lawyers and investigators backing them up, we agreed that it was better than either of us had first expected.

"I think we've touched all the right bases," he said. "The academic community, Congress, business and the courts. There's only one thing missing to make this a balanced team. Somebody from our end of things."

"I think this is all right," I said. "I mean, it's the Attorney General and his staff who'll be doing most of the dog work anyway."

"No. I want somebody else, even if you have to drag 'im in off the street. Four isn't enough. I want five."

I shrugged. "I'll try to come up with some more names."

He wheeled himself over to his desk and picked up what looked like a pamphlet and held it out.

"Now what about this?"

I could tell only that it was already open and half a page was ringed in red.

"About what?"

"This"—he shook it—"is the Twenty-fifth Amendment. You must have read it."

Oh, yes, I had read the Twenty-fifth Amendment. These past few weeks I must have read it a dozen times. I knew the history behind it, and I'd almost committed to memory every Presidential disability agreement on record—the very things it was supposed to replace.

"Sure. I've read it."

"Well, we've got to do something about it. Here, look at this." He rummaged around on the desk top for a moment.

"This is a copy of an editorial in yesterday's New York *Times*. Read that."

There was no need; I'd read it the day before. Given the uncertain state of the President's health, it said, he ought to—as soon as his strength permitted—waste no time implementing Section Two.

"And do you know that last night and this morning other people have told me the same thing. That Congressional committee that came to interview me, some of them mentioned it too. Now, I think we ought to have got together on this before . . . ."

My eyes were scanning Section Two: "Whenever there is a vacancy in the office of the Vice President, the President shall nominate a Vice President who shall take office upon confirmation by a majority vote in both Houses of Congress."

I wasn't really reading, nor was I listening. Instead, I was turning over possibilities. This matter of Section Two had bothered me ever since the swearing in. It would obviously be much harder for me if there was a bona fide Vice President in office. And while I still had no specific plan, I knew with the overwhelming certainty of instinctive knowledge that I must somehow keep that vacancy vacant. That was why I had deliberately not raised the question, but here it was, and it had to be dealt with.

". . . so, all in all, I'd say there's only one logical choice."

"Van Riebouw?"

He nodded. "Van Riebouw. Can't say I've ever cared for him, but after the way he took over when . . . when it all happened. . . ." His voice faltered for a moment. "Anyway, I think he's the one."

There was an inevitability to Van Riebouw that I didn't want to argue against unless I had to. And if I started out against him, I would only have to end up by supporting somebody else.

I wasn't going to do that for anybody.

"An excellent idea," I said. "He may not be your only choice, but I certainly think he's your best."

There was a pleased look lurking within the folds of the collapsed tissues of his face. It was no good trying to turn him against Van Riebouw. But it occurred to me that maybe I could turn Van Riebouw against the appointment.

"Would you like me to sound him out for you. He seems pretty happy in the Senate. You never know, he might not want to leave it."

He waved his hand genially. "You see him, then. You talk to him," he whispered hoarsely. "Then you send him over to see me."

Van Riebouw sat in his office like a god on a throne. From his lofty perch he apologized smoothly because I'd had to come to him.

"That's all right, Senator. I'm always glad to get away for a few minutes. It's a different world up there. Things seem more real, in a way, the minute you step out of the White House."

"Yes," he said thoughtfully. "I know what you mean. Still, it looks like we're getting back on an even keel. How's the President?"

"Better." I smiled. "Getting stronger every day."

"That's good . . . that's good."

"But he'll never really be himself again." It was a chance, but I had to take it, count on Van Riebouw's innate cowardice, trust he'd never repeat what I'd said straight to the President's face. He looked at me sharply over his glasses.

"No," he said in a flat voice. I couldn't tell if it was a question or an agreement.

"At least, that's what some of the doctors seem to think. Not being a medical man myself—"

He interrupted me. "It's just one of those things we'll have to learn to live with."

I breathed a silent sigh of relief. "And there's always the chance of a relapse. Or so I understand," I said.

He nodded his head gloomily and pursed his lips—the very

picture of the wise, elder statesman bravely acknowledging life's harsh realities.

"But that's not why I'm here taking up your valuable time, Senator. Although"—and I paused a moment—"it has a direct bearing on that." He was looking me straight in the eyes now. *He knows what's coming,* I thought. And that's why he insisted on my coming down here. It will be easier for him to say no here. I plunged.

"He wants you to be Vice President." I went deeper. "Because if anything happened to him—and we can't ignore the possibilities of some unforeseen complication or a relapse—then *you're* the man he wants to step in, take over again."

Already he was shaking his head slowly from side to side. "I'm afraid not. Not again."

"But, Senator," I protested, my spirits soaring while I tried to keep my voice sounding slightly puzzled, even a little shocked, "I don't understand. Why, if—God forbid—that phone were to start ringing and you picked it up to be told that he'd collapsed, you'd be Acting President again, anyway."

"That's true," he agreed grudgingly. "So far as it goes. But that's all going to be changed. We'll probably have a new disability statute before the Christmas recess. Let's just hope the President keeps on improving till then." He paused, then hastily added, "And after."

"But," I objected with inspired obtuseness, "there'd be no need for that if you took over the Vice Presidency."

"I honestly don't think there's much to be gained by it, for anybody. Oh, sure, I know what some people are saying. But you tell the President that in my humble opinion I can do more for him right where I am. I can fight for him in Congress. And it's not boasting to say that there's not many people who could get as much done for him down here as I can. Up there"—he waved toward the window—"I'd feel like some sort of ghoul—just hanging around waiting for something to happen to him. That's no good."

"Well, Senator, it's not my place to come down here and

presume to lecture you. I hope you understand that I'm here because I thought we ought to talk about it."

His whole body bobbed benignly. He understood perfectly, and I must understand his viewpoint, too. Would I give his warmest wishes to the President, and was there anything else?

"It's only my own curiosity, Senator, but could you tell me what sort of new disability statute you want to propose?"

"Let me ask you a question first. Who's the real number two in the executive branch? The Secretary of State. And after the Vice President he's really the most logical person to be standing at the head of the line. That's the way the disability laws used to be. I think we ought to get back to that. Let's face it. State's the number one appointment any President makes. The Secretary is also, let us not forget, the man who other governments—friendly or not—know best after the President. But he'll need Congress. So I think he ought to be linked up with the Majority Leader and the Speaker of the House in a kind of interim committee, with him as chairman, until the next election."

"And that's the kind of arrangement you think we're going to have?"

"That's for Congress and the President to decide. It's certainly what I'd like to see. That's why I'm so glad you came down here today. I mean, obviously I wasn't going to push something like this without talking to the President first. But you know how it is. Nobody wants to be overloading him with work before he gets his strength back."

I looked him over—the sleek gray hair, the pink moon face, the steely spectacles, the pale blue eyes—and I thought, *You spineless bastard.* I assumed my face was a mask, but there was evidently something there that made him first shift uneasily in his chair, then rise to his feet awkwardly, fumbling for words.

"But if there's anything else I can do, like that committee. . . ."

I found myself on my feet. "The commission?"

"Yes," he said. "Investigating the assassination. The President said he was having trouble getting people." He smoothed his hair down impressively. "Of course, I'm pretty busy, as

I told him, especially with the recess coming up. But you tell him that if he still thinks I might be able to help out there, I'll do my best. My very best,'' he emphasized.

I couldn't see much use in having him on the investigating commission. Almost all the actual work would be done by the commission staff and counsel anyway. On the other hand, he might add a bit more luster, and the President wanted five members.

''I'll tell him when I get back, Senator.''

''And there's another thing.''

''Yes?''

''I think you ought to give some thought to having it televised.''

I remember staring at him, wondering: *Doesn't this old fool have anything better to think about?* For an instant I thought I saw something, but before I could grasp it, my mouth moved mechanically and I heard my voice say, ''Televised?''

''Yes, son, televised. So it's all out in the open. So anybody who wants to see *can* see. Everything open and aboveboard. Let the whole world watch it this time. I think the Warren Commission was right. Oswald did it, and he did it on his own. But that commission made one big mistake. I've always believed they got off on the wrong foot right at the start. They didn't make it public. Don't you see? If it involved national security, okay. But it didn't. It was a murder, involving some miserable psychopath. And ten to one that's exactly what's involved here, all over again. Now, if this was just a private sort of murder, you'd at least be able to go down to the courtroom and see justice being done. Remember Blackstone—justice must not only be done, it must be seen et cetera? This time, I say let's do it in public.''

So this was to be his contribution to the investigation. Televised hearings. After the Ervin Committee experience there didn't seem much chance of that. And with Hutchison as chairman there was no chance at all. I shuffled my feet unobtrusively in Van Riebouw's thick pile carpet. Televised hearings indeed.

''A wonderful idea,'' I said, with a fervor that stopped Van Riebouw in his tracks.

"Well"—he smiled modestly—"I'm glad you think so."

"Oh, I think it's excellent," I said, and warmly shook his hand.

In the corridor outside his office I stopped for a moment at the water fountain while I collected my thoughts. If I could build Van Riebouw up in his attachment to the idea of televised hearings, get him to press noisily for it, he'd at least make a nuisance of himself, possibly even a fool. I had nothing to lose by encouraging him in a losing cause.

I went straight back to the White House, went over the afternoon appointments with the appointments secretary, cut ten minutes from somebody who'd been promised almost half an hour and told the secretary to hustle him out of there as soon as his time was up. Meantime, I was rehearsing my version of what Van Riebouw had said and wrote a memo for the record. Then I went over the rest of what I wanted to say to him, trying to imagine his responses and practicing my replies. At four I went in. I had ten minutes to make my pitch.

"Well, what did he say?"

"I'm afraid he won't do it."

He was surprised and a little put out. Like most people, he thought Van Riebouw was the Rock of Gibraltar.

"Are you sure he understood? He knew what you were there for?"

"Oh, he understood all right," I said with a hint of bitterness. "He just likes things better the way they are, that's all."

I could sense the confusion welling up in his mind. "And why not?" I went on. "He wouldn't say so, of course, not straight out. But it's obvious: He's having his cake and eating it too."

"Van Riebouw?" he said, bewildered.

"Yes," I said firmly, as if that were the end of the subject, and started to talk about something else. He cut me off.

"What did he say? I don't understand."

I could feel my heart pounding. "I don't want you to upset yourself," I said, betting that it was precisely like telling someone not to worry.

"What did he say?" He was getting waspish now.

"What he said wasn't quite so important as what he *didn't* say. But what it comes down to is that he's happy where he is, and if anything happens to you—say, you have a relapse or go into a coma or develop some serious complication—he's going to be Acting President anyway. He didn't go into details, of course, but that was the general idea. So he didn't see any point in doing anything about it. But he's thinking of working for a new disability statute so that the Secretary of State comes after the Vice President. Oh, and he's more used to you where he is. If you want my opinion, I think he just doesn't want to be Vice President. He's one of those people who consider it beneath them. Oh, he didn't say so, but he obviously thinks it's strictly for bench warmers."

Now the color was rising in his face. I had put as much sting as I could into my last remark. One of his cheeks began to twitch in an ugly way. He was trembling like a man with a bad chill.

"So what does that make me, eh?" he snarled. *Steady,* I thought. *The last thing I need is for him to pick up the telephone.*

"He didn't *say* that. But you know how it is—if somebody thinks something strongly enough you can pick it up pretty fast. But as long as they keep their mouths shut, they figure they're covered. I mean, you could call him up right now and ask him if that's what he said and he'd say no. And he'd be telling the truth. But I'd bet my life that that was what the son of a bitch was thinking."

"Backstabbing bastard," he mumbled angrily.

"Anyway, we'll keep working on the Vice Presidency angle. We'll come up with something."

"Anything else?"

"Well, I have a couple of ideas about the investigating commission. I think it ought to have televised hearings."

At first he wasn't enthusiastic. But I was ready for almost all his objections, using Van Riebouw's arguments to flesh out my own.

And suddenly he said, "I don't care about that. I want you

on the commission. You can take that up with them. But I want you on the commission, you hear?''

Fortunately I was sitting down at the time. There was a buzzing in my ears. I stared hard at the flags on either side of the window leading out to the Rose Garden.

''You hear?'' he repeated.

He wasn't asking, I realized. He was telling me. But why? It was a struggle, but I managed, despite the change in my breathing and the blood pounding through my head, to ask in a calm voice, ''Are you trying to get rid of me?''

''No,'' he said, and I thought he was embarrassed. ''It's not that. It's like I said, there ought to be somebody from our end of things.''

I started shuffling through the papers in my folder. ''Is that all?''

''Goddammit, yes, that's all!''

''And there's nobody else you can think of who'd do as well?''

''I can rely on you,'' he said. I could tell it was supposed to be reassuring, but it had exactly the opposite effect.

''If you insist, I'll do it, of course,'' I said. ''But who'll take over here?''

The pallid, gray-tinged flesh took on a decidedly pink hue. ''You'll still be in charge,'' he said huskily.

''Look, Mr. President, if I go on the commission, it means I won't be around here for long stretches of time. I can't run the staff on a part-time basis, and I can't run anything if nobody knows where they stand.''

He reddened some more and started to tremble. For a moment I was sure he was going to have another seizure. Half of me wanted to walk right out of there. But the other half was rooted to the spot. He tried to reach over and pat me on the arm but succeeded only in creating a mess on the top of the desk. This failure made him look, and probably feel, even more wretched.

''No need to take on so,'' he said soothingly. ''The subject came up, and we naturally thought of you, and. . . .''

''We?''

''Yes,'' he said stubbornly. Evidently he wasn't supposed to tell me whose brilliant idea this was.

"And you're absolutely certain this is the best thing for both of us?"

"As much as anybody can be," he said, with a definite lack of conviction.

We chatted briefly, and superficially, about the commission. But all the time my mind was racing. It was obvious that some sort of compromise about me had been reached. Somebody was trying to get me out of the White House. But he didn't want to give me up; at least, not all at once. Anybody else would have seen that it wasn't a genuine compromise he was buying. It was the kiss of death. Such an arrangement could have but one result—undermining my position. No doubt it was sold to him as a temporary arrangement, but the consequences were meant to be permanent. The commission wouldn't require much work, but it would demand a lot of my time.

How had they been able to sell him on this proposition? I racked my brains, but I couldn't come up with the answer. Why were they doing this? Another blank. Most important, who was behind it? Three in a row.

It was a strange day. I had checked Van Riebouw. But somebody else had checked me.

Chapter Six

Gloomily I studied the room's rich paneling, the high ceiling and the tall pillars. No doubt we were here in the old Senate Chamber, where the Supreme Court met until 1935, because the associations evoked by the other possibility—the hearing room in the old Senate Office Building—were too recent and too strong. It reawakened the McCarthy Committee in the minds of older people and the Ervin Committee, and the Watergate-Nixon fiasco, in the minds of almost everybody. Anyway, this setting wasn't particularly unusual. Most people have seen pictures of it at some time if only because it's a place favored by ambitious Senators who want a distinguished setting in which to announce their availability for bigger things. It was stately; it stirred no painful memories; it was convenient. Just the place for the Hutchison Commission.

"Does the most junior, but the most learned, member of this historic body approve?" asked a voice in my ear, chuckling good-naturedly. It was Specci.

"I approve." I laughed.

"Everywhere you go you bring out your mental tape measure."

"Okay, okay," I said and changed the subject. "This must all be pretty *déjà vu* to you anyway." He shrugged and smiled amiably. "But it's something else for me. I must have worked on a dozen committees and commissions of one sort or another. But this is the first one I've ever been on where I was up front. Even in high school and college I was always the guy behind the scenes."

Then I started to tell him about a high school in Texas where in the early sixties a group of sociologists had put the students in charge of almost everything, from arranging the menus in the cafeteria to scheduling classes. Everything worked smoothly, astonishingly so.

"The sociologists, the teachers, the parents, all were dumbfounded. Here was a committee of kids managing a big operation like that without any real experience and making it run like clockwork. What a triumph for democracy! they said. Then everything started to fall apart. They couldn't figure it out until somebody realized that the mimeograph machine was acting up. As the machine went from bad to worse so did everything else. But that didn't make any sense. Obviously the machine didn't run the school.

"Well, even a sociologist can't miss the point forever. It was the two sixteen-year-old girls in charge of the machine who were running the school, not the democratically elected committee. The committee thought it was in charge; so did everybody else. But while it was trying to reach agreement among a dozen people, these two girls already had clear-cut policies in mind. They had a realistic idea of what needed to be done, and they quietly went about doing it. They controlled it through the endless paper work. They modified policy by telling the committee what was physically possible within the existing administrative resources, and they made good use of their control over the dissemination of data.

"And they were running it all brilliantly until one of the machines went haywire. Then they started arguing betweem themselves about whose fault it was. They also had to spend too much time just attending to the mimeograph machine. So their control started slipping away. And once it did, all the latent antagonisms on the committee came into the open. As the administrative structure collapsed, the committee was torn apart by bickering."

"This really happened?" asked Specci.

"It really happened," I replied.

"That's an interesting story. And I get the point, but. . . ." His eyes twinkled, making him look like a friendly, ugly dwarf.

"But?"

"I still think it's about time *you* tried carrying the can for a change."

Then he excused himself. I looked around and saw Dalgleish and Carter chatting easily together, recalling mutual friends while they tried to size each other up. The Assistant Attorney General, Roderick Harrod, was sitting at a table going through his briefcase like a man who'd lost a hundred-dollar bill. I watched him out of the corner of my eye while I went over to the other two and briefly exchanged pleasantries with them. Harrod eventually found what he was looking for, appeared relieved, then awoke abruptly to the fact that he was failing in the social niceties. To help him out, I said, "Excuse me, please," to Dalgleish and Carter, and went over to talk to him.

"Well, how are you?" he said, pumping my hand.

"I'm fine, Rod. How long do you think this is going to take?"

He curved his mouth in an upside-down U shape, making him look faintly, and foolishly, pugnacious. Foolish considering the skinny frame, the thin—and thinning—blond hair and the Coke-bottle glasses.

"You can't be sure about something like this," he said. "But seeing that it all happened right on our doorstep, as it were, which cuts down the traveling, I'd say maybe a month for the hearings as such. Allow another five or six weeks for hammering out a report—assuming everybody does what he's supposed to and doesn't let his contribution sit in a desk drawer—and I'd say two to three months."

Three seemed more likely than two. And on any committee, three usually means four. That meant four months of being tied up with this business. Even if it meant only two months of real work for me, those two months could be crucial. By the end of the year I might find myself still in the White House but a long way from the Oval Office.

"By the way," he was saying, "how'd you ever get onto this thing?"

"Why, is there a door prize?"

"You know what I mean," he said. "This isn't exactly your kind of operation."

As nonchalantly as I could, I said, "The President wanted me here. So here I am."

Harrod looked at me, obviously unconvinced. "Well, you're certainly the dark horse on this commission." He tried to chuckle as he said it. I smiled. Both of us felt awkward for a moment, looking for something else to say or some way to break off, when the tension was scattered by the arrival of Hutchison.

As he came in, that sharply etched nose off a Roman coin cutting the air, we all, I thought, responded like boy scouts at the arrival of the pack leader. We fell as if trained to it into postures of unshakable admiration and warmhearted respect. Hutchison shook each hand with an easy smile and a sure firmness in his grip. "How are you? So glad to meet you. Looking forward to working with you. Glad to see you again. Now, what's the first item on our agenda?" At which we all sat down and quietly waited to follow his lead.

"Well," he exhaled. He looked to the two on his left, then to we two on his right, then over to Harrod and his team of assistants. He was all business now.

"Maybe I ought to say that I consider it a privilege to be here. None of us, I know, sought to be on this commission. Would that the need for it didn't exist. But the President and the country are looking to us for some answers. I don't doubt that we'll provide them as honestly and as fully as we know how. And if we can't we'll say so." *Here was a man,* I marveled, *who could make you think you'd never heard a cliché before.*

"I think the model we should keep in mind, if we're going to have a model, is the Truman Committee during the war." *That's interesting,* I thought.

"Now, there may not seem too direct a parallel there. I realize that. This isn't wartime, and we're not looking into government spending or the practices of big business. But we ought to try to emulate the way the Truman Committee did its work: It was a model of fairness, thoroughness and good sense. I know Harry Truman set them on the right path at the start. 'I want no smears,' he said, 'and no whitewashes.' I don't think we could do better than to take that for our own watchword as we go about the business of discharging our grave responsibilities." *God,* I groaned to myself, *what a grotesque and awful unintended pun.*

Having told us what we should do, Hutchison was now telling us what we shouldn't be, and I had a feeling that I knew what that was.

"None of us, however, can fail to be conscious of the shadow we're under, the shadow of the Watergate hearings. I don't want to rake over any old grievances. But we shall get this matter out in the open and settled in our own minds right away. Even if other people are confused about how we link up with those hearings, *we* need to be clear about it ourselves.

"We are, in the first place, a body created by the President. For that reason we are not, and will not become, antagonistic to the executive branch." He turned first one way, to smile at Harrod, then the other, to smile at me. "As I am sure these gentlemen will agree." We both self-consciously smiled back.

"In the second place, we are inquiring into a matter which is not, and cannot become, partisan. We might find ourselves with personal disagreements, but I do not doubt for an instant that either of our two great parties would be acutely embarrassed by the least effort to bring such a spirit to this inquiry.

"Third, if there is any personal advantage to be gained by service on this body," he said dryly, "I fail to see it." He deadpanned: "As, no doubt, do you."

"Finally, this is not an open-ended inquiry. Our brief is very precise: to investigate an isolated and specific event. If we find ourselves getting into matters beyond our explicit purview, I shall not hesitate to ask the President to do one of two things: Either rewrite the terms on which this commission is established or form a new commission."

Hutchison then went into a brief excursus on what he understood the structure of the commission to be. He couldn't resist saying that like Gaul, it was in three parts—the five commission members, a clerical staff and the legal staff. For this latter, and for all the assistance provided by the Justice Department, he was grateful, and he inclined his head graciously toward Harrod. "Now, Mr. Harrod, how can we best pool our efforts?"

Harrod made a few comments on how he saw his role. He—meaning himself and his assistants—would deal chiefly with legal and forensic questions. They would find witnesses, present evidence, seek out expert opinions on forensic matters, do legal research wherever necessary and carry out whatever field investigations or interrogations the commission delegated to them. He saw himself, he concluded, not as an independent operator free-lancing out of the Justice Department, but simply as head of the commission's legal staff. And he felt privileged to serve it.

After that the principal members of the clerical staff were introduced, and we soon found ourselves milling around, shaking hands, feeling that we were about to embark on some kind of team sport. An outsider just stepping into that room would never have guessed from appearances what serious business we were supposed to be about.

Then abruptly the chief thread to this net of good feeling was taken up and snapped by Hutchison, who said, "I think we can be sworn in now."

On cue, the Chief Justice entered to administer the oath to the commission members. From another door came photographers and journalists. We all solemnly swore in a galaxy of exploding stroboscopic stars. Hutchison made a brief statement, answered a few questions, then asked if we might be permitted to get on with our first formal session.

As soon as we were in our places, he began.

"What about procedure?"

For more than an hour we went into subpoenas, rules of evidence, right to counsel, depositions, the Fifth Amendment, and I waited and waited for someone to raise the question: public or private? Every time I was asked about procedure I went whichever way I thought the majority listed. But still no one asked. Surely they knew such a question existed.

I realized then that the other three were all waiting for Hutchison to bring it up. And if he didn't, then it would be settled. All taken care of without anyone's saying a word. Later on, if we were asked why we hadn't held public hearings, we could all honestly say, "Nobody ever mentioned that," and students of this commission could then wonder why not.

"Now, what else should we take up today?" He looked left, then right. *He knows exactly what he wants to take up next,* I thought, *but here's where courtesy pays,* because Carter used the pause to ask, "Mr. Chairman, I wonder if we might take up something that involves procedure, but not legal procedure, strictly speaking?"

Hutchison looked at Carter genially, but I had the sense there was a frown lurking there somewhere.

"Yes, of course you may. We're all feeling our way here."

"I'd like to suggest that we at least consider whether or not our hearings should be open or *in camera.* And if open, how much so."

Sagely, Hutchison tugged the tanned, lined flesh of his neck with thumb and forefinger. "Well, I've been assuming we'd probably have to have some executive sessions, if only because they touch on either security matters or methods of ensuring the President's safety. But I'd have no objections myself to having this chamber opened to the press and, say, a hundred members of the public." Then he looked over at Carter, as if Carter owned Congress, and added, "And any members of the Congress who want to stop by should be welcome to do so, of course."

From the faces of Hutchison, Dalgleish and Specci it looked as if the three of them were, in varying degrees, of the same mind. But Carter wouldn't desist. He'd obviously been talking to Van Riebouw. He'd sounded me out, and I'd encouraged him, but without committing myself. From the way he was acting now, I assumed he hadn't sounded the others out at all. What I didn't understand though was why he was so keen on television. He couldn't just be trying to keep Van Riebouw happy.

"I had something a little more public in mind, sir," he said.

The frown was now out in plain view. "Yes?"

"Yes, Mr. Chairman." Carter swept his arm through a right angle. "This chamber has ample facilities already available for nationally televised hearings. Not of everything. But let's say, of at most, half a dozen sessions of two or three hours each."

"What," asked Specci scornfully from next to Hutchison's left arm, "you mean like the McCarthy hearings? Or Watergate?"

He has got himself into an uphill fight going against these two, I thought. I didn't envy him. Then it occurred to me that there could only be one reason why Carter was pressing so hard. He didn't want to be on this commission in the first place, but now he was here he was going to try to get something out of it. As long as he was putting in time here, he wanted everybody to know it. *But now,* I thought, *he was letting ambition get ahead of him.*

"Your point is well taken, Mr. Justice." He wanted it to sound a lot smoother than it came out. "But I'm not suggesting some kind of a quasi-judicial circus, like the Watergate hearings. Surely you don't seriously think that anybody here is going to indulge in a lot of cheap theatrics in front of the television camera?"

"No, I don't," Specci answered. "But that's not my point. My objection is that I think television's both inappropriate to our task here and, because of that, it can only be distracting."

"If I may, I'd like to explain. Because that is exactly my point. I think it is *very* appropriate." Carter simply wouldn't quit.

Hutchison leaned slightly toward him. Specci sat back in the pose of a man dug in and awaiting bombardment.

"The Justice mentioned two lots of hearings, McCarthy and Watergate," said Carter. "The first was a shameful business, as I'm sure we all agree, and we as a people should never forget it. There's still a lot of disagreement over the Watergate hearings because they almost crippled the country. But what I have in mind are the *other* hearings, some of them held in this very chamber. I'm thinking of the great *educative* hearings. Hearings such as the first one I ever remember—the Kefauver investigation of organized crime. I was a child then. But they've stayed with me, because they were an unforgettable education on the darker side of our society. They were a revelation of brutality and lying and corruption.

"Then there were the Senate Foreign Relations Committee hearings that Fulbright conducted on Vietnam. I was in college then. And they were the education in foreign policy the whole nation needed. They made a big difference, not just to me but to a whole generation of students.

"So I have two questions I'd like to ask. The first is this: Is there anyone on this commission who doesn't remember those hearings?"

"Of course we all remember them," said Specci.

"Then I would also like to ask, with all due respect, if there is anyone here who thinks that *those* hearings should not have been televised?"

There was complete silence for perhaps ten seconds. Hutchison looked somberly at the papers in front of him.

"I'm not sure I understand the point you're making," he said.

"My point is that I think this commission has a responsibility to educate. The question we are really faced with is how well we do it. There's no doubt that one way or another, whatever we do is going to be more or less visible. But I think we ought to maximize that visibility, not minimize it. I have no particular desire to be seen on television. I have no particular need to make my name a household word. But only through the widest dissemination of these hearings can we hope to carry out to the full the job we've been given."

"Surely our responsibility is to determine, so far as we can, the facts about the assassination. It isn't for us to shout them from the rooftops," said Specci patiently.

"I'd say that perhaps such a view is too narrow," said Dalgleish, and I realized then that Carter actually had done his homework. If he hadn't sold that cherubic professor on it, he'd at least got him to think about it. "My view," Dalgleish continued when he saw he wasn't going to be interrupted, "is that we have two functions here, not one."

He was every inch the model of the modern jet-set academic. With a practiced style that mixed pomposity, false modesty and learning, he treated us to a minilecture in elementary social analysis.

"We teach our students in their social science classes to look at all institutions and procedures—even personal behavior, if you like—in a critical way. It's a way professors, like myself, and lawyers too, if I may say so, often forget as we get older. These students are taught to try to separate what we call overt or manifest functions from covert or latent ones. As I see it here, we have a manifest responsibility to get to the bottom of the assassination. But we also have a latent function. And that is, in fine, to reassure a frightened, grief-stricken people that they still have an orderly, responsible government capable of dealing with a national tragedy in an orderly, responsible way."

I marveled once again at the ability of academics to wax lyrical over the ordinary responsibilities of power. They found a poetry in it that I had never seen.

"Would you agree with that?" With a start I realized that he was addressing me.

"Yes. Yes, of course," was all I could say.

"Most illuminating," said Hutchison.

"And I can say with absolute confidence," said Carter, plainly relieved the reinforcements had arrived, "that there are in this building right now any number of men"—*one,* I said to myself—"who believe that our *real* predecessors, the Warren Commission, that is, made their biggest single mistake—the mistake that robbed their report of the credibility it needed—when they opted to work almost completely in private.

"The last thing I would like to say is that even though I'm sure the President would never dream of telling this commission how to conduct its business, I am confident he would have absolutely no objection to televised hearings."

This was supposed to be a cue, no doubt, for me. And Carter underlined it by trying to look at me, awkward though that was. Something stirred on the fringes of my consciousness. I felt tempted to back him up. But I couldn't quite grasp it. I held my peace, and Carter looked a little crestfallen.

"Most interesting," said Hutchison. "Shall we take a break?"

During the break I pretended to be busy with some paper work. I sipped my coffee slowly and tried to figure out, for the dozenth time, who was trying to torpedo me. I went over the log of telephone calls for the three days previous to the President's putting me on this commission. I went over the appointment cards. By now I must have read the writing off the sheets, but still nothing clicked. I had a feeling, though, that if I could only figure out the how, that would tell me who; and vice versa. But I still couldn't work it out. It was at my fingertips, literally, but. . . . I gave up on that one and started to work on Carter.

One of three things had happened. Either Carter had come onto the commission over his staff's advice, or they'd talked him into it against his instincts, or they'd all agreed he should do it but now he was having second thoughts. If, as seemed likely, he was trying to get himself ready for a run at the White House, it was probably this last.

There was no way he could turn it down without its getting out. And if the commission did a good job, he'd kick himself for not being on it. If it did a lousy job, we could blame it on the guys who refused to help out in a moment of crisis, like Carter.

If he was more blatantly a candidate for the nomination, he wouldn't have been asked. But he'd played it fairly coyly until now. I didn't expect that he was pressing for television so he could try to be the hero of the investigation. He was probably planning on the opposite: of behaving like the responsible politician—earnest, steady and conscientious. But most of all, he wanted people to see that he was there.

Why Dalgleish seemed to be supporting him I didn't understand. But that didn't seem important. Probably he just wanted to explain some social science to a national audience. Or maybe he had always wanted to be a talk show celebrity. Or something.

But suppose this thing came to a vote? Obviously Hutchison and Specci would turn it down cold. Probably Dalgleish would back up Carter. Which meant that I. . . . Then it hit me. I saw the whole thing. The idea that had been nagging at me from below the surface since that afternoon in Van Riebouw's office hit me with a force that almost made me choke on a mouthful of coffee. After that, I could hardly wait for us to get back into session.

When we did resume, Carter, the perpetual man in motion, came bustling back into the chamber, and we took up where we'd left off. I assumed he'd been out for a quick conference with his assistants. But whatever they'd decided, Hutchison had stemmed Carter's momentum, though only after allowing him to show his full hand. It would be pretty stale on a second outing.

"As I recall, we were discussing the possibility of television." Hutchison looked at Carter blandly, asking in effect if he had anything more to say.

"Yes, Mr. Chairman," he said. "But now that I've expressed my own opinion, I'd like to hear what the other members think." How feeble it was. How feeble it sounded.

I said, "If it's put to a motion, Mr. Chairman, I'd like to second the Senator's proposition."

Only a positive effort of will, I sensed, kept Carter from grabbing my arm and shaking my hand.

"I must admit I'd already heard some talk along these lines, but"—and I turned to him half-apologetically—"I didn't think it right for me to raise it myself. I'm sure you can appreciate why."

Of course they could appreciate why.

"But now it's out in the open, as it were, I think I ought to say straight out that I agree with every one of the arguments so forcefully expressed by my distinguished colleagues here.

"There's something else I would like to add, if I may. And that is this: We've had so many high-powered, top-level commissions and committees looking into one thing or another that if we're to have any real impact at all, especially after Watergate, we've got to put ourselves across in a dynamic way." I worked up to this point like a man driving home a nail. Having made it, I stopped.

Hutchison turned to his left, to Dalgleish, and said in his smoothest way, "President Dalgleish?"

There now, to my surprise and confusion, began a short, sharp, polite struggle to find out where Dalgleish actually stood; he'd started to backtrack. For no apparent reason he began to pick away at what he had led us all to assume was his position. Only gradually did I understand that when Carter had put the idea to him, he'd given it some preliminary thought, but nothing more. He was still arriving at a decision, but slowly, tentatively and circuitously. Carter, exasperated, began fidgeting with his pencils. I felt as he did but tried to mask my impatience. At least, I consoled myself, Dalgleish hasn't come out flatly against it.

But he did give me several bad moments, particularly when he virtually admitted to having no strong feelings on the subject and then started to gravitate in the direction of Hutchison and Specci, as a lighter mass does toward a greater. Despairingly, I found myself assuming that he would vote as they did. Carter made a gesture of giving up: He left his pencils alone.

Whether it was inspiration or desperation I'm not sure, but I asked if we might get Harrod's opinion. Hutchison looked solemnly at his empty pipe.

''Does anyone object to that?'' No one did. ''I assume,'' he said, looking me straight in the eye, ''that you are interested to know if televised proceedings would cast an extra burden on Mr. Harrod and his staff?''

''Yes, Mr. Chairman. That's it precisely.''

He bowed toward Harrod, who immediately launched into several funny anecdotes about the special hazards lawyers face on television. We had a brief excursus on Senator Sam Ervin and public expectations.

What's he stalling for? I wondered. But gradually I discerned a thread running through this waffling: Harrod was delighted at the idea of being on national TV, but he couldn't say so. It was run-of-the-mill vanity—an ego trip, no more, no less.

''So I'd say, sir, that it wouldn't be a handicap at all to us. If anything, it's conceivable that it might help. There is also—and this is my personal opinion—something to be said for this as a kind of living civics lesson. But I sure wouldn't like to influence the decision one way or another.''

''Thank you very much for your comments, Mr. Harrod,'' said Hutchison. ''Now, are there any more points before we put it to a vote?''

He looked at Dalgleish, who shook his head. He looked at me. *If it doesn't have the votes now,* I thought, *there's nothing I can do or say to save it.* I shook my head, as if saying farewell to my earlier vision.

"Very well, shall we vote on it?"

I voted first, for. So did Carter. Specci firmly said, "Opposed."

"President Dalgleish?"

He hesitated for a couple of seconds. "I think, in this case, for," he said.

The blinding light came back. "Point of order, point of order!" went a rasping voice. "Mr. Chairman! Mr. Chairman!"

"Television it is," said Hutchison. And from the tone of his voice you'd never have guessed he cared one bit about the outcome. "What's next?"

Chapter Seven

There was no doubt in my mind: I had found the third horn. Somebody, and by now I had a strong suspicion who it was, had attempted to force me into a damned-if-you-do, damned-if-you-don't situation—to impale me on the horns of a dilemma. Resistance to going onto the commission would bring me into conflict with the President's order and would weaken my position. But if I went meekly onto the commission, that would get me out of the White House for much of the time and would also weaken my position. In either case, my authority would be diminished. And once I'd been whittled down this much, I could then be whittled down some more. That was the general idea. But I had found the third horn.

Not that I'd discovered some midway position, some compromise between the two spikes that were meant to nail me to the wall. No, I wasn't hanging on by my fingernails. The third horn is a completely different spike. It's the one you nail the other guy with.

The third horn is the one other people usually don't see or else they underestimate it. Otherwise, they'd act differently. But it's always there, because no one can set someone else up without making a move. And any time someone moves he exposes himself somewhere. That's the place to put the third horn.

And once I'd found it, I could see at last how what I had

the will and the intent to do might just possibly be done. Perhaps if I hadn't been put on the commission, I would have found some other way. But in this new situation, an unforeseen possibility had been created. It was up to me to make the most of it.

Several points were already clear in my mind. The central objective of any attempt on the government must be to bring about total collapse. All the routine, orderly operations of the federal system needed to be brought to a halt, the more jolting, the better. It would be dangerous, but in that halt what things might not be shaken loose? And if I could somehow contrive a spectacular breakdown of government and make it come completely by surprise, the halt need not be for long. Most people would find their lives going on much as before: No one would suffer; no one would starve; no one would be killed. Yet an event like this would doubtless give people pause, and for an instant the structure would crack. For my purposes it seemed that twenty-four hours would be time enough, with time to spare.

What a day it would be! A day where there was both chaos and a vacuum, in the same place, at the same time. No one—well, almost no one—would know the truth of what was happening. All the established lines of command and control would have to be tangled, snarled, cross-wired. No one should be sure of whom to trust. No one should be sure of what to do. All the things our system was designed to prevent, or at least minimize, must be made a reality and be magnified even as the nation watched. If that did not induce a paralysis of the will to act, then nothing could.

But if these things *were* done, whoever knew the truth behind events, whoever knew the answer to the riddle, would alone be capable of effective action. That person alone would be able to impose a conscious order on events to reach a predetermined goal. Act quickly then, and all could be won. It would be a day when knowledge really came into its own, and with a vengeance. Knowledge would truly be power. Not armies or air forces, not artillery or tanks, but knowledge, data, facts, the truth—in the right hands, of course.

The preparation would be all. I would win or lose before the day ever came. Yet it would take the day and all it held to tell which it was.

I acknowledged to myself that because what I was about to do was very much a gamble, I should keep clearly in mind the necessary principles of action where deeds are known but intentions are not. Anyone familiar with Von Neumann's Theory of Games would have understood. It was essential to have a guide around which details could be coherently organized. It would maximize the chances of success while moderating the possible consequences of failure. No one could do better than that.

But to make any of it work at all, there was some clearing of the ground to be done. Complete freedom of movement was essential. It would take everything I had to see this enterprise through. I could not afford to have my nervous energies dissipated on the inevitable questions, accusations and recriminations that must follow each step. Yet if my wife got so much as an inkling of what I was about, she would try to make it impossible. It had become imperative that I put myself beyond the reach of my closest, most knowing, most effective critic. There was no way I could avoid this initial step. And if I didn't have the stomach for it, then I might as well forget the entire idea. This, I repeated half a dozen times to myself, is as good a time as any. Perhaps better, in fact, than almost any other. Carefully, quietly, I slipped out of bed.

A couple of hours later the room was dully gray with the weak light of a late fall dawn poking halfheartedly through the bedroom curtains. I was still wide awake when I felt my wife straighten out from the tortuous, lopsided S bend she insisted was the most comfortable way for her to sleep. I closed my half-open eyes. There was a gentle pressure on my upper arm, and I felt a soft kiss pressed lightly just below my ear. Slowly I opened the eye nearest her.

"You awake?" she whispered, sliding her long, bony fingers over my chest.

"No," I whispered back. "I always sleep like this when I'm horny."

She slipped her hand lower down.

"Are you really?"

"Aaaagh," I groaned dramatically. "Actually . . . if you really want to know . . . I just wanted to pee."

"In that case. . . ."

"No, no. Stay as you were."

"What for? There's no point in having my best efforts wasted."

"Best efforts?" I looked at the clock. "At this hour?"

"Some got it," she said with mock sulkiness. "Some don't."

I sighed heavily. "My mother was right. Not just about you, but about all women. She used to say—and I've learned how true it is, at bitter cost—'Son, all women are after just one thing you've got. It's the only thing they think about from the time they're old enough to know.' Mother was right."

She kept it light, but I thought there was a hint of frostiness behind her words. "Who was the one who wanted to give it one more chance?"

"Give what one more chance?"

She faltered momentarily, then said, "Marriage. You wanted us to try to stay married."

"Married?" I snorted with sham incredulity. "Who's talking about marriage? I'm talking about something far more important. I'm talking about sex."

"Sex?"

"Yes. Sex. It's about the only thing women ever think about seriously. Body-mad, virtually every one of 'em. And the few that aren't are neurotic, by definition."

"Women? That's a joke. You've got it the wrong way around. Ask anybody. . . ."

"Oh, no, you don't. I've heard all that before. That's got to be the greatest myth in history. You can't try to tell me, because I know better: I know from experience. Women," I said as insistently as I could, "are after one thing and one thing only. Once they've got that . . . well, it's all over. There's no more respect. No respect at all. They've got what they want and they're off. *Pht!*"

She started laughing.

"Go ahead, laugh. But I've heard about how in high school and college they're all down in the girls' locker room talking about how this guy has spots on his balls and that one can't get it up."

"That's ridiculous."

"No, it isn't. I know what they're like. They take what they want. Literally, mind you, they wring you dry, then cast you off like a squeezed-out lemon."

"Shall I stop—lemon?"

What could I say? I murmured something indistinct, and as we stroked, squeezed, kissed, shifting and rolling easily out of one embrace and into another, we spoke no more. Talk is an effort when the middle ground of breathing disappears, and we breathed huskily, noisily, wetly; we breathed slowly, we breathed quickly. But practiced in each other's pleasures, we needed no words.

Part of the practice for me was, as always, to fix my mind elsewhere. For if I concentrated on the dancing nerve ends, they would stray too far. I would melt away like a lollipop in sunshine. So mind went its own way while hands, mouth, groin and thighs worked on.

And I thought how lucky we'd been. And how unlucky. In my mind's eye I could see us making love like a team. That, at least, we still did like the team of old. For fifteen years we'd worked at our marriage. We were convinced that so long as we were together, we could handle anything that came our way, good or bad. And when I say "worked," I don't mean like reluctant employees. Rather, we were like two partners in a business bound by the conviction that each has half the solution to success and together they can grow rich, while each on his own would have nothing. Over the years we'd developed that almost unspoken language that sympathy creates. No slight disturbance could enter one's world without the other knowing it. What we had we shared, and not to share had become a type of cheating, even if the "it" in question was worry or bad temper. After spending the first half of my life without giving much, I had tried since my marriage to give all. Yet this past year or two everything seemed to go wrong. We, who'd shared everything, were becoming like strangers. And I, who'd spent my life trying to understand things, couldn't understand this. Marriages are supposed to break up over sex or money. Neither of us took much interest in money. I couldn't remember the last time we'd even discussed it, let alone argued about it. As for sex, I had a private joke about us being part of the sexually Talented Tenth.

Again and again it came back to my work. But that seemed absurd. She listened to my criticisms and complaints and told me to quit if that would make me happy. But I didn't want to quit. The reasons I gave Specci I'd given her a dozen times. But she turned impatient. *Then stop complaining and stop deceiving him,* she said. So easy to say, so hard to do. She didn't see him as I did, day in and day out. I suppose I was trapped for the first time in my life. And instead of trying to help, she was suggesting that I was a hypocrite and a liar, if not a fool.

I opened my eyes slightly and watched her face, feeling, as I always did, that it wasn't fair, but unable to resist. The same little furrow of concentration creased her brow that was always there when she was intent on something. Her cheeks were flushed from exertion, and her lips drawn back slightly. In the soft, diffuse light she looked closer to twenty-six than thirty-six. How much like. . . . My cheeks began to burn with shame, and memory. But I couldn't help myself from finishing the sentence . . . like Merrion.

Oh, my Merrion, my angel. How I loved you, darling. All that life now gone, ended at the age of eleven by a madman's bullet on a New York street. Go shopping with your mother and come back dead. You were the child we'd dreamed of having and could hardly believe you'd come true, and the older you got, the truer it was—beautiful, lively, intelligent, curious. All gone. And we would have no more. No more children for an insane world to devour. And no more bitter tears through a thousand ghastly nights. No more. We both agreed.

That was almost four years past. We'd survived somehow. Can I be blamed for thinking that two people who could come through that could go through anything together? Yet this last year, these past few months especially, something seemed to have gone irreversibly wrong. No matter what we did, we argued almost every day. She said I'd changed, become hard, she claimed, cold and distant. At first I thought she was imagining things. But when I realized she might possibly be right, how could I explain to her something that I didn't understand myself?

We had agreed to try a separation the week before the assassination. Then, that day after the funeral at Arlington, she was willing to give it one more chance. Here it was. And I was about to kick it all away. For a moment an anticipation of regret almost overwhelmed me. For the very last time I was tempted to turn back. We had loved each other once, so very much. With our lovely child we thought we were the perfect family. Yet in the end we had only ashes and each other. Soon that too would be gone.

As I struggled with these thoughts and feelings, trying to keep them from turning my willpower to sand, more memories came crowding in. I could see us again on the day I made fun of some new gadget she'd just bought. I'd teased her until, exasperated, she burst out, "You make fun of everything I have." When I started to disagree, she'd cut me off. "Everything I have except you—and you probably laugh at that behind my back." I'd collapsed on the floor, holding my sides.

Suddenly I heard my name. There were murmured endearments. Regret, memory, anticipation fell away. I hurried off to scale the peaks of sensation not yet blunted in the flesh of impending middle age.

On my swiftly diminishing member she bore down hard. Again and again, perhaps a dozen times in all. Then her spine and legs went rigid for a moment, before she began to shake in a driving, rhythmical way. Her nails raked my shoulder blades and the sides of my ribcage.

We sank back, out of breath. She stroked my arm and smiled at me. I reached over to cup a breast.

"Ah, marital bliss. Just like the book promised."

She smiled weakly at my weak joke.

"I think I'm leaking."

"You're lucky. I'm disappearing."

We showered together. I dressed slowly while she started to make breakfast and tidied up the living room from the night before.

"Just look at this mess," she griped.

"Nag, nag, nag," I griped back.

For a minute everything was quiet. I listened, but I couldn't hear her moving around. I felt my heart pounding slightly as I sensed her standing behind me. I turned around.

"I was going to hang your coat up."

"So?"

She held the coat up and turned one lapel slightly aside.

"What do you suppose this is?"

She pointed to a small, flesh-colored powdery streak. "And this." She opened her hand and flung an earring in my face.

Chapter Eight

My first inclination when I saw him lying there on the bed looking weak and ghastly was that I'd just have to chance it and trust him to back me up later. Half-apologetically I told him, "There's nothing from me personally that can't be put off for a while, Mr. President."

"Don't you worry about me. The doc says I can do some work this morning." He attempted an encouraging grin. "You're the one's gonna be in the hot seat today."

For almost half an hour we went over various problems involving legislation initiated by the late President, but still up on the Hill, and I was just about to send down for our Congressional liaison when he suddenly burst out, "Jesus H. Christ, you'd think they'd at least try to cooperate. Everybody knows how they bent over backward for Johnson. And I spent six years up there, you know. I used to work with most of those guys. You'd think they'd give me a break, wouldn't you? Forget it. If there's any credit for anything going around, they want it all to themselves." His eyes narrowed angrily. "If I was dying of thirst some of those selfish bastards wouldn't give me the sweat off their balls."

I laughed. "Well, you're not finished yet. And they know it."

"I guess so. Anything else for me?"

"There is one thing, but I really hate to bother you with it."

"That's okay."

"Well." I hesitated. "There are still quite a number of people who don't want the hearings on television. Who don't want them public, period."

Thickly he slurred, "I don't think this television business is all that important." Evidently he hadn't yet seen its potential impact. Then apparently inspired by the thought that I'd simply turned camera-shy and nervous, he tried to pep me up.

"Don't you worry about it. It's something new for you. But you'll do fine—just fine."

I bobbed my head appreciatively, trying to stifle a smile. "I only wish I was as certain as you are about them learning to live with it, that's all."

"What the hell else can they do? They've got nowhere else to go." He laughed at his own joke as he cracked, "It's the only one in town."

"But they could always try to sabotage the commission; try to give it a bad image, cast doubt on its findings before they even come out. Make it look like the Ervin Committee. That kind of thing."

The trembling in his hands became more pronounced. "Goddammit! Where's the reason?"

As emphatically as I dared, I retorted, "I wish somebody would tell *me*. Why would anybody fight so hard to keep these hearings from being public? In the end the vote was so close that they might very easily decide not to play dead."

"Now why in the hell would anybody want to do that?" He was suspicious now—but suspicious, I hoped, of everyone.

"For the same reason they wanted to have the hearings in private."

"And that is?"

I got up and started to pace. Then I went over and looked out at the traffic on South Executive Avenue—the picture, I was betting, of honesty baffled by unseen forces.

These last weeks I'd done as much as I could—as indirectly as I could—to create an atmosphere of siege. I was fortunate in one respect: There was no lack of material to work with. When was the last time anybody in this town had trusted anybody else? And how long since the country had trusted anybody here? We were only just getting back onto our feet again when the assassination occurred, and the recovery was too new and too brittle to survive such a blow.

The despair that was creeping in everywhere about our politics was by now eating into government itself. Government is a necessity of life, like breathing. But also like breathing, it needs a central and effective set of organs to work. After the Nixon disaster Congress did make a few self-conscious, highly publicized attempts to assert its independence. People started dusting off Woodrow Wilson's *Congressional Government*. And the ones who bothered to read it all the way through must have known what these new initiatives would amount to. Nothing. Because it still takes one man at the top. And what *Congressional Government* finally came down to wasn't the committees but the Speaker. It worked when the Speaker ran Congress. But who would allow that now? Congress was as full of emptyheaded self-indulgence as a beauty parlor, and about as capable of providing serious leadership. It reminded me chiefly of the Chimera of Greek mythology: a monstrosity with the head of a lion, the body of a goat and the tail of a snake.

The last couple of incumbents in the White House had made a great show of scrupulosity and openness. But that was a matter of their individual personalities. After the country had gone to the mat over executive privilege, nobody would want to touch the subject again for a very long time. I was betting that people had no stomach for another round. Only the media would be likely even to raise the subject. And there were limits to what they could do. Most of the time they were either running scared or whining ineffectively about their ineffectiveness. They *also* reminded me of a figure from the ancient world—the messenger who brought the bad news.

It was hard to find anything that seemed to be working as it was supposed to. There was barely a city, town or state that wasn't immersed up to its eyeballs in problems. We had the physical resources to solve most of them. What was lacking was the cohesion, the commonality of outlook, the self-respect and the determination to do it. The late President was just beginning to succeed in reviving the country's spirit when he was killed. Now all we had was a bad conscience, a sense of defeat and more social sores than any country should tolerate. Yet if people turned once again to the font of our political life, the Constitution, in search of a way out, what did they find?

I turned around and looked at him sprawled across the bed, pale and shaking, confusion and unhappiness etched into every line in his face. The Constitution—and its sworn defender, him? Carlyle's words came to mind: *"Extremely rheumatic Constitutions have been known to march and keep on their feet, though in a staggering, sprawling manner, for long periods, in virtue of one thing only: that the Head were healthy. But this Head!"*

Well, I had done all I could to make him sensitive to the current atmosphere . . . to make him feel like the defender of an embattled outpost with the cavalry nowhere in sight. I had given ambiguous orders to various people on the staff, muddled the lines of communication, inspired petty conflicts and generally made him feel that he was being served by a staff of idiots—except for me. I had never complained about being put on the commission and let him draw his own conclusions about the current deterioration in staff work.

But I had another—and more formidable—piece of leverage. I was no longer the only one who knew his true condition, but I was the only one who believed it, so far. I was certain I was the only person prepared to exploit its potential to the full.

"I don't know," I said. "I simply don't know. But I do know that no one puts up that kind of fight without a good reason. A very good reason. Otherwise, it doesn't make any sense."

"You know, some people might say I didn't ought to talk to you about the commission at all," he said wearily, indirectly begging me to drop the subject.

"Whatever you think, Mr. President," I replied, hinting remotely at cowardice. "But there's one thing we can be glad of."

He looked at me.

"That you put me on the commission. I think you were right. You *do* need somebody there to protect your interests."

"My interests?" he said, not quite comprehending.

"Yes," I said softly, "I think it's necessary."

"What the hell are you driving at now?"

"I'm not sure myself," I said helplessly. "A lot of little things. A whisper here. A rumor there. Snatches of conversation you overhear. Nothing you can actually put your finger on. But

I have a strong feeling that there really is something going on that we don't know about and aren't supposed to.''

''What sort of thing?'' he asked suspiciously. I could feel my heart pounding. *Oh, God,* I thought, *don't tell me he's suspicious of me. What if he asks for proof?*

''What sort of thing?'' he insisted.

''I hate to say it, but I think there's some kind of plot. A conspiracy, if you like.''

I could see his mind reeling as he groped for comprehension.

''Plot? Conspiracy? What for?''

''Who knows,'' I replied, ''until it breaks into the open, until they show their hand? I have a feeling that it all ties in with the assassination.''

''How?''

''I don't know. But I'd certainly like to find out.'' I saw his hands fumbling nervously with the bedclothes. ''Of course, I may be wrong,'' I said soothingly. ''There may be nothing to it. But even knowing that much would be worth something.''

''And you think all this . . . whatever it is . . . is mixed up in some way with the commission?'' He was utterly bewildered.

''Yes, Mr. President.''

''Maybe''—he thrashed about—''maybe there's some simple explanation, something else we haven't thought of.''

''Maybe there is. But the important thing is that we find out what it is.''

He lapsed into silence for a few moments, breathing heavily.

''Now, I want your word on this,'' he said unhappily. ''You're absolutely certain there's something. . . .'' He groped around until he'd found the word he wanted. ''Something . . . fishy going on?''

As expressively as I could without being melodramatic I urged, ''Yes, sir. I am. But what we really need to know is whether it's a minnow or a whale.''

Defeated and dispirited, he said, ''You find out what it is.''

''I'll probe as far as I can, for as long as you like. But the moment you want me to back off. . . .'' I let the sentence die away, leaving a heavy pause behind.

It was a medicine ball of a pause. But he couldn't leave it alone. Years of conventioneering, country clubbing, cloak-rooming pressed him forward, positively driven by Positive Thinking.

"Do whatever you think best. Don't you worry. I'll back you up all the way. One hundred percent." He enunciated each of the three words distinctly and repeated them. "One hundred percent."

"It might get a bit rough."

"One hundred percent," he said impatiently.

I pressed my luck. "They might start after you."

"That goes with the job," he snapped.

"So it's no holds barred?"

"No holds barred."

I reached over and warmly took his shaking right hand in both of mine. I squeezed it, a lump of very real emotion rising in my throat. "Thank you, Mr. President. Thank you very much."

He smiled at me with his eyes. And I could have sworn his cheeks flushed pink with pleasure.

"Rumpled elegance." I found myself turning the phrase over and over. "Rumpled elegance." Somewhere, years ago, I'd read that that was how the most self-assured of the British aristocracy used to look, leaving everybody below them to worry about looking neat and tidy. The phrase had stuck in a corner of my mind. And there was Hutchison bringing it back to life—rumpled, but in no way disheveled. Instead, he had a sort of careless ease, or he was modestly, unconsciously, trying to play down what was once an impeccably tailored suit. The rest of us, I couldn't help but notice, were all neatly scrubbed and pressed.

Both the television cameras were on, one panning us, the other surveying the spectators. We had agreed to a hundred and sixty seats, and every one of them was filled. So were the aisles at the back and down the sides.

"If I may, I'd like to say a few words," said Hutchison. There was a complete, immediate, almost breathless silence, broken only by the inevitable muffled cough.

"We have been commissioned by the President to conduct an inquiry into the tragic events relating to the death of the late

President. This is not a court of law. These hearings do not constitute a trial. But because of the possibility that indictments may follow the proceedings, every witness before this commission will have the right to be represented by counsel. All testimony will be given under oath. And if there is reason to believe that there has been perjured testimony, the Justice Department will take appropriate steps.

"But we are not principally concerned here with questions of law. We are here to determine questions of fact. If I may speak personally for a moment, I think the questions come under three different but related headings: First, how was this apalling crime—one which involved death and injury for many bystanders—carried out? In other words, how did it happen? Second, who was responsible for it? And third, how can we put an end to these assassinations? They can have no part in the political life of a democratic country.

"We are not here to sit in judgment save on these questions. Legal judgment will be for the courts to provide. It is for us to determine the facts of the matter, first for the President and, by implication, for the nation. We have sworn to do this to the utmost of our ability." Someone started to applaud, then thought better of it.

We had agreed in advance that we would start with the Secret Service, then go on to consider the FBI's report. Our first witness would be the chief of the Secret Service, who would be asked to explain the security arrangements for the President's arrival. He would also be expected to explain how they broke down.

As Danby Steele was being sworn in, I had a distinct feeling he was already hostile to the commission. He knew, as we all did, that whatever else we found, we would have to find fault with his arrangements for that night. What I hadn't realized was how bitter he was in anticipation.

The preliminaries were polite enough, until he was asked how many agents he had at Andrews.

"After taking into consideration that there would be approximately a hundred and fifty Air Force police in the immediate vicinity, I thought a screen of sixteen agents would be adequate between the President and the crowd. The crowd was already supposed to have been double-checked."

"Only sixteen?" asked Carter. "With the Cabinet and the Vice President to be protected, too?"

I felt a twinge of sympathy for Steele. If he had said fifty, I think Carter would have said, "Only fifty? With the Cabinet. . . ."

But Steele merely looked at him impassively. "Sixteen around the President and Vice President, Senator."

"So there were just sixteen agents to protect them that night."

"No, sir," said Steele emphatically.

An audible buzz started up among the spectators. Hutchison leaned forward. He hadn't said anything about orderly behavior in his opening remarks, and I'd wondered why not. Now I understood. He'd deliberately let them set themselves up.

"I would not like to order this room to be cleared," he said blandly. "But attendance at these hearings is a privilege extended by this commission. And disturbances of any kind will not be tolerated." He leaned back. "Please continue."

"You were indicating, Mr. Steele, that you meant to have sixteen agents on hand but that for some reason you didn't have quite that number."

"That's right, Senator."

"How many did you have then?"

"Altogether, we had thirty-four."

"Thirty-four?" Carter repeated it numbly. "Thirty-four. Well, where were these other . . . eighteen?"

"In the crowd."

The buzzing broke out again. Hutchison motioned with his hand that he wanted to speak and said, in the most businesslike, matter-of-fact way, "The next time there is an interruption this room will be cleared." He meant it.

Specci took advantage of the pause to take up the questioning. "Were they different from the crowd in any way? By that, I mean was there anything that identified them, set them apart from the other people there?"

With a heavily ironic bitterness Steele replied, "Yes, Mr. Justice. They were there to protect the President."

Specci was annoyed. "Was there a deliberate attempt on the part of your men to look like ordinary members of the crowd?"

"Those were their instructions."

"Instructions given by you?"

"Yes, sir."

"Now, I know that you have what is at best a very difficult job—a cruelly difficult job. But doesn't that have a hint to it of the *agents provocateurs?*"

"No, Mr. Justice, it does not," flared Steele. "Every one of those agents was there in a defensive role. They were under strict orders to be inconspicuous. They've been specially trained to be on the alert for anyone trying to use a dangerous weapon in a crowd situation, to disarm that person or deflect his aim, if possible, and to detain that person and, if necessary, protect him from other members of the crowd. I'd like to suggest that that's a long way from deliberately creating incidents."

Hutchison asked, "Is this routine practice, Mr. Steele?"

"Only when called for."

"And when is that?"

"When there's going to be a crowd and the President's likely to get close to it. After a while it doesn't make sense any longer to put more men between the President and the crowd. So you start putting some of them into the crowd. It's a long shot that one of your agents might be able to stop anything, but I think it's a chance worth taking under certain circumstances."

"Do you do this with all the people you are told to protect?"

"No, sir. Just the President. We don't have that kind of manpower."

"So altogether you had thirty-four agents at Andrews Air Force Base?"

"That is correct, Mr. Chairman."

"And in your professional judgment that was a number adequate to the task?"

"I wouldn't like to say that, Mr. Chairman."

"Why not?"

Steele took a deep breath that was as much as to say, *Here I am, a sorely taxed man, doing my best to explain a simple fact for the hundredth time.*

"I could have used fifty-four men, or a hundred and fifty-four. I don't have those kinds of resources. I don't always get the cooperation necessary to make the best use of my manpower. What I try to do is use the optimum number under the circumstances. That's how I define adequate—adequate to the situation. Not ideal, not perfect, but adequate."

"And we now know that adequate doesn't mean enough," said Carter.

Steele's cheeks went red, as if they'd been slapped.

"I think that remark's uncalled for, Senator," he said with forced evenness. But Carter wouldn't let go.

"Isn't the real justification for having a Secret Service the protection of the President's life?"

"Yes."

"Yet the President was assassinated. Doesn't that make it look, at least on the face of it, as if there was something wrong with your preparations?"

"Yes, Senator. You could say there was something wrong. But that doesn't mean the service was to blame for it."

Softly, almost gently, Hutchison interjected, "Who—or what—was to blame, Mr. Steele?"

"Sir, with all due respect, I'd say it was the President himself."

Hutchison looked up sharply, almost daring the spectators. Somehow they managed to keep quiet.

"That," said Steele, with an emphasis which bordered on bitterness, "is always the weak link in our chain of defense. If the person you're assigned to protect needlessly exposes himself to danger, there's not much you can do any longer, short of physically restraining him yourself."

"So you think the assassination was all the President's fault?" Carter asked sarcastically.

"Senator, I'd have put myself between the President and that grenade, if I'd had the chance. There wasn't one agent there that night who wouldn't have done the same—*if* he'd had the chance. But in the final analysis, we're not the President's ultimate defense. He is. He has to let us protect him—help us protect him, if you like. And I'll tell you this, Senator. If the President had done what he was supposed to do or if he hadn't charged out in front of my men, he'd be alive today.''

There was a solemn hush all over the room. But if we were trying to wish the past away, we failed.

Dalgleish asked, ''So it was really the President's own fault then?''

''Principally. But not entirely. There was the problem of the journalists and television people getting in the way, and—'' He broke off.

''And?'' prompted Dalgleish.

''The Vice President, sir, now the President.'' Steele looked over at Hutchison, as if to ask if we would listen to tales out of school.

Hutchison said, ''Yes, Mr. Steele?''

''You see—and I think the videotapes will bear me out on this—I think it might have been possible for one of our agents to have either knocked the weapon clear or to have caught it and thrown it clear. Unfortunately no one had that chance.''

''But that's all speculation, isn't it?'' I asked. ''I mean to say, we have absolutely no way of knowing if your agent would have done any better or if the results would have been much different.''

Reluctantly, Steele agreed.

''Had the Secret Service ever considered the possibility of a would-be assassin using a hand grenade?'' demanded Specci.

''That, and just about every other possibility you can think of,'' said Steele with obvious professional pride. ''You name it, Mr. Justice, grenades, thrown knives, booby-trapped dogs, mines, rockets, dangerous birds like hawks and falcons, bows and arrows—even blowpipes and poison darts.''

''I assume,'' interrupted Hutchison, ''that there's no need for us to go into the possible countermeasures you've devised for any of these things. But would you have any objection to telling us how your agents were supposed specifically to deal with a grenade or any kind of hand-held bomb?''

Steele thought for a moment. Finally, he said, ''I guess not, Mr. Chairman. In the case of this particular weapon the principal thing is that the chance of detection is very high. Our assumption has always been that a grenade is generally more difficult to conceal than a handgun. There just aren't many places you can hide a round or cylindrical object of some size in your clothes. You'd probably have to pad yourself out or have an artificial limb or something of that sort. Right there the chances of being inconspicuous go down pretty fast.

"On the other hand, you'd probably have to get in fairly close to throw it accurately, even allowing for its being an area weapon. And just pulling it out from wherever it was concealed would probably draw somebody's attention. You also have to cock your arm to throw it. In a crowd situation that makes you even more conspicuous to the people next to you.

"So in the case of hand bomb or a grenade we figured two things: It would most likely be carried in something like a lady's handbag, and whoever tried to throw it would almost certainly be seen. That meant the chances of detection were very high."

"But you couldn't prevent it?" asked Specci.

"Nobody can prevent it completely. All we can do is make it so hard that people won't be tempted to try. And we make it as certain as we can that if they do try they'll be caught. Our object was to keep the President far enough away or moving fast enough to make any sort of thrown bomb a minimal risk."

"Yet in this case you neither prevented it, nor minimized the risk, nor apprehended the person or persons responsible," Carter sneered.

Steele snapped, "This was an extraordinary case." Almost at once you could tell he regretted his words.

"Yes, it was," drawled Carter slowly, smugly satisfied at the chance to even the score. "It certainly was. Presidents aren't killed every day."

"If they're not—" burst out Steele, goaded now to fury.

But he was cut off by Hutchison, asking in his firmest, most polite way, "Would the chief like to explain what happened as he sees it?"

"Yes, sir," said Steele, calming himself. "As far as we can make out the suspect smuggled the grenades in. . . ." He faltered. "Somehow."

"Weren't ladies' handbags searched?" asked Dalgleish.

"Yes, sir. They were. So were briefcases. And anyone in bulky clothing was also patted down."

"Were any other detection devices employed?"

"Security included a number of metal detectors at the gate leading into the crowd area."

"And explosives sniffers?"

"Yes, sir. Those, too."

"Well, who operated these things?" asked Dalgleish.

It evidently pained him to say it, but Steele answered, "My men did, sir."

"And?"

"Well, sir, you have to understand that none of these things is a hundred percent accurate. Especially when you've got to move a lot of people through in a hurry."

"So how did this person manage to bring the grenades in?"

Steele grimaced. "I honestly don't know. But if we can look at the videotapes, I think we might be able to see one way that it could have been done."

Hutchison raised his hand to indicate that he had a question.

"Would the chief first like to show us on the chart where all your—what was it, thirty-four?—agents were? That ought to give us something definite to work from."

One of Harrod's assistants, standing at an easel, whisked a covering sheet off. Underneath was a six- by eight-foot diagram of the relevant area at Andrews with all the straight-edged graphic neatness of Artist's Conception.

Steele walked over to it and picked up a fistful of large blue magnetized disks. At the bottom of what was plainly the Air Force One steps he placed a large white one with a shiny dark blue *P*. Then one marked *VP* was shoved toward it. Half a dozen *C*'s were neatly arranged in a line. The crowd was represented by about forty green markers. Air police were blue with a diagonal white stripe. Sure enough, he carefully placed eighteen blue markers, each apparently with a name inked in, among the green.

"Of course"—he gestured at the greens—"there ought to be several thousand of these. But this should give the general idea."

It did indeed.

"Each agent will testify about his own position," he said, "but this is approximately correct."

"And where was the suspected assassin?" Hutchison asked.

Steele picked up a solid black disk. *Now who,* I wondered, *had thought of that?* He placed it not quite in the middle of the crowd. "About there, so far as we can tell."

"How far back in the crowd would you say that is?"

"Well, Mr. Chairman, it's hard to say. But judging from what happened after the first explosion, I'd say about twenty feet. No more than thirty, anyway, and certainly not less than ten."

We studied the positions of the blues in relation to the black. We were all staring at the black disk as if we expected it somehow to come alive, make a move.

"Then how close," asked Hutchison suavely, "would you say your nearest agent was from that . . . black one?"

"Again, Mr. Chairman, it's impossible to be precise. But I'd estimate that there were about three agents in that area no more than twelve feet away."

"So roughly twelve feet is the closest any of your men were?"

"No more than twelve. It's possible it was only eight or nine."

"Did any of your men actually see the suspect in the act of throwing the grenade?"

Steele pondered this for a moment, then replied, "Mr. Chairman, I don't think it would be proper for me to answer that question when the agents can testify on their own behalf."

"Quite right, Chief Steele. Your point is well taken." He looked around at us. "If you have no more questions for the moment?" We all shook our heads. He turned back to Steele.

"I think you've set the scene for us very well. Now, if we may, I think we ought to see the videotapes. But before we do, I'd like to ask the director of the Federal Bureau of Investigation to be sworn in. I think we've all read his preliminary report."

Yes, we nodded and murmured, we'd all read the report.

"Mr. Chairman?" I requested.

"Yes?"

"Would it be possible for the chief to remain at the witness table while we examine the tape? I think it might be helpful to have his comments along with those of the director."

"Thank you," said Hutchison. "Do you have any objections to that, Mr. Steele?" Steele had none.

I was elated. But I tried to look indifferent while I watched Pinchott Reedy sworn in. Reedy, the agent-made-good—by his own lights, the agent-made-God. But when he got to the top of the tree, he was hanging on by his fingertips. Half the people in government knew the late President had only been waiting for an opportunity to fire Reedy.

"Do you mind this procedure, Mr. Reedy?" Hutchison was so smooth.

"No, sir," responded Reedy. "The chief and I are old friends." He was wearing his best grim face as he said it.

"Now, are we to take it that these tapes are all that the networks have available?" asked Harrod.

"All that we've been able to find."

"Have they been edited in any way?"

"To the best of my knowledge, they have not."

"Let's have the first one, please," said Hutchison.

The lights went down, but not quite off. On a large screen, over to our left and slightly to one side of the magnetic chart, there was a quirky sort of flickering which soon resolved itself into a brightly colored picture. The crowd was being panned, but it seemed somehow unreal, artificial. Then I realized why. They were holding down the sound. It was a silent movie in color.

Air Force One rolls into view across the top of the screen. After a few moments the door opens, and suddenly he appears, waving and grinning. He comes down the steps, turns around, goes back for his wife. They come bounding down the steps again. Here goes the Vice President, hands outstretched. Handshaking and kissing all round. You see the mouths opening and closing but nothing coming out. They go to the microphones. Another shot of the crowd, writhing like a living thing but dumb. Eerie. You could feel the tension rise in the room.

Back to the podium. More soundless talk. Then he heads for the crowd. The camera swings around again onto the crowd. Hands and arms wriggle like multicolored snakes all over the right side of the screen. The three of them move forward from left to right. He half turns, looking straight at us, a big grin on his face.

"Stop!"

Almost everybody in the room jumped.

"Hold it right there," said Reedy. The picture stopped, thousands halted in mid-wave or mid-stride. Reedy moved over to the screen. I noticed he now had a pointer in his hand. He tapped the screen.

"Blow-up on this."

The operator zoomed in on the area Reedy was outlining. Even so, all I could make out was a forest of arms poking up at crazy angles over a cluttered undergrowth of heads and shoulders.

"Yes," said Hutchison slowly, "I see it."

I stared intently, but I couldn't see anything.

"This," explained Reedy, almost stroking whatever it was with the tip of his pointer, "looks like the suspect's hand."

The whole room craned forward.

"Can you magnify it further?" asked Dalgleish, almost pleading.

Reedy snapped his fingers. I bristled at the man's arrogance. The zoom came in tighter.

"That's as far as it will go," he said.

But sure enough, there was a hand, at the end of what appeared to be an orange-colored sleeve. And it was obviously bent around something.

"Let's have the rest of it, in slo-mo," commanded Reedy.

We saw the hand go back slowly. Back and back, so that it dropped out of view. You could feel almost everyone in that room literally holding his breath, as we waited for it to come back. And up it finally came, in a slow, lazy arc, reaching higher and higher this time, stretching well past its earlier apogee. The sleeve was definitely orange now, and the hand looked slender, with long white fingers. It was cradling something. Then, like one of those time-lapse films of flowers blossoming, the hand opened. Softly, gracefully something lifted slowly into the air. There was something about it which spelled Inevitability all over its dull spherical shell. Up and up it arched, while the arm went back down. But there was a strange jerkiness to the way the arm descended.

"Let's have that again," said Reedy. "This time I'd like to draw attention to the arm."

The tape came on again, but it was hard—impossible, in fact—to watch the arm and not look at that thing floating into the air.

"I'd like you to notice how the arm comes down in a way that indicates somebody was pulling it down."

So that's what it was.

"Lights." He snapped his fingers again. What a creep.

"That's about the best view we have—in fact, the only view we have—of the actual throwing of the grenade. If you gentlemen like, we can watch the rest of this, but we have a better film available of subsequent events."

"Also from the networks?" demanded Specci, sounding slightly suspicious.

"No, sir. One of our own."

"You mean a film the FBI made that night?"

"Not exactly, Mr. Justice. From one of the security agencies."

"Would you like to identify the agency for us?"

Reedy looked at Hutchison. "Is that necessary at this point, Mr. Chairman?"

"I suppose," drawled Hutchison, making a note on the pad in front of him, "we can always take it up later on if it seems relevant."

"Thank you very much, Mr. Chairman," growled Reedy in an unsuccessful attempt to sound gracious. "I think the important thing here is that it's a good quality film—regardless of the source."

The screen came to life once again. This time the President was seen from slightly above, but still from his right. And he was still moving toward the crowd. Near the right edge of the screen, if you looked closely, you could see the grenade in plain view, high in the air.

"May we have the sound, please?" ordered Hutchison.

The sound came up, loud, and clamorous. It was the unmistakable sound of a festive mob in full cry. He was reaching out toward them; they were reaching out for him. Suddenly a stocky man in a beige raincoat started sprinting in from the near side, heading for the President. The Vice President became aware of peripheral movement, looked up and noticeably went tense. On his next forward step he shrank a little as he flexed his knees. Then he sprang up, arms flailing the air. Just as the grenade fell to the ground and rolled out of the camera's line of sight, the President swiveled his head around. He swung to his left almost at the instant the man in the raincoat reached out to pull him down. There was a loud, tearing, most God-awful explosion. In the safety of my chair I flinched. I found myself trembling. When I went to wipe the sweat from my forehead, I found my perspiring hands balled into fists.

Suddenly I became aware of a cacophony of screams—the sounds of panic, of fear, of despair. But I was almost hypnotized by the sight of bodies crumpled in grotesquely unnatural positions. Some were twitching, a few seemed to be trying to crawl. Everywhere there was a sickening red oozing from heads and clothing.

The screaming now evoked a forest full of desperate small animals fleeing some terrible blaze. The camera swung back over the crowd. It appeared to have been lifted back en masse about ten yards. You could clearly see people trampling one another, falling down and writhing in panic and with hysteria. It was all screams and frenzy.

Then there came a rocking, muffled roar. Instantly the crowd seemed to bulge outward, like some variety of human balloon being blown up. And from the camera's elevated vantage point you could make out parts of human bodies hurtling through the air. A loud gasp of horrified shock filled the room. I heard someone murmur, "Oh, dear God! Have pity!"

The lights came up.

Most of the spectators looked grim and white-faced. Several were crying openly, unashamedly; others were weeping in a furtive, embarrassed way. The atmosphere was, for a moment, so thick you could choke on it. This was the first complete film sequence of the assassination any of us had seen. The networks had agreed not to add to the tensions by showing more than a fraction of their footage. But the second film caught everyone off guard. For a people supposedly inured to violence, I reflected, we were not yet brutes. We could still be moved by its horrors.

There wasn't much Hutchison could do after that but call for a short break.

When we resumed, Hutchison asked Reedy to give us a verbal summary of the main findings of the FBI report.

"Yes, sir. The principal conclusions are these: first, that the suspected assassin was a woman; second, that there is nothing to indicate that she was not on her own; third, that the grenades were introduced into the area by being concealed in her undergarments; fourth, that she detonated the second grenade when her apprehension seemed inevitable; finally, that this was a suicide mission, if you will, carried out by this person for reasons not known to us at this time."

"You have been unable to identify this suspected assassin?"

"Unfortunately, that is still the case, Mr. Chairman."

"What grounds have you for supposing that this person was a woman?"

"As the commission will recall from the last film, the hand does not appear to be that of a man." Reedy made a signal. At once an enlargement of the hand appeared in color on the screen.

We looked intently. And it was indeed white and slender, so far as you could tell.

"Also the orange sleeve," said Reedy. "It appears to be a raincoat." He dead-panned, "A man in an orange raincoat would be conspicuous." Somebody snickered.

"It might be a woman's hand, as you say, but isn't it possible that the bright lights in the area make it look whiter and softer—perhaps even more slender—than it really is, or was?" Hutchison wanted to know.

"Possible, but not altogether likely, Mr. Chairman. The bureau's considered opinion is that the general appearance of the hand combined with the appearance of the clothing points in the general direction of a woman. So does the weapon. And the possibility of concealing it in the manner suggested by the report."

"Even in these days," asked Specci, "don't you think a woman removing her bra—I assume that's what you mean by undergarments—in public would draw attention to herself?"

Again someone snickered, but Reedy ignored it. "To answer that question, under normal circumstances I'd have to say yes. But it might not have been a brassiere as you or I are accustomed to thinking of such a garment. It was probably made specially for this occasion, with some sort of release mechanism that would allow the contents to fall out whenever desired. . . .''

This time somebody among the spectators laughed out loud. Hutchison leaned forward, signaled to a Capitol policeman and indicated the offender. He was escorted from the room. Reedy picked up where he'd left off.

''As I was about to explain, this particular item of clothing was probably tailored especially for the occasion. The report suggests the weapon came out of the side of the garment it was carried in and rolled into some type of pouch under the suspect's armpit. Then it could be controlled by the pressure of the arm against the body and could be allowed to drop down into the hand at any time. That way, you see, there would be none of the attention-drawing movement that would be involved in reaching for it if it were in a pocket, for instance, or a lady's purse. It would also allow for quickly raising the arm as if to wave, then throwing in a rapid movement in the direction of the intended target.''

''May we now examine the physical evidence which supports this hypothesis?'' demanded Harrod.

''As Mr. Harrod is no doubt aware,'' replied Reedy with a vague malice in his tone, ''the evidence is in bad physical shape.''

''I think the commission members might like to see it even so,'' insisted Harrod.

Reedy scowled. ''Yes, sir.''

He motioned to an assistant sitting behind him. The assistant started to set plastic sacks on the table. Then he reached into a metal case and took out five thick stacks of shiny colored photographs. He walked over to the commission table.

''These are photographs of the scene,'' said the assistant as he gave them to us. I picked up mine and winced. My first thought was of a surgery textbook that I saw once as a child and was revolted by. My second was of a slaughterhouse, but with human beings in place of cattle. No wonder they weren't being put up on the screen.

''The photographs you are now examining are of the area where the second explosion occurred. That is the scene at which this evidence''—he gestured at the cold, shiny bags—''was gathered.''

Reedy's assistant emptied the contents of the first sack onto the table. It appeared to be a collection of multicolored shoe rags, all grubby and torn, but neatly tagged and labeled. The contents of the second sack were much the same, with different colored tags.

Reedy pointed to the first assortment. ''These were picked up within three feet of the explosion.'' He pointed to the second lot. ''These were from three to six feet away. In conjunction with the photographs they make it possible to identify most of the people and the approximate positions in the immediate vicinity of that explosion.''

I looked down at my photographs, idly noticing that I was already becoming hardened to them. And you could indeed see where some of the pieces of cloth had come from, match up this piece of rag to that lump of bleeding flesh.

''Which,'' asked Hutchison dryly, ''would you say is the suspect's clothing?''

Reedy opened the third bag. Out came a torn and crumpled orange raincoat with bands of thick white stitches.

''Here, Mr. Chairman.''

''And where was that found, Mr. Reedy?''

''Approximately seven feet from the point of the explosion. There are several possibilities. It may simply have been blown that far. Alternatively the suspect may have been trying to flee and the raincoat was pulled off her. Or she threw the second grenade in her attempt to get away but didn't throw it far enough to escape its effects.''

''So you found the raincoat, but nobody in it?''

''That is correct.''

''And you haven't been able to trace its ownership?''

''That is also correct, Mr. Chairman.''

''And the bra?'' asked Harrod.

Reedy went back to the table. He opened the fourth bag. Out came what seemed to be an old dishcloth somebody's dog had been chewing on.

''We think that this might be the garment in question.''

''May I see that, please?'' said Hutchison.

He turned it over in his hands, making a face. Specci and Dalgleish looked it over, then passed it back for Carter and me. It was utterly nondescript. Mentally I tried to picture it strapped across the body of a small or flat-chested woman, then swollen to a spherical ripeness by the two grenades to simulate pendulous breasts. I couldn't.

"What is it that makes you believe this to be the specially tailored brassiere?" asked Hutchison, obviously dissatisfied.

"Commission members may have observed," said Reedy doggedly, "that this does not appear to be a normal undergarment of any kind. Nor does it appear to be part of any known type of women's under or outer garment. Neither does it seem to be a banner or a handkerchief or anything else someone might carry in public. Yet it was found on the ground in the area; not on any of the bodies recovered, but on the ground as if it had been dropped there. It has been trampled on and somewhat torn by the explosion. But again, taken in conjunction with all the other evidence, it appears to be part of the assassin's clothing."

"You have left two important items out of your theory, Mr. Reedy," said Frank Specci.

"And they are, Mr. Justice?" hissed Reedy.

"The identity of this mysterious person who literally has vanished in a puff of smoke, and the motive for this crime."

"It has not been possible to identify all the remains as yet."

"But you haven't so much as hinted at the possibility of even narrowing it down to, say, two or three people. Yet everyone there was supposed to have a pass and some kind of official identification."

"Very true, Mr. Justice. But with so many passes—in this case about three thousand—some of them are bound to have gone astray."

"What about the identification then?"

"Again, Mr. Justice, you have to realize that in this area there are so many ID's issued every year that there's not a day goes by without some being lost and others being stolen."

"Well, Mr. Reedy, I'm afraid I don't think your agency has given us a satisfactory report on this matter," snapped Specci.

"And I'm afraid that I don't think the bureau ever *could* satisfy you, Mr. Justice."

"Thank you, gentlemen," said Hutchison calmly. "I do believe that we have now covered the principal conclusions of the FBI report. We've seen the relevant evidence. We've heard from Chief Steele of the Secret Service."

He glanced at the clock at the back of the room. I judged that he meant to wind this first session up in the next ten to fifteen minutes. I felt my blood pressure rise.

"Are there any further questions for the chief or the director on what we've heard so far?" he blandly wanted to know.

"Yes, Mr. Chairman," I quickly interjected. "I have several questions I'd like to ask."

He made a hint of a bow in my direction, then sat back.

"In the first place, there's the question of the murder weapon," I began. "I'd like some explanation as to how anybody could get hold of two brand-new fragmentation grenades. Ounce for ounce, I understand that these are about the most powerful conventional explosives we have. In this case, just two of them in a congested area killed nineteen people and badly injured more than fifty others."

"We have been unable to ascertain where the grenades came from at this time. Both the military and we ourselves are still looking into this matter. And with all respect, I would suggest that you take this up with the appropriate military representatives," said Reedy.

"I intend to put that question to them," I responded. "But it seemed to me that having theorized about how the assassin got into the area, how the assassin smuggled the weapons past the security checks, how the assassin carried out this killing, and, in a general way, who this assassin was, I thought you might just be able to give us one more theory—about how the assassin got hold of these weapons."

"No, sir, I can't."

"Perhaps, then, the chief might throw some light on how the grenades were brought into the area, now that he's heard the FBI's ideas. After all, his men were at the gate."

Steele looked embarrassed, even though he must have known the question was sure to be asked.

"I must respectfully say that I don't know."

"But you did say, didn't you, that when we'd seen the tapes and film, you might be able to suggest how it could have been done?" I reminded him.

"Yes, sir, I did. I can't say it did happen this way—only that it *might* have done. The assassin could have planted the weapons somewhere in the area at some time in the recent past, on the assumption the President would eventually be greeted there by members of the public."

"Isn't it true that this particular part of the base is constantly patrolled and searched?"

"Yes, sir, it is."

"And is it not also true that it was gone over by your men before the people were allowed in that night?"

"Yes, it was," he said lamely. "But it's always possible that the concealment was of a very professional standard. Under the pressures of time there's always the one in a thousand chance of its not being found."

"Well, Chief"—I sighed—"that's not much of an alternative to Mr. Reedy's suggestion, is it?"

"I'd say that was a matter of opinion."

"Either way, however, the Secret Service was caught with its guard down, wasn't it?"

"I'd like to point out that nobody has yet established negligence by me or my service."

"Moving on from the method of this assassination to the matter of identity, I'd like to ask what you think of this hypothesis of a woman in an orange raincoat?"

"I don't think there's enough evidence to support that idea. But I'd also like to add that I have the highest regard for the methods and the men of the FBI."

"Excluding Charlotte Corday, how many cases are there in modern times involving female assassins, Mr. Steele?"

"Not many." He hesitated, then took a guess. "Maybe half a dozen all told."

"I can't recall that many, even including Mary Surratt," I said. "But as a general rule, would you expect a potential Presidential assassin to be a man—or a woman?"

Steele clearly didn't like having to answer the question, but he finally said, "Speaking solely for myself, I'd have to say a man. But that doesn't mean I'd make any assumptions about the President's safety. And so far nobody's proved that it was a woman."

"Who do you think your agents would look at more closely in a crowd, the men—or the women?"

"They're supposed to check out everybody—including kids."

"And you don't accept the director's hypothesis?"

He vigorously shook his head. "No, sir, I don't."

"Yet while he offers somebody, you offer us nobody. So you can't do any better?"

"Only my best," he barked.

"Let me tell you what I think. I think that both the FBI report and your testimony today are about as useful to this commission as a motorcycle in the bedroom—it won't carry you very far, you can't sleep on it, you can't sleep with it, and on a chilly night it won't even keep you warm. About the only thing it does is make life a damned sight more uncomfortable."

Reedy shifted angrily in his seat, and Steele tried to interrupt me. But I couldn't allow him to cut me off, not at this point.

"Not so fast, Mr. Steele. You two gentlemen at the witness table have had your say. I let you talk without interruption. Now I want you to listen to me."

The whole room seemed to become alert.

"All we've got so far is an assassination by hand grenade and a hell of a lot of unanswered questions. With the best efforts of two critically important government agencies to help us, we haven't learned a single thing we didn't already know from reading the newspapers. If anything, we can't even be sure of what we thought we knew. He"—I pointed to Reedy—"says it was a woman in an orange raincoat; you say it wasn't. He says the grenades were smuggled in; you say they were planted and somehow overlooked. He says it was one person acting alone; you don't seem convinced.

"But through all the confusion, one thing is beginning to seem obvious: We've been down this particular path before. If anything, we were better off last time because at least the assassin had a name, even if he did end up dead. He also was supposed to have acted alone. And in that case too there were more loose ends lying around than you'd find in a spaghetti dinner.

"Well, I have a theory of my own. It accounts for the evidence—such as it is—and it ties up some of those loose ends that nobody else so far seems to be very concerned with. I am suggesting that there was more than one person involved and that those responsible for this crime are still at large."

I paused for no more than a second to let it sink in. There was a faint hum among the spectators.

"It was a suicide mission all right. But the assassin probably didn't know it was supposed to be. He—or she—had a partner. Each one had a grenade. That way, if the first one missed, or had a loss of nerve, or was caught, there was a backup. The second killer set off his grenade to do two things: kill his partner and increase his own chances of escape.

"But these are the small fry. Who was behind this effort? And what on earth was its objective?"

I paused for a moment. I was pleased to notice that you could have heard a carbon paper drop. Even Hutchison wouldn't dare stop me now.

"I'm struck by the fact that there is only one source for the weapons involved. Could you go into some shady pawnshop and buy them under the counter? No. A fragmentation grenade is a world away from your thirty-dollar handgun. There is *only one place* these grenades could have come from.

"Perhaps they were smuggled out of Army stores and into this Air Force base by some disaffected element in the lower ranks of the military—by some group as part of a political and social protest. But if their aim was a spectacular act of political terrorism, such as killing the President, then they succeeded. And have they come forward as terrorists always do and claimed the—pardon the word—credit? No. As the FBI report says, all we have are the predictable crank messages. And if it was some kind of suicide mission inspired by some deeply felt grievance, where then is the suicide note to tell the world why this act was necessary?

"I think it's obvious that whoever it was succeeded in killing the President but considered that in itself not to be success but *failure*. And the only way that makes sense is if the President wasn't the target or if it was the President plus some other person or persons. I am convinced it was supposed to kill the Vice President, too. And that accounts for the type of weapon involved.

"So I'd like everybody on the commission to consider these facts: The only source of the weapons is the United States Army. They had to be brought onto a military base. They had to elude the checks—including the chance of a physical shakedown—by the air police and the Secret Service. And *everybody* there had to have both an official pass and an official identification.

"These are the facts. So is it also a fact that when we turn to two of the most professional agencies in government to help us make some sense of these facts, all we get are far-fetched possibilities—theories with holes in them big enough to drive a Mack truck through. Specially tailored brassieres . . . ultra-cunning camouflage. But not *one single shred of persuasive evidence for either one*.

"We also had a film. Some kind of secret film, I gather. Probably we'll discover that the Army or somebody else in the military is spying on civilians again, assuming they ever stopped."

It was a guess, but from Reedy's reaction it was close to the mark.

Quietly Hutchison said, "A very interesting summary. But I'm not sure that you've managed to make your point clear."

"Mr. Chairman, what I'm saying is that all these items add up to only one thing: that there is only *one* adequate explanation for all of this—for how it was done and what its objective was. It could only have been carried out by means of a conspiracy, a conspiracy reaching into the highest levels of our government and our military services. And it could have but one objective: the paralysis of the government of the United States and the destruction of the Constitution."

There was a groundswell of muttering among the spectators, but Hutchison didn't try to damp it down. I raised my voice until I was almost shouting.

"It was a plot that came within an inch of success. It was meant to create a power vacuum by killing at one blow both the President and his elected successor. The result would have been a power vacuum such as this country could not survive. Thank God the plot failed—but only just.

"And now this commission is being bamboozled and deliberately misled. I've never seen an investigation stumble over so many red herrings in a single hearing as we have today.

"But I can tell you this, Mr. Chairman, I can promise you this: So long as there's breath in my body, I'm going after these plotters! Wherever they are, whoever they are, I'll track them down and identify them. I'll name them, each and every one of them! They're the guilty ones, far more guilty than the pathetic murderers who threw the grenades.

"This secret organization is betting on its powerful friends to protect it, I'm sure of that. But this is my warning to them. At least one person is on to you. Soon there'll be others. *And you can't kill us all.*"

Sweating and out of breath, I sank back into my seat. I could feel Carter looking at me, absolutely shaken. For the first time Hutchison was using his gavel.

"This hearing is now adjourned! This hearing is now adjourned!"

Steele bustled over and bent his head down, almost forcing his face up into mine.

"I don't know what your goddamned game is. Just because we lost one," he said bitterly, "just because we lost one, every wise ass in this town thinks he's got a license to kick my department around. But if you've got some bright idea about using this commission to fuck over me and my men. . . ." He stopped short.

"Yes, Mr. Steele?" I raised my voice loud enough to be heard halfway across the room. "Why are you trying to threaten me, Mr. Steele?"

His face reddened angrily, and he stalked off.

My desk telephone rang. I picked it up. A voice said, "You . . . you . . . I don't know what you're trying to do. But I know you tricked me, you did it on purpose . . . you conniving, rotten. . . ." The voice broke off. I recognized it. It was my wife's.

Chapter Nine

THIRTY YEARS ON: ANOTHER MCCARTHY? asked the headline over the editorial in the New York *Times*. THE FINGER OF SUSPICION POINTS AT—WHOM? wondered the Washington *Post*. Both, as you'd expect, worried about power without responsibility; both said the country was on the verge of a witchhunt.

I turned from the newspapers to the small sack of letters and telegrams that had already come in. Equally predictable: roughly four to one in my favor. In so many words, the general theme was "*I* knew it was a plot all along. But I didn't know if there was anybody there in Washington who had the guts, etc., etc. . . ."

Some time before, I had composed a reply to the editorials, in my head. I now spent a few minutes typing it out.

> In reply to the emotional charges that I am using the Hutchison Commission to launch a witch-hunt, I must admit to being guilty.
>
> It would be improper for me to discuss the work of the commission in any detail, but I can say categorically that I am determined to find out *which* of our security measures to protect the President broke down, to identify *which agencies* of government were responsible for this break-

down, to find out *which* steps we must take if there are to be no more political killings, and, most important of all, to identify *which* persons were responsible for this monstrous crime. I say "persons" deliberately, because I do not believe that this was—or could have been—the act of some lone, crazed assassin.

Other people are entitled to their own beliefs in this matter. All I insist on is the right to pursue mine—*which*ever way they lead. And I find it difficult at times to understand why anyone, or any responsible organ of opinion, would want to discourage me or put obstacles in my way.

So far, I have mentioned no names. Not one person has been "smeared"; no reputation—save my own—has been put in jeopardy. However publicly, however forcefully, all I have done is raise a few important questions and express a general opinion of the direction in which the answers are likely to be found.

The media and their usual allies and apologists have taken it upon themselves to decide that in doing so I have committed some sort of offense against public decency. What innocents they are! As almost anyone can tell them, they've been doing the same thing for as long as anyone remembers.

I read it through. Sufficiently literate, I decided, to help throw the suburban, college-educated middle class a bit off-balance by making them unsure of what they were dealing with. The unwashed, to judge from the mail, were already coming my way.

The buzzer on my desk sounded. Hastily, I corrected my typing errors, tucked the sheet into a folder and went down the hall to see the President.

He looked just as sick as the day before. Still, he'd insisted on coming down to his office. Vanity again, I supposed. He didn't want any repetition of having Cabinet members and Congressmen hovering around his bedside. Not if he could help it.

He growled, "I expect you already saw what the papers have to say."

"Yes, Mr. President. The major ones, anyway. And I've looked through the mail on my desk."

"Well?"

"Pretty much what you'd expect, all things considered—intellectuals and knee-jerk liberals against; ordinary, working people for."

"You were cutting up pretty rough, though, don't you think?"

"I'm very sorry sir, if I did or said anything that embarrassed you or made you think I'd let you down. The only thing I can say in mitigation, I guess, is that I don't have much experience from that end of a committee. But given what we may be up against here, I don't think I did anything fundamentally off base. I'm ready to stand by what I said."

Keenly, he scanned my face. *Had I rung false somewhere?* I wondered.

"I don't want you to misunderstand me now," he said. "I'm not saying you did anything wrong. It just didn't seem very tactful, the way you sprung out on 'em like that." He started to chuckle to himself. "Mind you, I think you scared the living bejesus out of old Hutch. And that Bud Carter looked about ready to crap in his pants."

"If it's the press coverage, Mr. President, and the way they edited the film for the network news programs. . . ."

He cut me off sharply. "Look, I know there's all kinds of rotten things going on around here. Maybe there *is* some kind of plot somewhere. There's sure a hell of a lot of crooked sons of bitches in this town anyway, up to God knows what. I know all that. But dammit all, do you have to lean so hard on the FBI and the Secret Service?"

So that was what upset him. I'd been fooling around with the sacred FBI and the even holier Secret Service. Neither of them stood so high any more as they had in the years before the Kennedy assassination and Watergate. But to people like him, whose faith in some institutions was simple and direct, nothing could bring it very low. He was the kind of believer who kept the church going through the Reformation. His was the kind of faith that kept Communists true to Communism despite Stalin.

Neither Reedy's obtuseness nor Steele's failure to prevent another assassination would deter him. They were irrelevant. What mattered was the noble institution. It wasn't for me to tell him he was living in a world of dreams.

I shrugged helplessly. "I'm sorry about that. But they're both so close to this thing, one way and another, that I don't know how it can be avoided entirely. There's a *prima facie* case of negligence involved there somewhere. And it isn't only me. The rest of the commission doesn't seem very happy with them either. You could see what Specci thought of Reedy."

He squirmed uncomfortably in his wheelchair. "But couldn't you . . . maybe . . . tone it down a little?"

"Whatever you say, Mr. President." There wasn't much more mileage to be had from them anyway.

Even in a situation like this the better side of his nature came through. He remained a man of clumsily generous impulses. For now, having tried to take something away with one hand, he was determined to give something with the other.

"But I don't want you to worry yourself about these press and TV people. Some of those jerks have made a whole career out of doing nothing else but knocking me and making fun of the things I've tried to do. It's about time some of them learned just where they get off. I'm tired of being pissed on by a lot of armchair strategists. I've taken this kind of stuff"—he gestured at the newspapers and the daily press summary—"for years." He made another gesture. "This time they can shove it."

His intercom buzzer sounded. "Secretaries Farb and Morrissey are here, Mr. President," said Madge, "and the Speaker and the Majority Leader are just coming up the drive."

"Okay, Madge. You send them straight in here." He turned to me. "Let's see what they have to say. Then we can see where we're headed on this thing."

I helped him tidy up some of the papers on his desk for a minute or two, until the door opened and in came Farb and Morrissey, followed by Van Riebouw and Czecky. It was obvious Farb was displeased; he was frowning heavily. Morrissey looked edgy and ill at ease. Czecky, I thought, looked ready to go a full ten rounds. And Van Riebouw was smiling beneficently, ready to save my soul or preside over my funeral, whichever came first. It was to be four against one, with the President as referee and scorekeeper.

"Mr. President," Farb began once the preliminaries were over, "I am afraid I must speak bluntly about the events of yesterday. I have been in contact with all those Cabinet members who witnessed the hearings, either live or broadcast. And it is the considered opinion of us all, as Secretary Morrissey will confirm, that the entire executive branch can only be brought into disgrace if there are any more histrionic outbursts of this kind. Let me also say that we are satisfied there was nothing more involved than an excess of zeal on the part of your special assistant here. But any repetition or any similar occurrence in the future can only leave the record of this administration in bad odor for a long time to come. It will almost certainly lead, in the short term, to a paralysis of government."

I could only admire Farb's courage. There was no equivocation in him.

"I appreciate the Secretary's frankness," I replied. "And I take it as an invitation to speak as plainly as he does. So why mince words—why not, if that is your view, Mr. Secretary, come right out and say that it stinks?"

"As you prefer," he said evenly, making his first mistake. I didn't need to look at the President to know his reaction to this.

"Either way," I continued, "it's really a matter of opinion. If we assume that beauty is in the eye of the beholder, then presumably odor is in the nose of the sniffer. And according to today's mail"—I reached around the side of the sofa, grasped a small mail sack, then put it heavily at his feet—"we're smelling of roses." I invited them all to examine the mail, which they did cursorily and with evident distaste.

"At least," I said, "we're smelling of roses right now. That's a fact. But how can you expect me to agree with prophecy? It's unfair; that's like trying to argue with God. Most of us couldn't tell you what the price of eggs is going to be, or if we're going to have a white Christmas. But Mr. Farb can forecast the contents of the history books. Perhaps he'd like to tell us how it's done?''

All men choke on something; Farb choked on pride. He'd counted on his enormous prestige as his trump card in this showdown. It was a prestige I had to deflate if I was to deal with him. And now his swarthy cheeks were crimson. He was being ridiculed by a mere special assistant, a man who only weeks before was a complete nonentity so far as he was concerned. Not only was he being ridiculed, but it was being done in front of the President. It was a gamble that his anger would upset his judgment.

''You know what I mean,'' he snorted, and turned to the President. ''Sir, I came here to give you the consensus of your Cabinet in this matter. I did not come here to bandy insults with members of your immediate staff. But because of this gentleman''—he pointed angrily at me—''half the country is currently searching under its beds for phantom conspirators. All Washington is in a frenzy because of this business. These wild, irresponsible charges have already done great harm. By all accounts, the Secret Service is so demoralized that half the agents there are considering a mass resignation. There's a strong rumor going around that Reedy's cooking up some melodramatic gesture to make himself out as an innocent victim who's being forced out of his job by a conspiracy in the White House. The media have shown how hard they intend to come down on us. And on top of that there's scarcely a general officer in the country who now feels he could look you in the face. Last, but not least, the reaction we're already getting from abroad can be summed up in one word: disgust. And all for what?''

Czecky could contain himself no longer. ''Yes, Mr. President, for what?'' he demanded.

''And I can tell you plainly, sir,'' Morrissey chimed in, ''that as far as the military's concerned, Secretary Farb is correct. There's not one officer of my acquaintance, regardless of his rank, who doesn't feel that people are now looking at him in an accusing way, wondering if he had any part in this imaginary conspiracy. I think we can expect some resignations in that department too.''

The President was looking from one to the other, miserable and irresolute. He wanted people to be happy. He wanted them to appreciate his efforts on their behalf. Yet all that seemed to come of it was squabbling and bickering. Such thoughts were written all over his ashen face. Van Riebouw, who had so far said hardly a word, judged the moment propitious for a summing up and a smoothing down.

"I think that what we're all trying to say, Mr. President, is that this particular hearing hasn't worked out the way some of us hoped it would. So far it's given this administration a bad image—a very bad image, in fact. But the situation hasn't gone so far yet that we can't repair some of the damage and get things back on an even keel."

The President looked at me. I said, "Now that you gentlemen have each stated your opinion, I'd like to explain if I may. Evidently my manner upset you. And for that I apologize sincerely. I have no wish to be rude or unfair to anyone. But my outburst, if that's what you'd like to call it, was an outburst of honest anger. As I sat there and listened to all that alibiing, and the attempts to evade responsibility . . . well, I simply got very angry. There was nothing more to it than that. It was bad-mannered, I suppose."

"It wasn't just the manner," snapped Czecky. "It was the whole damned business. All this BS about plots and conspiracies and secret organizations."

"To say nothing of the putative Hercules sent down from the White House to clean out the stable," said Farb.

"I must say it's remarkable how everybody's more worried about the image than about the substantive questions. My manner seems more important than the President's murderers. I would have thought that was the chief, if not the only, consideration," I said.

"Of course we want to find out who was behind the assassination," snapped Czecky. "We all do."

"But not one of you has so far mentioned it. Secretary Farb has scolded me. The Secretary of Defense calls me a liar. The Speaker is kind enough to suggest that I'm an irresponsible idiot. The Majority Leader speaks of 'damage' as if I were a species of political vandal. But at the end of it all we're not one step closer to finding the President's killers."

"We don't think your approach serves either that purpose or the best interests of the President," insisted Farb defensively.

"I think that's for me to decide, Mr. Secretary," wheezed the President.

Farb bowed slightly by way of excusing himself. Suavely he tried to pass it off. "We are only offering advice, Mr. President."

"I think that what's involved here goes a long way beyond that," I rejoindered. "You have all, very deliberately, decided to try to undermine my standing with the President and make him doubt my usefulness to him and this administration."

Farb tried to interrupt, but I overrode him.

"Oh, yes, you have. Why try to deny it? It's a normal part of life in this town. Cutting the rug out from under somebody else is something everybody does sooner or later. We all know that. But in this case you were in such a hurry you couldn't do it in the usual way, in easy stages, more or less indirectly. You want to break me right now, before I can do any more 'damage.' That's the whole reason for this meeting and why you insisted on having it right away."

What I said was true. And it was one of those personal, situational truths that, once openly stated, creates confusion among those it touches. It had registered, too, with the President. Half-heartedly, Morrissey tried to bluff his way through, but he soon ran out of steam. There was a brief but guilty silence. The time had come, I thought, to bring this particular confrontation to a head.

I pointed at Farb and Morrissey, "You two have tried before to get me out of the White House and limit my contacts with the President. It wasn't my wish to go on the commission. That was *your* idea."

Farb's face was impassive; but Morrissey looked over at the President, and the President looked away.

"Don't worry," I went on. "The President kept his word to you. But the attempt was so obvious it couldn't be mistaken. Nor could its motives."

In fact, it had taken me many hours to become convinced of what had happened and who was behind it. It became easy only when I'd figured out how it had been possible to get the President to order me on the commission. That could have been done only by framing me, which could not have been managed without leaving a telltale sign somewhere, and search as I might I could find none; or, by using something I *had* done or said to make the President think I might be disloyal. There were only three possibilities there: my wife, Specci, or Farb and Czecky. It seemed extremely unlikely that anybody would have bothered to bug me *before* the assassination. What could they possibly have hoped to get out of it? And since that evening at Andrews, I'd been very careful in my conversation. I didn't think I had much to fear—with one exception.

But I couldn't see Farb and Czecky simply walking in on the President and reporting what I'd said, even if they'd had a tape to back them up. All that might do was undercut my standing with him, but what would it do for them? For a long time I couldn't fathom it.

It wasn't until I grasped the identity of the third man that it became clear: Farb enlisted Morrissey, but without telling Czecky. Farb intended, with Morrissey's backing, to try to run the President, at least until another one was sworn in. Sane or crazy, he didn't trust this President to keep the country in one piece. In years to come a political scientist would no doubt be able to explain it all easily. Congress tried to reassert itself in the 1970's, don't you see, and failed. The Presidency was still in desperate straits, however. So we had the brief but very interesting phenomenon, in admittedly extraordinary circumstances, of an attempt being made by part of the Cabinet to assert control over the executive branch. Institutionally such an analysis might make sense and parallels could be drawn with eighteenth-century British government. But at the moment, I saw it all entirely in terms of personalities.

Farb and Morrissey had probably told the President just enough to make him doubt my commitment to his interests. With Morrissey there they'd have been able to mix in a little hocus-pocus about national security. But they were smart enough not to try to sell him too much all at one go. They probably shook him up, then offered a way out of his dilemma: put me on the commission. That way, there would be no danger of my isolating him the way some aides had isolated Presidents in the past. But I'd still be able to serve him on a daily basis, and that way he'd be able to judge the depth of my commitment to him. If I were sound, it would show up. Or so they'd told him. And he'd bought the whole package.

"I'm not sure you're being entirely fair," said Morrissey defensively, with gestures to match.

"Well, if you're trying to say that it backfired on you," I said, "you're entirely right. You wanted me to be on the commission. I didn't, nor, I suspect, did the President. But you sold him on this deal. How I neither know nor care to know"—Farb looked up at me angrily, but I went on unimpressed—"and now you're squirming because you don't like the consequences. One thing's pretty obvious though: One way or another, you're determined to get me out of here, and you were determined to do it before this commission ever came along. I'll let the President draw his own conclusions from that."

The President, who was by now thoroughly shaken, clearly didn't know what to conclude. But I was certain that at least one point must have gone home: *Somebody was out to get me*. It was only a short step from that to concluding somebody was out to get *him*.

Farb, who was probably seething, started to explain calmly that he was trying to help the President and insisted that we were becoming distracted by "personalities." Morrissey, on the other hand, looked as if he wanted to flee.

"My only regret is that you misunderstood our motives, then and now," said Farb.

I felt my hand was now strong enough for me to spurn openly this attempt at reconciliation, and, in truth, Farb was offering very little. He neither conceded that I was right nor apologized for attempting to undercut me.

"There is only one other thing for me to say," I remarked.

"And that is that I am personally and unshakably convinced that there was, and is, a plot to destroy the government. Call it wild and irresponsible if you like. But from what we know so far, that is the only explanation that brings all the available facts together in a logical and coherent way. The idea may seem repugnant to you. It is to me. But this is also a rare kind of political situation—one where the proposed answer is either completely right or completely wrong. If my hypothesis is wrong, then only one person is going to suffer for it—me. And I'm highly expendable. For a while the country is going to be a little jumpy, that's true. But that will also pass. In the meantime I'm prepared to make a solemn promise to you: that I will name no names until I have enough proof, and strong enough proof, to satisfy a court of law."

Morrissey shifted nervously, and Farb looked thoroughly outraged.

"Suppose, however, that I'm not wrong, that there really is a secret organization, involving powerful figures, determined to seize the government. Then the whole country is at stake. The Constitution, this administration, our whole way of life, are resting on a knife-edge. One slip, one moment of indecision, one bad guess, and we all go under. Let me ask you one question, Mr. Secretary Farb: Will you give the President, and the people of this country, an absolute assurance, in writing, that there is no plot, no conspiracy, involved in the assassination of the late President? Will you give a public guarantee that I am wrong?"

I fixed his eyes with mine. And as someone said during the Cuban missile crisis, we were eyeball to eyeball—and the other guy blinked first.

"No, I can't do that," said Farb softly.

"Then perhaps Mr. Secretary Morrissey can give the President and the nation that assurance?"

Morrissey shook his head and murmured, "No."

I turned to Czecky. "That's an impossible guarantee to ask, and you know it," he said. "And I still think the way you behaved makes the commission look like the Inquisition at work."

He was as tough as ever. Yet it seemed to me that even with him there was now something in his tone that pointed to a weakened confidence in the ground he stood on.

"I have apologized both to you gentlemen and the President for my display of anger," I said. "But if the Speaker wants some kind of tame, sham, fake hearing for the sake of calm and decorum, then I must say that I won't have any part of it."

"Why not let the commission go ahead in the way most people expected, though?" inquired Van Riebouw, conveniently forgetting his own role in getting the hearings on television. "At the same time we could get the intelligence community to make another, more intensive investigation behind the scenes, along the lines you suggest."

The President looked up at this proposal, which meant I had to head it off.

"In the first place, I don't think Hutchison would be party to a charade. The moment he heard about it, he'd resign. We all know that. That would make a fine mess, wouldn't it?

"I also think that going after these assassins openly is the best way of frightening them off another attempt. At the same time we're assuring the country that there aren't going to be any whitewashes or cover-ups.

"And finally, now that the question of a conspiracy *has* been raised, I don't think it's realistic to expect that people will forget about it."

"All right. I've heard enough," whispered the President.

We all looked at him. He was trembling, and an ugly twitch was leaping on his face.

"Get out. Go on—get out!"

The four of them started shuffling shamefacedly to the door, uncertain of what else to do.

"Yes, Mr. President," Farb said weakly. "We're sorry to have imposed on you like this. But we were only trying to give you our best advice."

Chastened, the other three joined in hesitantly, agreeing that this was so. And on their faces was a look of amazement as they saw the President of the United States thrashing about in his wheelchair, ordering them out and mumbling incoherently about "no respect." I started to leave with them.

"Not you," he croaked. I ushered the four of them out, murmuring, "I'll let you know what the President decides. Thank you for coming."

"Coming here, telling me what I do stinks." He was almost choking with rage. "Bastards. They wouldn't have dared—wouldn't have *dared*—with anybody else. My Cabinet. They're not *my* Cabinet; they're *his* Cabinet. They used to laugh at me before. I know that. But I didn't take their resignations. I kept them on. And this is how they treat me. Walk in here, tell me what I ought to do, how I ought to run my staff. They want to protect their own little empires, that's what it is. They don't think I can handle this job. Even if I hadn't been hurt, they'd still think I wasn't up to it."

He ranted on in this vein for some time, making vague threats of retaliation, recalling countless small gestures his four visitors had made in the past—gestures, he was certain, of contempt for him personally. He remembered words he'd heard uttered and rumors of words, all holding him up to ridicule. I listened attentively, glad that Farb and the others had caught a glimpse of his true condition and how he responded to stress.

When I left him I set up a meeting with his military aide, Brigadier General John B. Homan.

Chapter Ten

We sat, looking grim, in a small, soundproof, ostensibly unbugged room in the White House basement. There was a particular tone I wanted to establish, and this gray room made for a good beginning. The atmosphere was hushed and conspiratorial. Homan attuned to it at once, putting aside his usual breezy affability. It was like whispering to someone and having him whisper back.

"I feel I ought to apologize for dragging you down here, General. But this was the only place outside the West Wing where I could be certain we could talk freely. And it would get around pretty fast if we met in the West Wing."

He examined my face, a frown puckering his brow. Puzzled when I pulled him to one side in the mess a couple of hours earlier, he was more than puzzled now. He was worried.

"Would you like to give me a quick rundown on what this is all about, sir?"

"Yes, General. It's to do with the assassination—and those who might have been involved in it."

He bit his lip and answered slowly, "I was afraid it might be that."

"But don't worry," I tried to reassure him, "this is outside the work of the commission. I'm here on behalf of the President."

He pulled out a note pad and pen. "Do you mind if I make notes of our conversation, sir, as we go along?"

"Please stop calling me sir," I said. "I appreciate why you want to take notes. But I also hope that when we've had a talk, you'll understand why it might be a good idea to either destroy them or put them somewhere that's very, very safe."

He looked somber and wrote something down. I continued, "What is your personal opinion of the hypothesis that there was a plot to kill the President and the Vice President in a single attack?"

"It's plausible," he replied noncommittally, scribbling in his note pad. "But I don't think I'd like to say any more than that."

"I don't like to press you on this," I insisted, "but do you also think it possible that these same people having failed the first time, might make another attempt—only this time trying to seize the government outright by force? In other words, a coup d'état?"

Homan studied the backs of his hands and his fingertips for a few moments, plainly troubled. But I also sensed very strongly that he wanted to answer the question and answer it honestly.

"You know, I've spent twenty-two years in the Army. In most of that time I'd have had no hesitation in saying that a suggestion like that was ridiculous. You remember that book *Seven Days in May*? Well, I thought it was pretty good. I enjoyed it. But to me it was fun the way science fiction is fun. Not to be taken seriously.

"Even after Vietnam, when everybody was down on the Army, I'd have said the answer to your question was no. And it still seems far-out to me. I can't honestly say I can picture it in my mind. But"—he exhaled unhappily—"it is *possible*. Christ, these days almost anything seems possible. But I'd also like to say that I do not personally know of a single officer whom I would suspect of disloyalty. I can't help you there."

I liked Homan. He was a brave and honest man—intelligent, ambitious within the rules, conscientious and unquestionably devoted to his service and his country. These were the very qualities I was counting on. And as he sat there, on the other side of the plain, government-issue desk in that austere little room, looking up at the neon lights through wispy gray aureoles of Dutch cigar smoke, I was genuinely sorry he would have to be destroyed and his career turned into a shambles. For the gently waving hair, the large, noble head, the straight back and gangling frame said far more eloquently than uniform and stars could ever do that this was one of nature's own aristocrats. On his chest was no splashy announcement of campaigns and battles fought, no beribboned steps to echo the rungs up the ladder of a successful officer's career. He wore only his Combat Infantryman's Badge, his pale blue Infantry lanyard and his Master Paratrooper's wings. A plain soldier and a good one.

"General, I believe that a coup is not only possible, but imminent. What's more, I think that you and I are among the handful of people who can prevent it or at least keep it from succeeding."

He was writing hurriedly. Without raising his head he firmly demanded to know, "Why me?"

"Because I know you. The President knows you, and we both trust you. We are going to have to rely very much on your judgment in assembling a force to prevent this coup."

"Impossible," he retorted. "I'm afraid that goes beyond the range of my responsibilities."

"I'm not going to presume to tell you how to do your job, General. . . ."

He interrupted me. "Jack."

"All right, Jack. Will you at least hear me out before you decide whether or not you'll help us?"

He sat back, but kept his pen poised.

"The President ought to be able, in a crisis like this, to go to the Joint Chiefs. But this thing is potentially so big that he can't be sure that one, maybe more of them, isn't already involved in it. Maybe he should go to the Chief of Staff of the Army and tell him he wants soldiers brought into the District. But suppose he gets the wrong soldiers?"

Homan was suspicious now, if not downright incredulous.

"I'm not saying any of these officers is implicated. All I'm saying is that we can't be sure they're not. And even if they're not, if this plot is as big as we think it is, some of their friends and protégés might be mixed up in it. We both know how strong the temptation would be to warn their friends off. They'd also be likely to help their guilty friends cover their tracks and then justify it on the grounds they were protecting the good name of the service."

Homan was writing again, and he said emphatically, "I don't want to see the Army dishonored either."

"General . . . Jack, I think we both realize that the Army's going to be under a cloud for as long as this business goes unresolved. These officers, whoever they are, have already disgraced the uniform. Better, I would think, for the Army to help clean up its own mess, and to do it as quickly as possible, than let it drag on and have somebody else do it."

With a slight, wry smile on his face, he asked, "How do you know I'm not one of *them*?"

"I don't. I'm trusting to my judgment that you're not. The President and I have to trust somebody. We're betting on you."

"I think you've got the wrong man. And I'll tell the President that, if you like."

For a moment I was worried that perhaps I had indeed got the wrong man.

"What sort of shape do you think the President's in these days?" I asked him.

"Not good," he said.

"But you've seen him, though; you've heard the rumors going around this building all the time. . . ."

"I don't listen to rumors."

"But you agree that he's not . . . very strong?"

"Okay, so he's not completely recovered. But I'm a soldier, not a doctor. There's not much I can do for his health."

"No. But you can protect him and the Constitution."

"Does he know about this interview?"

"Yes," I lied.

"I still don't think I'm the right man for you."

"Perhaps you don't appreciate the seriousness of what's involved."

There was a long, drawn-out, fervent reply of "Oh, yes, I do."

"Jack, all I'm asking you to do at the moment is put me in touch with the most reliable general officer, known to you personally, who has a combat command within the continental U.S. but not in the immediate vicinity of the District."

Scribble, scribble went the pen.

"You're serious about this." It wasn't so much a question as a realization.

"Let me reply by asking you another question, if I may." He put down his note pad, which I took for compliance.

"Do you think I'd be so much as hinting at this impending coup and asking you to stop it, if we—the President and myself—weren't convinced that the threat was real?"

He mulled this over for a while before asking, "What proof do you have?"

"All circumstantial."

"Then how can you be sure?"

"We can't. But so long as we act discreetly, we don't need a whole lot of evidence. What we do have to have, however, is a way of spoiling this attempt when it's made. If, for whatever reason, there's *no* attempt, then we disband, and that's that. I suppose we'll breathe a sigh of relief, break open a bottle and have a good laugh at ourselves."

"And that's all?"

"That's all."

He doodled on his pad for a full minute. "I still don't like it."

"I can't say I'm very enthusiastic myself. But all I'm trying to do is come up with a minimax strategy to counter these people."

"I've spent a long time in the Army," he mused, talking more to himself than to me. "I've worked pretty hard at it, and I've been fairly successful. Hell, I like the Army. It isn't simply a job to me. I want to be in it for a while yet. But if this thing isn't on the level. . . ." His voice trailed off.

"Jack, I don't see you as some grubby careerist. I don't doubt that if, for some crazy reason, you had to go out on the South Lawn and wrestle an alligator to save the President, you'd do it.''

We sat there, looking at the desk, the walls, each other, for a minute.

''I guess you're right,'' he eventually conceded. He wrote something on his note pad, ripped off the page and pushed it across the desk to me. He'd written: ''Maj. Gen. William C. Taggart, 101 Abne. Div., Ft. Campbell.''

''I'd stake everything I've got on Bill Taggart,'' said Homan. ''If there is a plot, and Bill Taggart's in on it, then there's not much hope for any of us. You can kiss the Constitution good-bye.''

Chapter Eleven

Five days later I was just another fish swimming—at times, struggling—along in the roaring tide of tourists, servicemen and Mexican workers that swamped the Friendship Bridge joining El Paso to Juárez. I looked down and saw, in the fitful lights from both shores, a swirl of muddy brown water racing down the mere gully that the grandly named river becomes at this point. Where the crowd erupted from the bridge like a bursting boil onto the main street everything looked more garish, more frantic, more prosperous and more desperate than ever. A town living forever on and at the end of its wits.

I dodged and twisted my way for about a hundred yards until I came to a bar on the right-hand side called Bermúdez. Most of its clientele was, most of the time, Mexican. There was little here (except perhaps local color) to interest the tourist. I elbowed my way into a table near the window and ordered a drink in my tentative Spanish. As bored and as impassive as the others there, I waited. Yet all the time I was studying the ever-changing, shifting crowd on the sidewalk, trying to sort out each individual from the mass, but examining clothing, not faces.

After at least twenty minutes a short, powerfully built man in an aloha shirt walked slowly past the window, looking intently toward the street. I finished my drink and strolled out into the crowd.

It had taken five days to set up this meeting with Taggart. Homan, I must admit, had worked hard, and secretly, to bring it about. He had kept his notes, but he'd also promised to say nothing, even if asked, without my or the President's permission. And without Homan there would have been no meeting with Taggart. The airborne general had eventually agreed to meet me here, only after I confirmed by coded message that it was the President's wish that he do so. He already had a commitment at Fort Bliss for the Saturday afternoon.

Ciudad Juárez was a wonderfully convenient place for us to meet. In fact, it was ideal. We strolled down the main street of the Revolución that Saturday night, fending off the peddlers of all that gringo tourists are presumably after, from somebody's untouched sister to a pair of handmade sandals, declined taxis at almost every street corner and talked as freely as if we'd been in a bathysphere at the bottom of the ocean. We could be followed, we could be filmed; but no electronic listening device yet known would have been able to pick out our conversation from the general noise and bustle—not as long as we kept moving and didn't talk too loud.

Taggart's first words were: "I hope we can keep this short."

"So do I, General."

"And I sure hope to hell the President knows what he's doing . . . with all respect."

Taggart's hostility almost radiated from his muscular bulk like a magnetic field. I could also tell that what repelled him was me.

"I gather you don't much care for me personally, General, but. . . ."

"Let's just say I don't rate you as a television star," he growled. "But that's irrelevant."

"Yes, it is. I'm glad we agree about that."

"Now, what is it that's so hot we've got to meet like this, but it's so hot nobody can talk about it?"

"There's a coup being planned. An attempt to seize the government by force."

Taggart stopped and spun around violently, almost knocking an old Mexican woman, loaded down by plaster religious figures with orange day-glo halos, into the street. "Bullshit!"

His eyes were gray and hard. Stopped there, he reminded me of a granite rock on a craggy shore with the sea breaking around it. With difficulty I got him moving again. When he next spoke, he said, ''This conspiracy talk is the biggest load of horse manure I've ever heard. And let me tell you, mister, that I'm glad I've had this opportunity to tell you so to your face.''

''I appreciate your sentiments. But I think you ought to at least listen to what I have to say, especially after all the trouble we've gone to get here.''

He was silent and stone-faced as we walked along or, rather, made crazy little arabesques as we pushed our way down the street, saying, ''No . . . no, thank you . . . not interested . . . no . . .no . . . ,'' perpetually shaking our heads. Every so often we stopped to look in a window or at something, anything, back along the sidewalk. That way we could keep anyone who might be following us sufficiently far back that they couldn't overhear.

''Okay,'' he said stiffly. ''What does the President have to say? Because when you talk, I expect to hear the President speaking.''

''Fair enough,'' I said. ''We believe there's going to be a coup attempt. We don't know when. We probably won't until a few hours, at most, before it happens. But we think it can't be far off now.''

''What kind of grounds do you have for believing this . . . this fantasy?''

''We've monitored some pretty strange meetings involving the Chiefs. There's an RCT that's been doing some very unusual training. Somebody's also managed to get two armor battalions very close to the District, for no apparent reason. When we've asked for explanations, all we've got back is a lot of double talk.

''We've also got part of a message, but we still haven't managed to crack the code. And this last week, since the television hearing, there seems to have been a sudden increase in activity all the way around.''

Bitingly, Taggart snarled, ''What kind of proof is that, for crying out loud?''

''Look, General, you wouldn't be able to make any more sense out of the physical evidence we've got than we have. But I was also told to tell you no more than the essential minimum—for everybody's sake. We might—we just might—be dead wrong on this. So . . . least said, soonest mended.''

Taggart's weather-worn face—it looked like something you'd keep tobacco in—was sunk in a thunderous scowl. The crowd drove us apart, then brought us back together.

''So, what do you want to see me about if you can't tell me anything?'' he demanded.

''Because I . . . that is, the President, wants you to spoil this coup when these people make their move.''

''If they make it.''

''Okay, if they make it.''

''And how, precisely, am I supposed to go about kicking my career right up the ass?'' He was hard as nails, but he was starting to come my way.

''Our best hope is to smash this thing the minute it breaks into the open. They're probably assuming we won't make a fight of it if they get in the first blow.''

''So you want to get in first?''

I shook my head. ''I wish we could. But we don't have a force big enough. And without you we won't have a force at all.''

''So?''

''We want you to parry that first blow and give the government at least a chance to fight back.''

We resisted a spotty-faced adolescent who tried to drag us into a brilliantly lighted store full of bullfighters and madonnas painted on velvet. It gave Taggart a chance, however, to consider what I'd said.

''I'm listening,'' he grunted as we got back into the crowd.

''How many men could you airlift into the District in a hurry?''

''Without clearing it up the line first?''

I nodded my answer. Taggart was suddenly enthusiastic for

a taco from a hole in the wall near the Golden Palace. When he'd finished it, he wiped his mouth with his handkerchief and through gritted teeth said, "One battalion, probably. I've got direct control of enough aircraft for that. If I can bluff the Air Force a bit, maybe two battalions."

"How long from the time you get the word till you'd be ready to fight?"

"Are you talking now about a real, honest-to-God fire fight?" His voice sounded hushed and slightly tense.

"A real, honest-to-God fire fight, with real, honest-to-God casualties. Let's just pray, though, that it doesn't come to that."

"I don't believe it," he said fiercely. "This isn't some two-bit Arab country. You're talking about the United States of America."

I tried to make my voice sound subdued, saddened, but still loud enough for him to hear me clearly.

"I'm talking about trying to keep it that way, General." I repeated my question. "How much advance warning would you need?"

"To the DZ?"

"Yes."

"And where is the DZ?"

"West Potomac Park principally, also around the Washington Monument and—if that's not enough, and you're willing to try it—along the Reflecting Pool and down the Mall."

"You've gotta be kidding."

"General, I don't have that kind of sense of humor."

We walked along in silence for a few minutes, declining a proposition from a Mexican queer (at least, he said he was) to come along and see how handsome his friend was.

"That's quite a drop zone," he finally said. He fell silent again for a minute, then said, "If there's no real hitch, we might be able to load the aircraft in about thirty minutes. Then allow an hour and a half for us to get there. I'd say about two and a half hours before we'd be ready to fight—or whatever. But that would be pushing it."

We walked along some more, then a thought struck him with

a force that brought him to a near halt. "I hope the Air Force isn't in on this, because if they are, then there's not a damned thing I could do for you. We'd be sitting ducks."

"Let's hope it isn't. As far as we know. . . ." I left the sentence unfinished.

"That's great, isn't it," he grumbled bitterly. "It's just the Army . . . the goddamned United States Army."

"Will you help us, General Taggart?"

We were moving back toward the bridge now. We agreed that he would go first and I'd leave a few minutes later. Unless I was very wrong, I reflected, there were now several hundred feet of film of us somewhere nearby; doubtless there was also an agent or two, with a camera, itching to get the film back to Washington to be developed.

"Listen, I've got a couple of things to say to you. In the first place, I don't necessarily assume that you and the President have got this thing figured right. There's probably a simple explanation for everything. In the second place, I'm not commiting myself till I've heard more of the details about this so-called conspiracy. And I want to hear this request for troops from the President himself."

Here, at last, was the request I'd been waiting for. I sympathized with Taggart's demand. I could only hope that he'd buy my answer.

"I'll get you an order in writing."

With barely any hesitation, but very politely, he replied, "Negative. It's got to come from him personally."

He was certainly going the limit. There wasn't anything higher than a direct verbal order from his Commander in Chief—and that's what he wanted.

The bridge was now no more than a hundred yards away. Its looming proximity helped put a nice edge on the increasingly insistent tone of my voice.

"Believe me, General, we've considered that. But with the President the way he is now, there's no way of arranging a get-together between you two without somebody finding out. We figure there'd be maybe one chance in three of a leak to the wrong parties. And it might easily act as a trigger; they'd have nothing to lose at that point. If they did preempt us, we'd be caught with our pants down—and no way in hell of getting our asses covered up again. So . . . I'm sorry, but it's no dice. We've got a zero margin for error. We can't afford the risk."

"I'm sorry, too. I can't help you."

It looked like a stalemate. We were both morose as we shuffled slowly along the bustling street, swiveling our necks like ventriloquists' dummies, resisting entreaties to buy. But I had one more card left. It was really the card I'd come here to play.

"How about this: I'll try to get a written authorization from the President for you, to be shown only in an extreme emergency or when this thing is over. When you get my signal—we can work out a code word—you put your men in the planes. But you don't take off until you get a verbal Okay from the President himself." I was all restrained desperation. "What do you say?"

Taggart was uneasy. "How can you be sure of your communications security?"

"We can't be positive, it's true. But we've got at least one backup system in the works."

"But what happens if your communications get the chop?" he insisted.

"Then, I guess, you'll just have to disembark your paratroopers. You can say it was an emergency drill. In the meantime, the whole country will be going right down the tubes," was my embittered and halting reply.

We stopped. The Mexican police in their sand-colored uniforms and Sam Browne belts were only a few yards off, at the entrance to the bridge. We stared hard into a store window full of cut-price, tax-free liquor.

"And then it's all my fault, eh?" asked Taggart wryly.

"I didn't say that . . . and I wouldn't."

"Yeah. Well . . . who knows? Maybe you wouldn't." He fidgeted in his pockets for change to pay the toll. "Anyway, I'll think about it. I'll let you know."

He strode off, past the policemen, to be caught up in the stream of revelers already calling it a night on this side of the bridge, zigzagged into and out of the toll booth. disappeared into the darkness and anonymity on the hump of the bridge.

I walked across the street and down to the Bermúdez where I asked the waiter, "*Cerbeza, por favor*" and felt pleased with the way I pronounced it.

Chapter Twelve

The next morning, Sunday, I'd had only a couple of hours' sleep when the telephone shrilled. It was Specci, expertly managing to sound determined and apologetic at the same time.

"Sorry to have to call you so early." I glanced at my watch and groaned melodramatically. Not yet seven o'clock. "It's just that this seemed the best time to get hold of you and have a talk."

Normally I was up at this time, but now I was very tired. "Can't it wait till Tuesday, Frank?"

"If I thought it could wait, I wouldn't be calling you like this."

"All right," I said, "what is it?"

"If you don't mind"—undeterred by the obvious fact that I did—"I'd much rather see you about it than discuss it over the phone."

"What is this, Frank? Some kind of put-on? Go ahead, talk. If you like, I can set up a scrambler."

But Specci was not to be denied the fullness of a face-to-face confrontation.

"You haven't had breakfast yet, have you?"

"Oh, sure—but only in my dreams."

"I tell you what," he said, as if the idea had only just occurred to him. "Why don't you come over here and have breakfast with me? Joannie's off to mass in a couple of minutes. And I can promise you, you'll be well bribed: I make the best Lady Effingham's Eggs you've ever tasted."

"Whatever they are, they'd better be. See you in twenty minutes." I hauled two hundred pounds of lead into the shower and sprayed it with cold water. So Specci had finally called, I mused. I was glad, too, that he'd insisted on seeing me in person.

As I pointed the car up North Glebe toward Chevy Chase, I remembered to call the White House switchboard to let them know where I'd be. When I put the telephone back into its magic box, I found myself looking off to my right as I crossed Chain Bridge, looking down the Potomac toward the Capitol. This was the best time, I thought, when there was hardly any traffic, hardly any people about and the capital of the world all groggy with sleep.

A line of poetry came unbidden to my mind—"And all that mighty heart is lying still!" *Tennyson,* I murmured, shifting into third. *No,* I corrected myself, shifting down, *Wordsworth.* Anyway, that was a different world. But scarred and battered though it might be, what a mighty heart is here! Of khaki-colored walls and green roofs, of green-moldy statues charging, skirmishing, marching, peering, of fresh gray ferroconcrete and gleaming white stone—but most of all, of power.

This place, I thought, *must be unique among the great capitals of the world.* It's the only one I know that came into existence for no other reason. Even Brasília is an integral part of a program of regional development. But Washington was the result of a straight political trade-off between North and South. All it was was a swamp. It was to be a place from which to rule, and still is. Nobody doubts where it stands on everything: Its museums are good, not great; local theater and music, for all their showcases, are competent; it has a dozen colleges and universities, all mediocre.

Not culture, not learning, not the civilizing arts of society, but power—that's what Washington exists for. I expect that if it were ever withdrawn, then Washington would become nothing but a torpid, down-at-the-heels Southern town of moderate size, living on and off the memories of its golden age. But I love it.

As I pulled into Specci's driveway, it struck me how much this house told about the man who owned it—neat, old but not too old, expensive without being showy. That wild storefront lawyer always had a bigtime judge inside him struggling to get out. I walked around to the side and found him in his breakfast nook trying to coax an elegant silver chafing dish into a short, but useful, life.

"So, how's my favorite Sunday chef?"

"Laugh all you want, but it's a lot more interesting than washing the car."

"Oh, I'm not laughing." I laughed. "I'm looking forward to this. What is it, Julia Child's recipe of the month?"

"You'll see." He had the flame at the height he wanted. In went a large dollop of butter. "Two eggs?"

"Please."

He squeezed a couple of oranges and started making toast, giving the water in the chafing dish time to heat up and melt the butter. Four generous slices of Emmenthal went into the dish. He proceeded to break four eggs, very carefully, onto a plate. With even greater care he maneuvered them, one at a time, onto the slices of the now softened, buttery cheese.

"Everything you always wanted to know about heart disease, but were afraid to ask!" I said triumphantly.

"Do you want to start buttering that toast, please?" he said, still manipulating the eggs, then splashing some of the hot butter over them. By the time he'd got the coffee and I'd sliced the buttered toast into fingers the eggs were cooked and set. He sprinkled them with salt and paprika.

"Two for you, and two for me."

"Thanks." I started eating. "Frank," I said after my first mouthful, "these are the best Duchess of Who-is-it's eggs I've ever eaten, anywhere." And they were, in truth, delicious.

"Bit too much paprika," he mumbled through a mouthful of toast.

"Be sure to get me on the panel of judges when you have the first annual United States Supreme Court cook-off."

He smiled. Perfectionist he might be; but he liked to please, and he liked to be thanked. We finished breakfast, made a gesture in the direction of washing up and took our second cups of coffee into his study. Three Presidents and a Rembrandt drawing looked down. All looked as if they belonged there.

"We're old friends, aren't we?" he asked lightly.

"Yes," was my cautious reply.

He blew hard across the top of his coffee cup, creating a miniature storm of rising steam and tossing waves.

"What are you up to?" he wondered, as casually as if he was asking the time of day.

"I don't think I . . ." was as far as I got.

"Oh, come on now. There's something going on, something really important, and you're obviously mixed up in it. If you're in a jam . . . well, if you're involved in some kind of embarrassing situation and you're trying to cover up by dragging a lot of red herrings across the trail, I thought maybe I could help."

"There's no mess, Frank. No scandal," I said, hoping I was keeping my voice steady. "And I'm not mixed up in anything."

"You don't seriously expect us to swallow all this conspiracy guff, do you?" he said, still calm and friendly.

"I don't expect you to do anything."

He changed course. "Did you know that Hutchison was thinking of going to the President and telling him to make a choice—either he goes off the commission or you do?"

"If he feels that strongly about it, why doesn't he?"

"Because I told him I'd talk to you first. See what you have to say. And see if there's something we might do to help you."

This meeting with Specci was not unexpected. Nor was the way it was going. Even so, I felt like an adolescent being lectured by his favorite teacher for cutting up in class. Lying to Frank was harder than lying to anybody else I knew. It went against the grain of practice built up over more than ten years. So I was deeply apprehensive that I might, by some careless word or gesture, betray myself.

"What do you mean by help? You think I'm cracking up?"

"No," he said, almost laughing. "But you have been under a lot of strain. You were at the airport, which was a pretty terrible thing in itself. Then having to relive it with those films. And the work on the commission on top of your responsibilities in the

White House. Anybody might start to get a bit groggy under a load like that.''

''I'm sound of mind and body, Frank.''

''Accepting that, then, why didn't you tell me, or Hutch, that you thought there was a conspiracy? We had a couple of executive sessions, and you didn't even hint at it. Why wait until we were being televised?''

He was still patient, still calm, but he was becoming Mr. Justice Specci, bearing down on an appellant's lawyer with a shaky brief.

''Because it didn't all fall into place until the other afternoon, when you were putting it to Reedy and Steele.''

''As Macaulay said, that's all sail and no anchor. But why, now that you're hot on the trail of this plot, didn't you come to yesterday's session—because it *wasn't* televised?''

''White House business. I sent Hutchison a message. So long as there are four of us there, the commission can do its work. And I stayed up last night reading the transcripts.''

''Tell me something. If you were in my shoes, do you honestly think you'd find any of your answers convincing?''

I had become conscious of a latent trembling below the superficial tenor of my speech. If I couldn't keep it under, it seemed advisable to disguise it when it broke through.

''Oh, knock it off, Frank!'' I barked. ''That's one of those questions like 'If you had a cross-eyed, albino stepbrother, do you think he'd like cheese?' That kind of question's impossible and unfair, and you know it.''

''So, I would like to suggest, are some of yours,'' he said, unruffled. ''Do you remember, though, why we require that the prosecution proves guilt instead of making the accused prove he's innocent?''

''What is this, law school?''

''Come on,'' he insisted. ''Why do we?''

''Well, if I had to put in a brief I'd say something like this.'' As if reciting a formula, I intoned, ''It is an unfair burden in law, philosophy or debate to be asked to prove a negative case. There is less evidence, and far less reason, for those things which have not happened than for those things which have. Thus the burden of proof on lawyers, philosophers and debaters must lie with those who make the affirmative. Something like that."

"Fine. Good. But all of a sudden you turn around and start demanding that people prove they weren't part of a plot to kill the President. But damn it, man! You haven't even proved that this plot exists. You seem to expect everybody else to prove that it doesn't."

"So I got a little carried away."

"I don't believe it. You never get carried away. You were too good a lawyer, and you've got too sharp a mind, to charge into anything without thinking about it first."

"Okay. Suppose I told you that there *is* a plot, then, and that I'm the mastermind. And the object of this particular plot is nothing less than seizing the government of the United States and making myself dictator. How would that do?"

"Don't be ridiculous," he responded with asperity, sounding impatient for the first time. "Do you know what I think?"

"No, what?" I asked, sullenly swilling the dregs in the bottom of my coffee cup around.

"I think the President's a very sick man—a lot sicker than most people realize. I also think there are times when he. . . ." Specci had to force the words out. "When he's not in complete control of himself. Acts irrational, shall we say?"

"Why not say crazy?" I snorted.

"Anyhow, whatever it is, you're in a better position to know than anybody. Better, I expect, than his wife or his doctor. He might be able to pull himself together when he's around them. But you see him all the time. He has to rely on you. When the pressure's really on him, nine times out of ten you're the one he'll turn to. I'd say that if anybody knows what his real state is, it's you. Am I right?"

"You're not even warm."

"Well," he persisted, "let's just say, for the sake of argument, that the President is unstable—with a good chance of getting worse before he gets better. Let's also say that one of the symptoms is a paranoid tendency. . . ."

I blinked. "Paranoid?"

"For want of a better word, if you like. And this sick man has the whole burden of the Presidency thrust on him in a tragic way, after a lot of people—let's face it—have called him stupid, and a clown, and a lot of other things. Over the years, when the name-calling's as vicious as it's been in his case, it's bound to result in a lot of resentment boiling away inside. The only reason he got to be Vice President was that he could deliver California in a close election. So there he is, sitting in the White House, knowing that hardly anybody thinks he belongs there. And on top of that he's got this brain injury that lets all this . . . venomous stuff . . . break through. Once it starts, you know, it's going to happen more and more, and each time is going to be worse than the last."

"Very interesting," I drawled. "But I don't see where all this is taking us."

"Don't you? I would guess that he's the one who thinks there was a conspiracy involved in the assassination. He's the one who thinks there's some kind of plot now. And you feel you ought at least to oblige him by raising it on the commission. You're deliberately making him think you share his paranoia. Of course, that can only make him more dependent on you. But it's all a dumbshow, being put on for the sake of a sick President by an all too-devoted chief of staff."

He swiveled gently from side to side in his revolving chair and lit his pipe.

"So Mr. Justice Specci has it all figured out, while everybody else in town is still trying to decide what I'm up to?"

"I didn't say that. But it makes more sense than anything else I've heard or read about you lately."

"I wonder if, while you're at it, you'd also mind explaining where you got this paranoid stuff? That's a pretty strong word to be using seriously when you talk about the President. At a guess, I say that most people would say he's about as paranoid as a newborn baby. That's one of the reasons people make fun of him—they say he's too extroverted."

"Is, or was?" He studied his pipe for a while, then said, "Somebody, I can't say who. . . ."

"Hutchison, probably." It was a deliberately bad guess.

He shrugged amiably and continued ". . . saw him recently. Said he twitched and slobbered most of the time, but seemed rational. Until your name came up."

"My name?" This was interesting. "This is the first I've heard of it."

A door slammed. I started.

"That'll be Joan," said Specci. "She won't bother us in here. Studius Specci: Sanctus Sanctorum." He puffed energetically on the pipe to make a glowing dottle in the bowl.

"Well, when your name was brought into things, he came on like gangbusters. You were the greatest. You were the only one who was really loyal. You were the only one who'd risk his neck for him—the only intelligent person who had any real respect for him. And so it went."

"That's a bit exaggerated, I suppose. But that only shows he appreciates all the work I put in for him. What else is it supposed to prove?"

"Not much. But that was only half of it." He leaned down into a drawer and took something out. "He was like this."

He passed a heavy gold disk across the desk to me. I took it: a gold five-franc piece, beautifully made, dated 1804. On one side it said "Republique Française." I turned it over. There was a garlanded head, beneath which was inscribed "Napoléon-Empereur."

"Okay," I asked, "what was the other side?"

"Oh, treason, plots, nobody could be trusted, nobody had any respect for him, but he was on to them, and he was going to smash them—that kind of thing," he said in an affable, lighthearted way.

I could feel my heart beating faster. My pulse was up. So he'd been talking to Farb.

"How long did it last, this tirade of his?"

"Maybe a couple of minutes." Specci thrust his head toward me, and his voice suddenly took on a gritty tone. "But he was serious, absolutely serious. He really believes people are out to get him. Christ, he thinks everybody's out to get him but *you*."

I desperately tried to look somber and, I hoped, worried. But the adrenalin coursing through my body now was not from worry but excitement. I'd known that sooner or later Farb would realize I'd been telling the truth. He'd seek allies. First Morrissey, now Specci. But what would they do?

"If he's only half as sick as I think he is," Specci was urging, "then it's our job to get him out of there—not to cover up for him."

"Thanks for the advice on how I should do my job, Mr. Justice."

Specci eagerly tried to disarm what he thought was genuine annoyance. "Don't misunderstand. If anything, you may be doing your own particular job only too well," he said soothingly. "But you've got to take a broader view of it, if he's too sick for the job. You can't do it all for him, you know. And you're not there all the time. And if you try to keep him under wraps and go around making out there's a plot here and treason there, then you're only encouraging him in these delusions of his. You're also making it that much harder for anybody else to try to help."

He paused a moment for this to sink in, then made his final point. "All we need, of course, is for him to get on the hot line one of these days and start to come unglued. God knows what would happen then."

"And you think it might actually come to that?"

"I do. In fact, I'd bet on it if something isn't done soon."

"You've talked to Hutchison about this, I assume."

"Only in a very roundabout way."

"Nobody else?"

"Not yet." He was lying. I had found my respect for him diminishing slightly when he accepted my lies. When he lied and I knew it, my respect diminished still further.

"But you're going to?"

"Only if I have to. But unless you can give me a good reason not to, I don't think I have much choice. I can hardly drag him out of the Oval Office and down Pennsylvania Avenue with my bare hands, can I? But if it came to that . . . don't bet I wouldn't try it. In the meantime, somebody's going to have to be told, and we're going to have to work out some way of defusing him. Right now that man's a walking time bomb just waiting to go off.''

''And do you have anybody in particular in mind for your bomb disposal squad?'' I started to suggest names, hoping that some, if not all, would stick. ''Farb, no doubt, as the number one man in the Cabinet. And Morrissey, if you're so frightened about the hot line situation. Oh, and Van Riebouw of course, as the replacement. And if you're thinking of getting that Disability Committee reconvened in a hurry, you ought to get hold of Dave Cżecky. And why not include the Chief Justice, for good measure? That'll make it look more legal, I would think.''

''That's a good list to start with.'' He was frostily forbearing.

''Why not really do the job right—hire the Kennedy Center and issue tickets?'' I said sarcastically.

''In the meantime, I don't think there's anything else that needs to be done,'' he said, ignoring my last remark.

Nothing? There was a slight buzzing in my head. Nothing? That would be fatal. They had to do *something*.

''What do you mean, nothing?'' I asked.

''Look,'' he said in a lecture-room voice, ''it's pretty obvious to me that you're trying to provoke somebody into doing something. Who I don't know. What I don't know. But you're strutting about like some bantam cock just looking for a fight. So, as I said, I think maybe everybody should cool it for a while.''

So that's the advice he'll be giving to Farb, I thought. The question then must be how long Farb and the others would follow it. If they follow it for too long. . . . He interrupted my train of thought, saying, very calmly, ''I'm really disappointed in you.''

I was sincere when I replied, ''I'm sorry about that, Frank.'' I stood up, ready to go. ''Do you think Hutchison will resign from the commission?''

''I don't honestly know,'' he said, rising. ''But I expect he will if you press him much further. I think he might try to scratch the TV coverage for Tuesday.''

''Would you tell him something from me?'' Specci looked at me. ''There won't be any more outbursts. But that doesn't limit the questions I can ask.''

"I think he'll accept that."

We went downstairs. I exchanged a few pleasantries with Joan Specci and made my departure with a great show of friendliness all around. As we strolled out to the driveway, Specci warmly shook my hand to say good-bye.

"Still friends?"

"What kind of question is that, Frank?" I protested.

He looked up into the dazzling blue of a late fall sky and squinted hard. "I love my country, you know."

"So do we all."

"I guess so." He lowered his gaze, bringing his eyes down to meet mine. "I really feel bad, though, that we don't see eye to eye on this thing."

"Yes."

"If you change your mind, or if there's anything I can do—anything at all—give me a call. Okay?"

"Okay. But I have to tell you it's pretty unlikely." We stood there awkwardly, vacillating, torn by disagreement but bound by old ties. "And if I don't, you're not going to let it drop, are you?"

He stood uneasily on the razor-sharp verge of grass where it met his driveway and in a voice brought under a heavy burden huskily said, "You know I can't."

Chapter Thirteen

When I arrived at the White House, I went straight upstairs to his bedroom, nodding a brisk "good morning" to the boyish-looking warrant officer who sat in the hall, a thin black briefcase flat across his knees. In recent years the "football" had been moved away from the immediate reach of the President. But now, because of this President's precarious health, Morrissey had insisted on moving it back. And to look at that warrant officer, you'd think he hadn't a care in the world, sitting there with plastic sheets of numbers and letters that could incinerate the world. He held the key to something that could reduce to fleeting vanity the thoughts of Socrates, the conquests of Caesar, the teachings of Confucius, the journeys of Columbus, the crimes of Hitler and Stalin. And he knew it. Yet still he sat there, calm but alert, probably thinking of something mundane like buying shoes for his children.

His composure made me recall the early days of nuclear weapons and the commonplace hyperboles about "scars on the heart" among those with fingers close to the button. Maybe we'd grown callous. But all I'd ever noticed since I came to Washington was that it made the people around the White House a little bit nervous in a crisis. Nothing more. The only weak hearts seemed to be those among the disarmers.

The Sunday papers were sprawled all over the big bed, spilling their fat guts onto the floor. I waded through a sea of business sections and Sunday color supplements. He was leafing listlessly through the NSA *Black Book* with its translations of the more important intercepts made in the past twenty-four hours.

"Would you have somebody come and get this?" He sounded very tired.

I turned to the door and called for the NSA courier, gave him the folder and walked back into the room.

"It's a beautiful morning, Mr. President." I waved out toward the Washington Monument, and my gaze fell on the ring of flags set fluttering by a slight, air-clearing breeze. Suddenly I was wondering just how dangerous it would be to drop paratroopers there. Would they be able to dodge it? In my mind's eye I saw a fatigue-green helmeted figure smash heavily into one smooth gray side about twenty feet above the line where the newer stone meets the older; then another went smack up against an angle and crumpled in a heap. I winced. "Absolutely glorious."

When I turned back to the bed, I started to pick up the papers, out of some compulsion to tidiness. Habit made me careful not to get the New York *Times'* parts mixed up with the Washington *Post'* s, careful not to put the Chicago *Tribune'* s "Parade" where the *Chronicle'* s "California Living" should be. For one fleeting moment I felt a strong temptation to mix them all up, just for the hell of it. Then I decided it was not the sort of thing he'd appreciate. Stooping, rising, dumping, I said, "I talked to Homan again. He wasn't much help. And his friend wasn't all that more forthcoming, either."

"So you struck out."

He's sour this morning, I thought. "Not completely. But you know how it goes: They want to protect their friends. There. I think that does it. You finished with these?" I was holding a stack of newspapers about a foot high and heavy.

"Put 'em over there," he ordered, nodding toward a small table. I carried them across.

"Yech!" I shook my hands, gray-streaked with newsprint. "A nation of engineers, scientists and inventors, and we've still got this.'' Simultaneously I was asking, with body and eyes, for permission to use the Presidential bathroom. By the same means he granted me that courtesy.

When I came out of the bathroom, I remarked lightly, ''That's only one more of life's great mysteries. It's like the garbage. You buy four bags of groceries on a Friday, and sure enough, next week you have five bags of garbage. I've never yet figured that one out. And here we are: We've invented everything from the cotton gin to the telephone, and we can't even get the ink to stay on our newspapers.''

I was trying, as best I could, to cheer him up, help him shake off the melancholia that he wore like an extra blanket. But I didn't succeed.

''So did they tell you anything or not?'' He really was in a bad mood. I adjusted my own accordingly, all business, no-nonsense, yes, sir.

''They wouldn't admit to knowing anything personally, of course. They also denied knowing anybody they thought might be involved. But . . . on the other hand . . . they're willing to help.''

''And for that you had to take off for a whole day?'' I could barely recall when he had last been so waspish, at least with me.

''I think it was worth it,'' I replied, firmly but easily.

His eyes scanned my face, tried to fix on my eyes, failed and slipped down and away. He stared hard at the big window and Harry Truman's porch and, without looking back at me, made a downward motion with his hand to tell me to sit down. I pulled a chair over to the side of the bed. In a husky whisper he said, ''I can't handle this job. It's too big for me.''

When he swung his head back around, I could see the tears brimming in his eyes, now shiny with emotion. I sat there, my mouth half-open, probably looking like a fish out of water. I was completely surprised. So I sat for a moment, mind fumbling, groping. I had to say something. But I couldn't.

''I've really tried my best. But I didn't know how many . . . how much. . . .'' He broke off, voice thick. He couldn't go on, but I had now had a chance to pull myself together.

"I'm sure every President must have felt like that at some time," I said soothingly. "There's really no way to prepare for it, there's nothing that can really train you for this job. But everybody appreciates that. So long as you do the best you can, nobody can ask more of you than that. It's a ballbreaker of a job—everybody knows that. You're just being a bit too sensitive about it, that's all, too conscientious."

After buttering him up for years, I was sure I knew the right tone to put into my voice, knew which arguments to stress, knew how to chide him—gently—knew how to flatter him—indirectly. I was rapidly assuming that this was a fleeting fit of depression, much like many others I'd helped coax him out of over the years.

"I'm going to resign."

I was stunned. For a moment I had the sensation of drowning. I found myself swallowing hard and fighting desperately against a rising panic.

"Resign?" I echoed dimly. *He can't resign,* I silently screamed to myself.

"They were right," he moaned. His whole body, once proud, now frail, shook heavily. "I can't handle it. Maybe before, I could have. I don't care what they say . . . I think I could have done it if they'd given me a chance. But I can't go on like this." He turned his tearstained face to me.

Mechanically, I urged him, "You can't do it, Mr. President." I leaned heavily on "President."

"It's the only right thing I *can* do, don't you see?" He was all despair. "I'm not saying it was anybody's fault . . . but we let ourselves get carried away. I wanted to take over as soon as I could. I admit it. But so did the Congress. So did Van. So did the media. And so did you."

I did? That was hilarious. I was the only person who'd tried to discourage him. But what he was saying was generally true. A little more caution and a lot more courage all the way around, and this situation would have been avoided.

"Everybody wanted me to be sworn in. They *wanted* me to be okay," he was saying. "So we sort of charged in." Almost at once he started to backtrack. "And it might have worked out, you know. It could have. When you get these injuries it could go either way. We were unlucky, that's all."

His voice, already weak, was pleading and urgent. It dropped even further as he concluded confidentially, "I'm one very sick man, you know. I mean, really sick."

I protested, shocked that he would speak of himself in this way, "Mr. President, just because your recovery's a little slow—"

He didn't let me finish. "No. It's a whole lot worse than that. There's some things I haven't even told the doc."

If he wasn't going to be persuaded he was better than he was, then it was up to me to make other things seem not so bad as they were.

"All right, let's say you're in terrible shape—though I've got to say you don't look so terrible to me—and let's also say we acted hastily. That still doesn't mean you have to resign." The last word was delivered as a verbal lash, and he felt it.

"It's not as if I *wanted* to," he pleaded.

"Then don't do it." I shrugged. "Look, you're probably only feeling a bit down today. Tomorrow . . . who knows? You'll probably feel a lot better."

He sank back into his pillows and slowly rolled his head away from me, then toward me.

"I never feel good anymore," he said bitterly. "And I keep seeing his face . . . and the look on hers. Oh, God!" he groaned.

For an instant I was about to call the doctor. Almost as quickly I changed my mind. For one thing, I wanted to see if this was simply a mood. For another, I didn't want him talking resignation with anybody else.

"Don't you think you could just hang on for one more year?" I gently asked.

"No," he cried. "And it's more than a year."

"It's almost Christmas now. If we tried, we might be able to get the next inauguration moved up to, say, four weeks after the election."

"Don't you understand? I can't take it anymore. Every time I turn around there's so much work, so many people to see.

And everybody wants something. I'm tired. I feel lousy. I want to be left alone. It doesn't matter what I do, it's always wrong," he concluded sourly.

"If you delegated more work to your Cabinet, I'm sure. . . ."

"*My* Cabinet." He sneered. "It's not my Cabinet—it's his. Ever since I tore up their resignations, I've seen how their attitude to me's changed. You saw how they marched in here the other day and tried to push me around." He choked as he said this. "They wouldn't have dared try that on him." He was almost gagging. I patted him on the back and held up a glass of water for him. He sipped feebly.

"If you're really as bad as you say you are," I said slowly in a voice laden with feeling, "I suppose you don't have a lot of choice after all. But it's an awful pity. You might have brought so much to this office."

"You agree with me?" A trickle of spit-thick water dribbled down his jaw. With my handkerchief I dabbed it away.

"There are times when I think of you really as a friend. You know that. And it looks like this is one of those times. I don't want you to kill yourself for the sake of a job—not even for the Presidency."

"So it's okay with you?" He looked near death, but it was only the burning down, not out, of his strength.

"As far as your health and your life are concerned, whatever's best for you is what I want. You know that."

He grasped my hand in friendship and gratitude. I should have felt some reciprocal emotion. But I didn't. Only cold and remote. And I felt cold and remote even from myself.

"The only thing is," I said, "I don't think we ought to rush into this. You think we acted too soon before. We might only make things worse by acting too soon now."

"But I can't go on. I really can't," he implored.

"I'm not saying you should. What I am saying is do it, but don't rush things. The country's still in a state of shock, you know. If you drop another crisis on them before they've recovered, then almost anything might happen. What I'd suggest is that we wait until Congress comes back from the Christmas recess. In the meantime, we can try, discreetly, of course, to get things ready for the transition. Then we get Van Riebouw and that committee back up here and sort out all the whens and wherefores."

"You think we could do that?"

"Sure," I said blandly. "Then you and I can go back to California and watch the sun go down from Tamalpais each night and sail around the Bay and generally have a good time while you get better."

"You'd come back with me?" He sounded surprised.

"Why not? There's nothing for me here once you leave." I shrugged and stood up.

We looked at each other, moved, until he said, "It's a deal." He extended a shaking hand. I took it.

"There're only two things I have to ask of you, though. First, don't say anything about this until we're ready to actually take concrete steps."

"All right," he agreed.

"The other thing is, I'd like to get on with this investigation. If we can get this thing cleared up, I think that in itself will make our few months here worthwhile."

"You keep it up."

"And I think I ought to call the doctor." I picked up the telephone.

I went back down to my office and worked for a while. The doctor came down to tell me that he'd ordered the President to rest for the day and given him a mild tranquilizer. He also tried to impress on me that the President had reached a certain plateau of recovery but didn't seem able to go beyond it. He found that worrying. I admitted that it worried me, too. Then I told the switchboard that I could be reached in my car for the next couple of hours, and I was off.

Now the race was on. Between me, his health and the military. One of us would have to crack first, and it had to be the military, I said to myself over and over again; it had to be the military. "Washington," a *Life* reporter once said to me, "is really a military city." And he was right. It's full of military men, military monuments, military uniforms. The doctor I'd just been talking to was a brigadier general. Every time I went through the Capitol

I was more and more struck by overbearing military motifs: walls and ceilings bristling with painted and sculptured pistols, cannon, swords, muskets, glorious death, vigilant eagles. Whenever the President drove into or out of the White House, he saw General Sherman. But it was all of a piece, I reflected, with the atmosphere: Southern small town, not Northern big city.

The streets were busy now, with parties of tourists in full cry.

I drove past the old State Department building, turned onto the MacArthur Parkway and headed for Montgomery County. It was still a lovely day. I felt like a kid who'd just got out of school, instead of a grown man plotting.

I drove past Camp Bennett just off the Brookville Brighton Road near the Triadelphia Reservoir. I made a mental note to try to find out what sort of facility it was. Off Hawkins Creamery Road near 108 I stopped for a minute, made a large rectangle on a note pad and wrote "Davis Airp't." then drove on. I stopped again near Montgomery County Airport, wrote a few numbers down and drove near the Atomic Energy Commission building on my way to Loudon County across the river, in Virginia.

By now I was getting hungry, so I stopped for a few minutes at a drive-in. I thought of Specci and his chafing dish—of the way he was coddling burgundies and bourdeaux in his basement, waiting for the right "age"—and bit appreciatively nonetheless into my corned beef on rye. We may not have a great national cuisine, but we make appetizing fast foods. I treated myself to a Tastee-Freeze.

It was such a nice afternoon that I drove around haphazardly, looking up at the sky from time to time. There were a lot of planes out today. I had no way of telling which was which, though once a small helicopter with "R. B. Crop Spraying — Orange, Va." seemed to be following me.

At the junction of Monroe-Madison Highway and Whites Ferry Road there was a small landing strip that I estimated to be almost half a mile long. I took the highway down to Leesburg Municipal Airport. Half a mile away, in Lawson, I drove past the FAA building. Two miles farther south I stopped and made another note. Evergreen Mill Road took me to another spot where, right in the junction it made with the Lee-Jackson Highway was an X-shaped landing field. I was about four or five miles north of Bull Run, and the air was rent by the screaming of big jets coming into and out of Dulles two miles to the west.

Turning south into Prince William County, I passed Camp Upjohn, a few miles above Quantico. I made another mental note to check on "U.S. Military Reservation" at the end of 687, just off Route 1. I then completed my great arc of afternoon driving by continuing north, back across the Potomac into Prince Georges County, Maryland, passing not far from the Globecom Radio Receiving Station.

After checking into the White House once again, I worked for a couple of hours, then left, satisfied, with a good day's work behind me, but with one worrying cloud on the horizon.

Chapter Fourteen

Late Monday morning I sat in the basement room where I'd met Homan exactly one week before. It was supposed to be regularly debugged. Yet it was impossible not to wonder. I thought of Juvenal's famous taunt in the *Satires: Sed quis custodiet ipsos custodes*—"But who will watch the watchmen?" I tried to bring it up to date, putting into Latin "And who will bug the buggers?" I was just getting on top of it as Homan entered.

"Hello, Jack." I was as casual this time as I'd been conspiratorial the last.

"Good morning," he replied breezily.

We might have been meeting on the beach or in a bar to discuss nothing in particular, certainly not anything important. He seemed without a care—a different man, almost, from the one I'd met a week ago. I had a feeling Homan had come to a definite decision, or at least a clear-cut set of alternatives. He would proceed to follow through on whichever one he finally chose and never look backward. He'd make no complaint, either, if his choice ended badly. If it was his choice, consciously made, that was enough. I envied him that kind of composure, that suspension of self through action and result.

"I've heard from Bill," he said. "That's why I wanted to see you at once."

"That's good," I responded, thinking, *It's too soon.* I tried to hide the tension I felt rising inside me. If he and Taggart had reached a decision that fast, it seemed all too likely to be a firm negative.

"He wants me to speak to the President first. Then I'm to give you my decision."

I made a steeple of my fingers and examined the resulting architecture of opposing bony buttresses with care. I adjusted it. "And so you shall," I said. "You certainly shall. You must be seeing him some time soon in the ordinary way of things. We don't want it to look unusual; that's all."

"That's the problem. I don't get to see him in any routine way."

"No awards or promotions coming up?" Mentally I was reviewing the President's appointments for the next week. There was nothing I could recall that Homan could suggest as a plausible cover. Or had I slipped up?

"Not for nearly two weeks."

The inner tension at once began to drop. "And it has to be right away?" I asked.

"If time's as important as you say it is." It was a fair point.

I pulled open a drawer in the desk. From it I withdrew what looked like a cast-iron telephone inside a bread box: an ugly, clumsy-looking contraption, but nonetheless a most sophisticated piece of work—the KY-15 Pulse Code Modulation scrambler. Into a narrow slot I pressed a metal and plastic disk whose surface was embossed with dots, as if meant to be read by the blind.

"Will this do? If I take you in to see him, it'll be all round the building in no time," I explained.

For a moment Homan was pulled up short by surprise, but he quickly regained his self-possession.

"Sure. That'll do fine."

"There're only a couple of things I'd like to ask first."

He sat expectant, while at the other end of the line I could hear the short bass sounds that indicated another disk was going into place.

"Don't go into a lot of detail. Try to keep it short. Ask if it's really okay with him for you to help me with this 'special project' — something like that. He'll know what you're talking about. And for God's sake, try not to say anything to upset him. Okay?'' I could hear the voice at the other end of the line saying, ''Hello. Is that you?''

''Okay,'' Homan said. I handed the telephone part of the apparatus across the desk.

''Hello, Mr. President. This is Jack Homan.''

Homan's entire persona underwent a visible change as the words crossed his lips. Perhaps it would be more accurate to say that he not so much changed as massed the quintessential parts of his whole personality. He was sitting at attention, respectful, deferential, zealous to be of use, even to a man he'd known for several years and probably didn't think much of. But it was not the man he was addressing now—it was the office.

''I'm sorry to impose on you like this, sir, but you can appreciate how it is with a . . . a special project like this. . . . Yes, sir . . . that's right, sir. I simply wanted you know that I'll do whatever I can. . . . Yes . . . well, your special assistant's with me now, and I think we're making good progress. . . . Thank you very much, Mr. President.'' He waggled the phone and raised his eyebrows: Did I have anything to say. I shook my head. ''Good-bye, sir.'' He put the phone down almost reverentially.

''The President doesn't sound too good, does he?'' His question had an emotional force that spoke how strongly he was now torn between wildly mismatched feelings of relief on the one side and concern on the other.

I was able to use the procedure of putting the scrambler away to dissemble my own sentiments. I kept my head down and my voice low.

''He's not a well man, Jack.'' Banal, but true.

Relief began to get the upper hand over concern. Homan started to take great encouragement from the call to the President. I had known that if I refused to let him see, or even talk with, his Commander in Chief, he would have walked out of that room feeling satisfied, thinking he was well out of it. But now he was not only satisfied, but enthusiastic. Duty called.

"Bill sent a message by his wife to my wife. Suzy—that's Bill's wife—called my wife early this morning and said that if I'd let Mary buy a hundred-dollar dress, then Suzy could have one too. They can't figure it out; they think it must be some new kind of Christmas gag."

"So what are you going to do?" I asked.

For the first time, I saw Homan laugh out loud. "This is gonna cost me a hundred bucks."

"Taggart, too," I reminded him.

He roared. The sound of his laughter reverberated off the cold concrete walls. "That's right. Him, too. Hoisted on his own petard."

I should have felt happy and confident after my meeting with Homan. But I didn't. Even though Specci had managed to get most of it wrong the previous day, he had stumbled onto part of it that was right. Building on that small part, he could ruin everything I had set out to do. The past twenty-four hours I'd been worrying myself into an increasingly debilitating feeling that it was hopeless. I was fairly sure of what he was probably doing and saying at this very moment. Yet every effort I made to think of a direct counter drew a blank.

It was intolerable that just as everything started to go smoothly in one direction, they should start running into problems in the other. Of the two or three counters that did occur to me none of them was something I could do on my own. I began to fear that the lack of willing, witting allies was going to prove an insurmountable handicap. A small voice lodged at the back of my mind could be heard rehearsing excuses, chiefly on the theme that one person can only do so much.

It was in a grim mood that I started in to clear up the worst of the mess among the staff work. But I quickly became sufficiently absorbed in unsnarling the tangles I had myself created that for most of the afternoon and evening I was able to avoid thinking consciously about Specci at all.

I was glad that Madge, the President's secretary, posed no problems. She was a harmless, loyal, competent drone. She ran the other secretaries with a tight hand. But she knew that all she could say to me or the President was "yes, sir," or "no, sir," and "thank you very much, sir." If she wanted to lose her job quickly, all she need do was express an opinion on something that wasn't her business or start to take the side of somebody else.

I had made it my concern when I first went to work for the President that he get rid of the busybody who was already his principal secretary. I made sure that in the gubernatorial campaign she'd had more work to do than she could manage in the time available. She'd have to cut corners or confess it was too much. But she was jealous of his reliance on her. She'd also worked hard at convincing him she was superlatively competent. Soon she started hiding things from him. Her files also turned out to have mysterious gaps in them. After that her days were numbered. I waited until the campaign hit a rough patch, as all campaigns do; then I gave him a choice—her or me. One mistake after another was traced to her desk. It was not a hard decision for him to make. And Madge had heard enough of her predecessor's fate to make her cautious.

The real issue at the moment was how far the problem of access had got out of hand. It was essential that those who could see the President took in only problems that he alone could deal with. Almost as important was that they did not take up more of his time than the matter warranted. As I leafed through the files, it was obvious that several people were already trying to reinterpret the range and nature of their responsibilities. There was nothing that could be taken as a direct and overt challenge, but the sharp edges of my control were being blunted.

Usually, in a case like that, the best thing would be to come down at once on anything that resembled excessive ambition. But this was different. It had served my interests better to stay my hand for a while. They could only tax his strength, wear him down, try his patience, confuse and depress him. He would find himself reluctantly but inevitably being drawn into the pettv ego clashes, the jurisdictional rivalries and the morass of detail from which I had sheltered him for years. My purpose had been well served. But the time had now come to reassert control.

A cursory study of interoffice memorandums showed that several people who should have known better were burning up one of the two most valuable resources he possessed—his time. The press secretary was going in to see him four and five times daily, on the smallest excuse. The appointments secretary was seeing him even more often. Staff members from the National Security Council were in and out of the Oval Office as if it were a bus station. Whole files that should have been reduced to two- and three-page summaries were going in there on almost anybody's say-so. I'd given them their heads, but they'd not had much call on the other resource—information—which I'd managed to control quite effectively. And without it, these other people had gone out on a limb.

I wrote out a memo directing that any document for the President's consideration must, regardless of the subject or the source, be no longer than three pages, double-spaced. Further, any documents addressed to the President must cross my desk first. I stressed the importance of the President's health.

I called the appointments secretary and the press secretary into my office. I asked them to each write out in no more than three hundred and fifty words specific explanations for the sudden upsurge in their demands on the President's time. They were annoyed, but when they got the point, I told them I wouldn't insist on their statements. At least, not yet.

I called the special assistant in charge of the NSC staff and told him to exercise more control over the people under him. I suggested that if he didn't, I would have to ask the President to decide which one of us should go, that I couldn't do my job effectively if people from the NSC were free to do as they pleased. As he was a holdover from the late President's staff, I didn't expect him to want to force a showdown with me. He promised to be more sparing of the President's strength in future.

I went through a backlog of materials that had gone in to

the President the past three weeks. More than half were self-serving productions being circulated by some vested interest in the federal bureaucracy. I had always believed that one of my most useful functions was to spell out to him the reality behind what other people were asking. I made it a rule never to take anything in to him without demanding more information than was initially offered. Indeed, I usually made that a condition of doing anything. But it was clear from the material in front of me that most of it was propaganda. And it was easy to prove it. I returned masses of material with critical comments written in the margins and demanded more information, less opinion. The really atrocious specimens, however, I kept to one side and took them with me when I went upstairs to have dinner with him at about eight o'clock.

He seemed calm, if a little moody. I referred to some of the files I'd been looking through. Wearily, he begged off.

"Paper work. There's no end to it."

"Anyway," I said soothingly, "things are back under control, I think."

"You can take care of it, can't you?" He sounded like a humble petitioner.

"I think so, Mr. President. Now everybody knows where he stands."

"Good," he said, relieved.

After dinner I was ready to do some more work. But he didn't want me to leave. He wanted to watch a football game.

"College or pro?"

"Let's see the Trojans," he said, with more enthusiasm than I'd seen him show for anything in several weeks.

I called downstairs to the basement and had them bring up a videotape of the last USC game of the season, against Notre Dame. We lifted him onto the couch, and the two of us settled back to watch the game. But while he was absorbed in it from the kickoff, I found my mind wandering.

After a slow start, and having conceded their opponents an early touchdown, his beloved Trojans started to fight back. By the half it was 10–10. And because he loved every minute not only of the game but of everything connected with it, we had to watch the whole of the half-time show. When Southern Cal's mascot, a white horse called Traveler III, came charging around the track skirting the field, I thought he was about to fall off the couch with excitement.

"Look at that, will you! Isn't that the greatest damned mascot you ever saw?"

"Fantastic."

"Aw, come on. This is a lot of fun."

I smiled at him, humoring him. And he knew it. But far from resenting it, he enjoyed it. Nothing could shake his faith in football.

In the third quarter the Trojans started to make mistakes. Notre Dame scored another ten points and made it look easy. He wasn't worried anyway: He already knew the result. Sure enough, SC scored a touchdown. Then a field goal. Then another touchdown. But with three minutes left to go, the Fighting Irish came storming back. In the closing seconds of the game they scored. They had to go for the two-point conversion or embrace ignominy. With the packed Coliseum holding its collective breath, their quarterback rolled and twisted his way clear and threw a short pass to his All-American tight end. He took the ball on the three, then fumbled it away just as he crossed the goal line. Trojans jumped about wildly. The disgusted tight end angrily kicked at the base of the goalpost.

"Beautiful, beautiful!" shouted the President, rocking about on the couch.

But I barely noticed it—I was rocking about excitedly myself. That was it! The solution to my problem was staring at me. It was right there on the screen with that furious tight end taking a savage swing at the goal post. Action speaking louder than words. My feelings of relief and joy were too strong to be contained or masked.

"See," he chortled happily, "it even got to you. What a hell of a game!"

"Marvelous," I said, and this time I meant it.

The next morning I set off early for work. When I turned onto Connecticut Avenue, it was a few minutes before seven thirty. I called the White House to tell them I was on my way down. I drove slowly, looking at the traffic gradually building up to its rush hour peak.

When I stopped at the lights where Macomb comes in from the right, I pulled a small piece of paper about three inches square out of my shirt pocket. On it was typed:

896 004 528 907   065 881 764 927
535 762 438 045   962 008 693 131
881 375 196 857   089 160 787 643
973 568 115 008   307 692 187 434
023 781 649 174   927 535 160 883

466 198 057 100   826 381 477 138
964 125 738 246   432 003 535 486
651 066 745 588   917 349 215 857
853 764 101 635   079 528 450 099
936 272 833 581   692 187 438 358

I set fire to it with the lighter and very carefully lowered it into the ashtray. I had purposely used the heaviest typing paper I could find. It looked all right. I could see that at least half of it had broken into only two large fragments. As the light changed, I snatched my fingers violently away from the ashtray and slammed it shut.

Chapter Fifteen

After a light lunch and a few words with the President, who seemed to have plunged back overnight into unshakable melancholy, I went down to the Capitol for the second of the televised sessions.

I left the government limousine on the north side of the Senate. Even so, I had to battle my way past half a dozen reporters and photographers. Did I expect the hearings to resolve the question of the assassin's identity? Did I have any proof linking any person by name to the conspiracy behind the assassination? Would the President be watching on television? Could I comment on reports that. . . . To all of which I responded politely by saying that I had nothing to say that went beyond what I had said already, and thank you very much, but you must excuse me.

I made a beeline for the President's former office—the Vice President's room behind the Senate Chamber—to pick up a couple of books for him. A guard told me that Carter was right next door, in the Senators' Reception Room. I sidled in. He was billing and cooing with a group of Colorado mining and property development millionaires and their wives. While I waited for him to get rid of them, my eyes roved over the ornate gilt wall medallions, each surmounted by an eagle. I studied the large center panel; as unadorned as on the day Constantino Brumidi died. Probably as well, I thought. Brumidi never did know when to stop. If it weren't for his premature death, the Capitol wouldn't have even this solitary oasis of comparative artistic restraint.

"Well, well," said Carter expansively after showing his guests out. "If it isn't the fellow who dropped a bombshell, then dropped out of sight. Got any more of the same today?"

The words may have sounded malicious, but his tone wasn't. He wasn't even annoyed at having been upstaged. Once the shock had passed, he was left with no sentiment but curiosity. That was our man Carter.

"I don't know, Bud. Depends on what shows up today and tomorrow. You guys got through a hell of a lot of work without me. Maybe if I just keep quiet, this thing'll be over in no time."

Carter was not to be easily shaken off. "But you really think there was some big plot? Huh?" It sounded less like a question than a dare—roughly, dare to say yes.

I dared. "Yes. I think there was a plot. Or plots."

"Or plots?" Dare and double-dare you. "You mean, *more* than one?"

"That's what the plural usually means, Bud." He looked at me blankly. "First a conspiracy behind the assassination. Now another one to cover it up."

"And the President's still backing you?" I thought he seemed a bit envious that one man in politics should stick his neck out so far for another.

"So far as I know."

"Let me tell you something," he said, as if ready to spill the secrets of his soul. "Those fellows that were here just now, they think you're on the right track. Fact is, there's a lot of people back in Colorado that do. You ought to come by and take a look at my mail some. Or if you like, I can have some of it brought over."

I tried to turn down this pathetic offer without laughing. Poor Carter. If he could make a friend of anybody, he was willing to try.

"That's very kind of you," I said. "But I'm literally swamped with a backlog of mail already. It's gratifying to know that the country hasn't lost its common sense, though.'' And it was true. The last ten days a flood tide of support—by post, by telegram, by telephone, even by hand—had poured into the White House, encouraging me to fight on.

But I almost lost my composure when Carter proceeded to offer me fatherly comfort and advice. ''Listen,'' he said conspiratorially, ''this thing still might get too big for you to handle. You know, if the tide of opinion turns and the President ever decides *not* to back you up . . . well, it's not my place to say it, I suppose, but you've made a lot of enemies—and I mean really powerful enemies—faster than anybody I ever saw.'' Then, evidently impressed that I didn't give a fig about popularity among the powerful, after he had spent a lifetime courting them, he said, ''You've sure got guts. I'll give you that much.''

It was in a carefree, cheerful mood that we made our way around the outside of the modern Senate Chamber to the corridor which led to the old.

Hutchison, I was pleased to see, came fully up to my expectations. I'd tried to anticipate how he and the rest would greet me. I didn't care for what Carter or Dalgleish said or thought. I'd already seen Specci. But I found myself overwhelmed by curiosity about Hutchison's reaction. Would he be icily contemptuous? Politely hostile? Overtly nasty?

In the event, he greeted me politely, calmly, almost exactly as he'd greeted me before. Yet I did not doubt for a moment that in his heart he held me in contempt. But he was not a petty man or a rash one. He would try to destroy me, but as a gentleman would. Even as he struck me down, he would be polite and calm. He would shed no false tears nor beat his breast in triumph. And even as he savored my fall, he would be saying ''Please'' and ''Thank you'' and ''Glad to have met you.''

Dalgleish and Harrod weren't in the same class. They wanted me to make no mistake about their disapproval. To my greetings they forced out tight little hellos. Specci seemed sad, but friendly.

At the previous week's executive session they'd reviewed all the earlier testimony, clarified a few obscure points and tried to tie some of the looser ends together. From there they'd gone on to screening some of the key witnesses, mostly Secret Service agents and air police. From the scores that Harrod's staff and the FBI had interviewed they'd talked to a dozen. Of that dozen, we were to question the most promising ones at length, on live TV. From there we were scheduled to move on to the question of the origin of the weapons used.

When we pressed into the chamber, the atmosphere was electric. We had an even larger crowd than before, though I wouldn't have thought it possible. One of the staffers whispered to me as he passed, "Who's minding the store?" With his head he gestured at the Senators and Representatives who'd virtually monopolized the seats.

For the most part, there was a monotonous regularity to the questions and answers:

"Where were you?"

"I was here." Pointing it out on the board.

"What did you see from your vantage point?"

"I didn't see very much."

"Did you see the murder weapon?"

"Yes . . . sort of."

"Would you like to explain what you mean?"

"Well, I saw it. But after it was thrown—while it was in the air."

"Did you see the person who threw it?"

"No, sir."

"Did you see the second grenade?"

"No. I only heard the second explosion . . . and the screaming. Everything was very confused when that happened."

"Did you see a woman in an orange raincoat?"

"I can't really say."

"Why not?"

"There were so many people wearing bright-colored clothing. I might have seen her, but I don't remember."

"Did you see anyone acting suspiciously?"

"No, sir."

"How would you describe the security arrangements that night, from your own point of view?"

"Extremely tight, sir. We took every precaution."

These same questions and answers were gone through again and again. It became wearying. At one point I remember gloomily noting that there were five of us on the commission, plus Harrod, plus the witness and his counsel: that made eight. And eight bell ringers "accomplishing the extent" had forty thousand, three hundred and twenty changes to go through. I sat back, silent—no ardent campanologist I. But when it seemed they were about to dismiss the first witness, I signaled to Hutchison that I had a question to ask.

At once the atmosphere—which had become all glazed eyes and benumbed brains—was recharged. And as it dawned on the witness, a chubby-faced air police captain, that I had a question for him, I could see the man tense.

"I won't keep you, Captain," I said. "I have only one question for you. My question comes down to this—What do you really know about the assassination?"

In the man's eyes were fear and loathing. He seemed momentarily thrown by the question, however. And when he replied, in what was no doubt meant to be a tone of fierce defiance, there was a hollow ring to it.

"I already told you what I saw."

"That's not what I asked," I said patiently. "I asked, What do you—as a responsible officer of the security forces at the scene—know? In other words, What is the whole of your knowledge of this matter? Not just what you saw."

"I only know what I saw," he stammered in confusion, his intended defiance crumbling.

"And that's your answer to my question?" I tried to sound vaguely incredulous, but not melodramatic. But the lawyer from the Air Force JAG Office decided the captain was in need of protection. Appealing to Hutchison, he objected, "Mr. Chairman, this is badgering the witness."

Before Hutchison could frame a reply, I retorted, "I'm not badgering this man. I'm simply not satisfied with his answer. But . . . oh, let it pass."

I then lapsed back into silence and inactivity. After a few

more desultory questions, and even more dispirited answers, the captain was dismissed.

The next witness was the senior Secret Service agent present at Andrews that night. He had seen only what he'd seen, but he was highly articulate and described it in great detail. Yet though his was a different vantage point from the captain's, he'd seen pretty much the same thing. No woman in an orange raincoat, no throwing of the grenade, no persons acting suspiciously. Again the hearing became heavy and listless. Again I waited till he, and the rest, seemed about finished before I indicated that I had a question.

"Yes?" said Hutchison.

"I would like to ask this witness just one question." I looked straight across at the man. He stared right back.

"What do you really know about the assassination?" I challenged him.

"Just what I said," he snapped, digging in.

"I'm sorry, then, but I didn't hear what you said—I must have missed it in all the picturesque description."

He bristled at the taunt and glared belligerently. "I already explained. . . ."

I didn't let him finish. I bore down relentless now, driving each word home like a nail. "What do you really know about the assassination?"

"I can't answer that question," he barked, exasperated.

"Why not? It's the one question this hearing's all about."

"Because," he gritted through clenched teeth, "I don't know anything except what I saw." His knuckles, I could see, were now white. His hands were clenched fists on the tabletop.

"So you also—another of the key security people there—don't know anything about the assassination. Certainly nothing that will help this inquiry. Thank you very much for your assistance." I sat back in my chair in wordless disgust.

The third witness was one of the rooftop marksmen. A qualified sniper, he had the properly phlegmatic qualities of his calling. Time meant nothing to him. And nothing that was said could break the man's stride.

I found him fascinating, because he saw the assassination not merely from a different physical angle but from one that was mentally and emotionally worlds away from the rest of the witnesses. He talked of it with complete dispassion. He appeared to view it from the assassin's position—and then, only as a challenge to his technical competence. He saw it through a professional killer's eyes. Yet he was not an unsympathetic figure. He was no slack-minded connoisseur of weapons and violence. At one juncture Dalgleish, aghast at what he took to be the man's heartlessness, asked him point-blank, "Doesn't this impress you as an appalling crime, Sergeant?"

The man replied coolly in his soft Southern drawl, "It does in a way."

Dalgleish was by now a victim to the humanitarian rage boiling in his veins. "Am I to understand, though, that you are not personally appalled by this assassination?"

Still unfazed, the marksman lazily replied, "I don't think I was asked here to express personal opinions, sir. But if you want to debate the metaphysics of political killing and all the collateral questions of ethics and personal outrage, then I'll be glad to oblige you in some other venue of your choice, Professor."

Hutchison wasted no time moving in to save Dalgleish from being ground into little pieces on national TV. Indeed, after that exchange Hutchison and the rest wanted nothing better than to finish with this man and move on to the next witness. He sat there, tanned and fit-looking, reminding me of a lizard sitting on a rock out in the desert sunshine . . . waiting. But admire him as I might, I couldn't let him become an exception to the pattern I was establishing. I made a gesture with my pencil to catch Hutchison's eye.

"Yes?" he said.

"I have a question." You could feel the whole room tense. In fact, I felt a bit tense myself. And I could tell at once that the sergeant was waiting; he thought he was ready for me . . . ready to shoot me down. I had to give him a different target.

"Sergeant. . . ." I stalled. "Sergeant . . . how easy is it to get hold of M-4d's?"

If I'd fazed him, he didn't show it.

"That depends."

"All right. Let me give you a specific example. Let's say you and I wanted to kill somebody using these grenades, could we get hold of them?"

His professional honesty—not pride—led him to say, "I don't know about you, sir. But I could."

"Easily?"

"Easily."

A little voice whispered in my ear, *Now*!

"What do you really know about the assassination, Sergeant?"

He looked at me, unmoved. I couldn't crack this man—not if I had all day to do it. But at least I'd got my question out and scored another, albeit peripheral, point.

"I guess I know a lot about it in some ways, and not so much in others. But probably not as much as you do . . . sir." There was a brief appreciative sniggering among the spectators. I flushed slightly but couldn't be deflected because I'd been scored off.

"What is it that you do know a lot about?"

"Oh, what you might call the technical side."

"What about what you might call the organizational side?"

"Not a thing."

"Please understand that I mean no disrespect to the honorable rank you hold or to the work you do, Sergeant. But maybe you weren't in the know because you don't have enough rank?"

"Maybe so," he said, completely unruffled. "I couldn't say."

"Just one last question: If you *had* seen the assassin about to throw that grenade, what would you have done?"

"I'd have shot him—or her."

"Even though firing into a crowd you might have missed and struck somebody else?"

He calmly, almost coldly, replied, "I wouldn't have missed."

After that Hutchison thanked the man and called a break. We stood up and stretched our limbs. I was simply glad to see that marksman's back.

During the break I saw Hutchison and Specci whispering together animatedly. And I noticed that as soon as I started moving toward them, they stopped talking.

"How long do you think we'll run today?" I asked Hutchison offhandedly.

"Another hour or so. What do you think, Frank?"

"No more than an hour, I hope," said Specci, looking glum.

We stood there, feeling slightly awkward, looking from one to the other. Then Hutchison asked, as if it were of no particular interest, "Were you ever a prosecuting attorney?"

"No," I replied evenly.

"Well," he said, still sounding bland, "you have that particular knack for using a question like a club." He smiled. "Mind you, defense attorneys use it too."

"Sometimes it's necessary," I said, shrugging my shoulders. "And my question is the root of what we're getting at here."

"Oh, to be sure." He was still smiling at me. "Never lose sight of the essentials."

"That's right," I said.

A few minutes later we reentered the chamber. I'd expected some falloff in attendance, but no one seemed to have left, or if any had, others had taken their places.

Harrod had apparently been told to keep things brief because we managed to get through three more witnesses—two of them Secret Service agents and one a low-ranking civil servant—in a little more than an hour. And as before, I waited until each of the Secret Service men was finished before I asked, "What do you really know about the assassination?"

I found myself leaning heavily on "you," pausing, then bearing down on "know." I also noticed that the witnesses and spectators were waiting for the question. In fact, the witnesses started to frame their replies to the other questions so as to cover themselves when I asked mine. There were all manner of qualifying clauses—"All I know is," "I only know what I saw," "I really don't know anything" and so on—long before I spoke to them. Yet each time I bore down on them. But I didn't say a word to the one "civilian" we interviewed that day. By not doing so I did not break the pattern: I gave it definition. And it seemed to me that it did not go unnoticed by the spectators or the other people on the commission.

When we called a halt for the day, it was late afternoon. The weather outside was cold, gray, rainy. But I went back to the White House in good spirits. After I watched the television news, I felt even better and looked forward to the next session, when I would be able to question the Army.

Chapter Sixteen

Hate at first sight would be the most accurate description. The four Army officers who appeared on the next morning behaved much as if I was the sole member of the commission. Yet it was not my doing that brought them before us. It was the indisputable fact that the assassination weapon was a fragmentation grenade.

As on the previous day, we had a full house. *How,* I wondered, *was Congress going to be able to wind everything up by the weekend if most of its members were playing hooky?* I noticed that even Czecky looked in for an hour, though the demands on his time in these last days before the recess must have been enormous.

So far as the Army officers were concerned, the general ground they would cover had been worked out the week before. But somehow everybody assumed that he was to be questioned chiefly by me. The others on the commission by and large showed only a *pro forma* interest in interrogating them. It would be tedious to reproduce the full transcript of my exchanges with these men. The questions and answers ran very much along the same lines in each case. But these were some of the highlights:

"Now, Colonel, is there any record of the number of M-4d's lost or stolen in the past year?"

"No, sir. No separate record."

"You mean no record relating only to these particular items?"

"That is correct."

"What records do you have?"

"An amendment to the normal annual inventory."

"And does that break the losses down?"

"No, sir, it does not."

"So you have no way of knowing how many grenades, or rifles, or machine guns, or artillery pieces are lost, missing and stolen each year?"

"Well, the heavier weapons are itemized. But bullets, grenades, loose shells and the like are not."

"So you have no idea, no record of what deadly weapons are lost or stolen?"

"No overall record."

"Are you indicating that there is some other record?"

"Well, every unit from company upward has its permanent files, sir. But we only collate certain items in our overall accounting systems."

"Have you searched for lower level records on these grenades?"

"Yes, sir."

"And did you find anything?"

"Yes, sir. There are several instances of M-4d's being reported missing."

"But—"

"But these are only fragmentary."

"You mean they form no accurate overall picture?"

"Yes, sir."

"And is there anything to link any of these missing grenades with those used to kill the President."

"No, sir. There is not."

"Tell me, Colonel, why are these grenade loss records so fragmentary?"

"They just are, sir."

"Have they always been that way?"

"I suppose so."

"But you don't know?"

"I've never had cause to look at them in so much detail before."

"But they're not very helpful, are they?"

"No."

"Yet the Army has—how many miles of documents?"

"I don't know. That isn't usually the way we measure them."

"Hundreds, isn't it?"

"It might be."

"Yet even after forensic experts have reconstructed more than half this weapon and have given you seven out of the eight digits of its serial number, the Army still can't tell us where it came from or how it got out of the Army's control?"

"Is that a question?"

"Yes, it is. I'd like you to explain to us how this situation came about?"

"I'm afraid I can't."

"Colonel, are you telling us all you really know about this assassination?"

"Yes, sir. I am."

"You have no personal knowledge of a conspiracy to kill the President?"

"I have no knowledge of any kind of conspiracy to do anything, period."

"So you know nothing about the assassination?"

"Nothing."

"Even though these weapons came from an Army arsenal?"

"Nothing at all."

The colonel from the Pentagon's Records Section left as he had come, angry. The next witness was a lieutenant colonel who was an expert on weapons security. He looked like a man who spent his life eating sour apples.

"So your job is to discover ways to keep weapons from being lost or stolen?"

"Yes, sir. That's right."

"And how many weapons does that involve?"

"Millions."

"Does that include all weapons?"

"Most standard weapons. But I also work on how to secure new ones when they're being issued to field units."

"Standard I take it means standard infantry weapons, including grenades?"

"You take it correctly."

"So in a sense you are responsible for all these weapons."

"I hope you're not implying that I ought to go around every night to make sure all the rifles are locked up."

CHAIRMAN. "There will be no outbursts of any kind. There is nothing funny here. Please continue."

"But you agree, there was a security breakdown?"

"You could call it that."

"I do, when not one but two of these very powerful grenades get out of the Army's control—despite your efforts to prevent it."

The lieutenant colonel went on to protest that he knew nothing about the plot to kill the President. He also objected to the tone of several of my questions. I reminded him to concentrate on the words. The next witness, a captain, was an authority on urban terrorism. He had written a widely quoted handbook on the subject. I asked him, "From what we've heard so far about this assassination, do you think it has the characteristics of a military operation?"

"A *military* operation?"

"Yes. It involved penetrating a very heavy security screen. It involved a surprise attack with deadly weapons. It included a murderous diversionary or cover-up tactic. In short, it was a cold-blooded exercise in the use of violence to achieve a highly specific objective. Now that's not terrorism. That's virtually a textbook definition of the military function: the management of violence for specific ends. Isn't it?"

"It could be so described."

"But you still don't think this assassination partook of the nature of a military attack?"

"The military has no absolute monopoly on the use of deadly weapons or surprises or diversions."

"But this was a long way from holding up an armored car,

say, or gunning down passersby on the streets, wasn't it?''

''That's a matter for conjecture.''

''Let me put it this way, then. Given the security screen, wouldn't it have been a lot easier for a trained group of soldiers to carry off an attack like this than for a bunch of disgruntled civilians?''

''It would have been less likely for military personnel than for anybody else.''

''But as an exercise in the use of violence, they would have the best chance of success, wouldn't they?''

''I don't know. That's all speculation.''

I didn't ask the captain what had now become *the* question. Again, not doing so helped give it shape and form. To use it wildly or recklessly—to spread its power thin by using it everywhere—would rob it of its usefulness and might even be turned against me. By now, however, as this session drew to a close, it was a useful instrument. On its own, judiciously employed, it was like a powerful accusation. An accusation, furthermore, that most people would clearly prefer to avoid. Those it touched left that chamber under a cloud.

The last witness was the airborne lieutenant colonel whose battalion had held the perimeter at Andrews that fateful night. I bore down on him very hard. I made him explain the Army's rationale of ''prepositioning'' troops. He went into much detail on how useful a technique it was—how it had a calming rather than an inflammatory influence on crowds, how it discouraged the unbalanced, how it made apprehension of wrongdoers more certain. He clearly believed that he and his men had no cause to apologize for what happened. Why, I wanted to know, did they fail to apprehend the assassins? How could he be so confident that no one, absolutely no one, had been able to leave the area after the explosions? I asked him why, if the security screen could be penetrated one way, it could not be penetrated the other? Finally: ''What do you really know about the assassination?''

''Nothing beyond what I've already said.''

''So you are not a party to the attempts to cover up for this crime?''

''No, sir. I'm not a party to anything.''

"And you expect us to believe that as the principal Army officer there, commanding a force of eight hundred paratroopers, you spoke no evil, heard no evil, saw no evil. You just stood around and watched the President of the United States, the First Lady and the Vice President get blown up?"

"I will not be smeared by you."

"I'm not smearing anybody. I'm asking you a question and waiting for your answer."

"My answer is, You can go to hell."

Someone started to applaud. Hutchison came down on him hard. We finished on a calmer note, and the last witness was dismissed.

In the cloakroom Specci came over to me.

"I think you've done it now," he whispered.

"Done what?"

"I think Hutch is going to tell the President he wants to be taken off the commission."

"He can't do that," I objected. "If he goes, the whole thing collapses."

"You'd better tell him yourself then." Specci looked worn-out and depressed.

"I said there wouldn't be any more outbursts, and I kept my word."

He stared at me. "There might be a difference of opinion about that," he said grimly.

I looked around for Hutchison. I couldn't get through for the mass of bystanders, Capitol police and press people milling around, but I managed to get hold of his secretary and told her to set up a meeting for me right away—that evening, if possible. I then got back to the White House as fast as I could. I told the switchboard that if Hutchison called, the call was to go through me. I rang up the President and talked to him for a few minutes about how it had looked on TV. Then I opened a bottle of scotch, and waited.

What had they made of my gamma pad (or what was left of it and reconstructed from the ashes)? Where, I wondered, was it now? Could they make this Phoenix fly?

Perhaps at this moment it was being passed around by the Joint Chiefs in their bilious-looking "tank" with its mustard carpet and turquoise walls. No, most unlikely. It was probably over at NSA, good old "Never Say Anything," and they were saying, "Sorry, Mr. Secretary, but it can't be broken. Even if we had the original intact, we couldn't break it. You see, it's been used for this one message only. The next sheet on the pad has a different lot of numbers, from which the key, which he's memorized, forms an entirely new code. So even if we got hold of the other copy of this pad, we probably couldn't crack it. These four squares make it pretty tough. We don't have any indication where the message begins or ends. The problem is that you make up a new code each time you send a message." And that would be the last stage of its journey, unless they let the Christians in Action have a crack at it.

But no doubt it had already been mulled over at Fort Holabird, pondered by the Counterintelligence Analysis Division at the Pentagon, passed on to the DID Code Section at the FBI and shown to the Protective Research Section of the Secret Service. That was enough to qualify me as a "Person of Interest." Perhaps I had gone into *The Compendium*—the Army's blacklist on civilians. I was among the immortals.

In all the passing to and fro of these reconstructed ashes and some intriguing film footage, a new fraternity was being born. All in secrecy and darkness two groups of men were stumbling along, parallel to each other. And according to the laws that govern parallels, when they reached infinity they would collide. They must surely link up, feeling more secure in augmented numbers, exchanging information, comparing notes, developing theories, trying to make an intelligible whole from a handful of suggestive parts.

But though they were now bound, each to the other, these two groups had different ways, with words and logic being strongest on one side and things and action on the other. Specci would say, *Caution!* And so long as it was a matter of words, he would prevail. But that contained the seeds of defeat, for the other side was more impressed with the tangible, the concrete. And it seemed to me the solution was not to persuade Specci that he was wrong, but to convince the others they were right. Theirs was an intelligence that understood things, not thoughts, deeds not words. But not until I'd grasped that point was it possible to find the right counter. And the gesture of a frustrated football player awoke a memory of Dr. Johnson's encounter with the arguments of a philosopher who maintained the insubstantiality of matter. Johnson, on most occasions a man of words, kicked violently at a rock and rebounded heavily. "I refute it, thus!" he said, and stalked away.

That was the answer: something tangible, something concrete, something the others would understand. Physical proof, if only ashes. It had not been so very long since the Secret Service put a threat uttered in a bar, a stolen uniform and a missing police car together to come up with a conspiracy to assassinate a President. Not only did they conclude that, but they acted on it. What was there to show that things had changed so very much since?

I could see them somewhere, perhaps in the north basement of the Pentagon, dusting off the old plans, like "White" and "Cabin Guard," with one eye on their alibis. They'd be careful to weave a chain of mutual and individual protection, with overlapping and dovetailing justifications. To make it all legal and aboveboard they'd probably bring in the Army's general counsel, swearing him to the deepest pledge of secrecy the man could utter. He'd then dig out all the legal precedents, the twenty occasions in the history of the Republic when federal troops went into the streets, mostly in the past two decades. He'd point to one unbroken thread at least, of putting a federal judge in among the soldiers. That's where Specci would come in. And between them they'd all solemnly agree that what they were about to do was what Washington himself would have wanted: They'd be acting only as "the *dernier* resort."

They'd all promise to support each other. Steele would point to the legislative heritage of the Kennedy assassination, making the USSS the one and only authority as to what constituted a threat to the President's safety. He was thereby empowered to call for whatever assistance he judged he needed from any federal agency and from the armed forces of the United States.

The Army would dust off the "Selma Proclamation" as a justification and precedent for bringing in troops where no violence had occurred, justified because of "a substantial likelihood that domestic violence may occur." They would remember to cite the precedents for "prepositioning" troops going all the way back to 1966. Already it was accepted practice, they would argue, to move in the troops *before* any disturbance had occurred and before there was any breakdown of the local police power. *But shouldn't we tell the District's director of public safety anyway?* somebody would probably ask. Yet they'd want to keep this as much an all-Army show as they could, and the answer would probably be no.

There would have to be a survey of the fifty thousand troops in the vicinity of the District. How about the two airborne divisions? No, they'd decide. It looks as if one of them's involved in this somehow, though I'd never have thought a guy like Taggart would get mixed up in this kind of thing. But if one of those divisions is tainted, the other might be too. Besides, we don't want to have to bring the Air Force in any more than we have to.

So it would come down finally to two questions: Do we have enough men? and How long will it take to get them here? They could count on the elite Third Infantry from Fort Myer, the Ninety-first Combat Engineers from Fort Belvoir, the Sixth Cavalry from Fort Meade. There were several thousand marines who might be brought in from Quantico, and the Monks at First and I. But let's not ask for them unless we have to.

They'd find that it took thirty-six hours to get thirteen thousand soldiers into the capital after the 1968 riots triggered by the assassination of Martin Luther King. As then, they'd be committed by doctrine to planning for maximum manpower, minimum firepower. So they'd go over it again, wrestling with the classic staff problem of how to get there firstest with the mostest. And the handful of staff officers brought into this affair would grumble to one another about having to do something so delicate in almost total darkness.

Couldn't they simply *tell* the President? they would ask. And someone else would derisively reply, Tell the President? He'd think we were faking the whole thing. He'd probably believe that we *were* plotting first and were now trying to cover up. Anyway, he's likely to fall apart at any moment. It's come down to a question of who cracks first and who's best prepared. It's obvious what's going on, but our chances of convincing the President are about zero. Let them make their first move, and we'll nail the bastards to the wall.

But someone else, perhaps Farb or Morrissey, would have second thoughts and might ask, Don't you think that maybe he's being too obvious? And they would all think again. By now the evidence had a logic of its own. It coalesced, with their actions and theories, into something that had come alive. And it would take a morally brave and intellectually certain man to kill it in cold blood. It would, without their fully realizing it, have begun to take control of them, and one among them, an intelligence expert perhaps, a man who could expound at length on "East Wind—Rain" and express strong opinions on whether they were right to wait for the last of the Japanese intercepts to be decoded, would point out the veracity of fragments. Something whole would be suspicious. But all they had were fragments, the sort of stuff that always comes into the intelligence net through someone's carelessness, haste, inexperience or simple accident. But that indicates that it is, in all likelihood, the merest tip of the iceberg. What other meetings have there been that we *don't* know about? What other officers have been suborned who we don't know about? How do we know that some foreign power is not involved in some way? We only got the fragments of the gamma pad because, as the film showed, the light changed and he burned his fingers. We could easily have missed it.

Having woven a fine mesh net of sense around themselves, spurred in their work by anger, frustration and the press of time and danger, they would draw it ever tighter, choking themselves with their own logic. And at some point Taggart would probably provide some corroboration by having an unexpected alert—nothing that couldn't be normally passed off as routine, of course, but interesting all the same. From logic back to premise they would shuttle, then back to logic. Each time they came to a stop they'd find themselves looking down the same road, leading to one great event—an event for which their training, the logic of their organization and the logic of events urged them to be ready. They would be ready. They'd make sure. . . .

The intercom buzzed. "Mr. Hutchison's here, sir." I jumped up, put my glass away and hurried into the corridor.

Hutchison had not even tried to call the President. He'd come over here, determined on a showdown. And he faced me with a choice: I could either refuse point-blank to let him see the President or could let him in. If I refused, there would be an unholy rumpus. The President might read in tomorrow morning's papers that Hutchison had resigned and had to do it this way because I had kept him from seeing the President. On the other hand, if I let him in—who knew? Things might work out.

"Hello, Mr. Hutchison." I greeted him in the corridor as if we were nothing less than the great man and his public. He responded in kind, though there was now a marked gravity to his entire demeanor, a gravity that sounded in his words and informed his gestures.

"Good evening. I'd like to see the President if I may. I hope this isn't inconvenient."

"Not at all, not at all. It's . . . simply unexpected. Would you like to step into my office for a moment?"

I could see that even the normally unflappable White House secretaries were alive with anticipation. I tried to edge Hutchison toward my door, but he resisted—or at least sent up wordless signals of resistance—and somehow kept his body pointed, as if it were an arrow, toward the corridor leading to the Oval Office.

"Oh," he said smoothly, "I don't think there's any need to take up your valuable time. I only wanted to see the President for a minute or two. Do you think you could squeeze me in?"

I had the appointments secretary summoned from just down the hall and made a show of trying to work out how Hutchison could be gotten into the President's office in between other commitments.

"Look," I told him, "if you take five minutes off here . . . and another five from this guy, and switch these two around, you should be able to get the chairman in at ten to six."

He mumbled deferentially, but not so deferentially that his sense of self-importance was impaired. Then I asked Hutchison again to step into my office. Now that I'd arranged for him to see the President in another few minutes, it was impossible for him to decline again without seeming unctuous or rude or uncertain of his ground. He accepted at once this time.

"Cigarette? A glass of sherry perhaps? Or would you like something stronger?" I offered.

He thanked me and declined them all.

"How do you think the hearings went?"

"Much as I expected," he replied, without a hint of sarcasm.

"Do you think we'll be able to wrap things up shortly after the New Year?"

"Perhaps."

I toyed for a moment with the idea of asking him point-blank what it was that he wanted to see the President about. But this once, it wasn't in the cards. Almost anybody else, about almost anything else, I would have asked the question and received an answer. But not now, not this time. We both knew why he was there. And we couldn't discuss it. So we made up things to talk about while the clock stole on toward six. We considered the problems of Christmas shopping, or why college football was more exciting than the pros, or the difficulties of studying Chinese and if intensive courses were best. He skillfully kept the talk away from the hearings—so skillfully in fact, that it was impossible to get back to them. Yet all the time we talked there was another conversation going on. And he was getting the better of it the longer it continued. I was almost relieved when the intercom sounded.

"The President is free now."

I tried to joke. "He may be free," I said as I steered Hutchison toward the door, "but he's no pushover."

He looked at me blankly and didn't even bother to reply. We trod the thirty-two steps to the Oval Office door in total silence.

I felt as I hadn't felt since I'd to go to see the principal in high school.

The President looked frail and gloomy, but he tried to muster some cheer in his greeting.

"Hello, Hutch. Jeez, you really look good on television, you lucky son of a gun."

"Thank you, Mr. President."

"And what do you think of my boy here?" he said, with a show of exuberance, motioning to me.

"He's inimicable," Hutchison dryly replied.

This threw the President offstride momentarily. "Yeah . . . he certainly is. Now, what can I do for you? What's the all-fired rush?"

I held my breath, and I looked at the President. He really—and I was both surprised and yet not surprised at the same time—didn't know what was coming. I had the sensation of watching an accident unfold in slow motion before my eyes: a terrific collision, yet everything shown clearly and in close-up.

"I'd like you to take me off the commission, Mr. President."

He blinked, uncomprehending.

"At once, if you please, Mr. President."

Now it began to penetrate, but the President still looked groggy, as if once more his brain had been pulped by flying metal. All he could say was, "The commission. . . ."

"Yes, Mr. President, the commission. I'd like your permission to resign." He said it patiently as if explaining the alphabet to a slow-witted youngster.

"You can't resign," said the ancient child in the wheelchair. The words were intelligible. Yet there was something about them that indicated incomprehension behind them still. "You mustn't resign."

"I'm afraid I must," Hutchison said, with emphasis on the "must."

"But why? Tell me why." The President was the very picture of confusion.

"Because of your special assistant, I'm afraid." He really did sound as if he regretted it.

"I don't understand. He's getting to the bottom of this. I saw him. He's got 'em squirming now. He's. . . ."

I saw Hutchison slowly, but eloquently, shaking his head. "No, Mr. President. He's only obstructing the work of the commission."

"But you're wrong . . . I saw him. . . ."

"No, Mr. President." The head was still shaking. "What you saw was an attempt to divert attention away from the real work of the commission and use it to spread fear and suspicion. In two weeks this man has done irreparable harm—not just to the commission but to you, to the government, to the country. Now, if you don't mind, I'd like to put some distance between him and myself."

"But you can't do that. You've got it wrong." He turned to me, pleading. "Tell him. For God's sake, tell him he's wrong!"

"I know he's wrong, Mr. President," I said, "but he won't believe me." I turned to Hutchison. "Will you?"

"No." He said it nicely.

"But if he resigns, what happens to the commission?" The President was beginning to grasp the scope of this disaster.

"I'm sorry, Mr. President, you'll simply have to find somebody else."

I tried to repair the damage. *At least,* I thought to myself, *try to hold things together for a while longer*.

"Maybe," I said as genially as I could, "maybe we could work something out."

Both men looked at me, one with eagerness, the other with suspicion.

"A compromise?" prompted the President.

"Something like that. Obviously"—I turned to Hutchison—"if you just step down without warning, the whole commission collapses. That won't merely embarrass the administration or humble me—if that's what you're after. It will make it that much harder to find out who assassinated the President. And you surely can't want that result."

"Not particularly," he said.

"Suppose, though, that you go ahead and resign. But first

give us a week or two to find somebody else to take over as chairman. Then we could announce your resignation and the new appointment at the same time. What do you say?''

I looked at the President.

''Is that the best you can do?'' he asked peevishly. I shrugged my shoulders in a gesture that could be interpreted as Take-it-or-leave-it or Let's-see-you-do-better.

''Is that what you want?'' Hutchison asked the President.

''I guess so,'' he said miserably.

''And that's what *you* want?''

I brightened up a little. ''Yes, Mr. Hutchison. I think that would be the fairest compromise for all concerned, everything considered. Though it's still going to be an awfully bitter pill to swallow.''

''Well,'' he said, all gravity and courtesy, ''that makes my mind up more than ever.''

Now the President began to see a glimmer of daylight.

''So you'll do it?''

''You misunderstand.'' He turned to me. ''It seems to me that every time somebody agrees to one of your proposals things only get worse. So before I came here, I promised myself to do exactly the opposite of whatever you wanted. That way I couldn't possibly go wrong. If you'd asked me to resign, I'd have refused.'' He turned back to the President. ''You'll have my resignation tomorrow. I'll expect to see it in Friday's papers. Thank you, Mr. President, for your confidence in me in the first instance. I'm sorry that things worked out so badly.''

He was already moving toward the door. ''And thank you for squeezing me into the President's very busy schedule. Good evening.''

He was gone. I was still trying to grasp it, and he was gone. The President and I looked at each other, openmouthed. His face was distorted by a grotesque twitching, the muscles provoked by anger and shame into frantic leaping.

Stupidly, I announced, ''He's gone.'' The President seemed to shrink in his wheelchair. The twitch grew wilder, his cheeks colored, and tears stood in his eyes.

"What are we going to do?" He was a wretched man. "What are we going to do?"

I dropped onto the couch and rubbed one well-stuffed arm. "I don't know."

"This is a mess," he moaned.

"Yes." I waited for him to start railing at me, blaming it on me. But he didn't.

Instead, he said, in a tentative, fearful way. "Say, do you think he's one of . . . *them?"*

I could have laughed, but I felt more like crying with relief.

It was the voice of sorrow more than anger that replied, "Not a chance. He's simply been misled."

Hutchison's resignation was a check to my growing confidence. Stepping down without warning, giving as his reason a "profound disagreement" with unnamed "elements" on the commission, he dealt a blow straight at the President. But I was under no illusions: It was really aimed at me. By removing himself in this way, he intended to bring the commission down. As it collapsed, he meant for me to go down with it. Perhaps he hoped the President would be forced to abandon me. If so, he had miscalculated the emotional needs of a prematurely aged, mentally unsound man to whom this latest stroke was a crushing defeat.

He broke into uncontrollable bouts of weeping at all hours, on the slightest pretext—a harsh word, a slammed door, an unsympathetic gesture, the memory of a grievance—almost anything. I was thankful that with the Christmas weekend approaching, the demands on his time and attention were subject to a natural surcease, however modest. But I dared not let him spend more than fifteen minutes with anyone. And after each appointment I looked in to make certain he was still coherent before he saw his next visitor. Even so, a lot of people left the Oval Office looking sad, if not bewildered.

This most recent catastrophe only encouraged him in his determination to resign. I assured him the preliminary steps of transition were well in hand, that they would be finalized as soon as Congress reconvened in three weeks time. I told him not to worry about the future of the assassination inquiry, pointing out that Van

Riebouw could set up one of his own once he was Acting President or Congress could create a select committee if it wanted. The important thing was for him to stop worrying himself sick over it.

Thursday I released a statement, to coincide with the outgoing news of Hutchison's resignation. The President accepted the latter with deep regret. His opinion of Mr. Hutchison was in no way diminished. There had been a painful misunderstanding of the commission's scope, which the President also regretted, but he respected the chairman's sentiments when that misunderstanding became clear and was gratified that the chairman had acted decisively. The President expected a further announcement involving the commission to be issued early in the new year.

While I was working on this statement, indeed, while I was doing anything that day, my attention was drawn back insistently to one question: What now? I had several bad moments of near panic when I felt defeated.

Hutchison could not possibly have known that the President expected to step down in a month or so. And the President would not have abandoned me under those circumstances, even if he had leaned on me less heavily than he did. To discard me now would have been not just superfluous but foolish, considering that I was responsible for managing the delicate operation of transition.

But Hutchison had raised a new threat to my efforts all the same. By a single gesture he had put himself in the forefront of everyone who thought me mad, bad and dangerous. He provided what my opposition was lacking: a statesman to head it. And I mean a real statesman, not a fake one, not a Van Riebouw. If he were not already a party to what was going on, he soon would be. And all my plans were based not on fighting someone of great popular renown and admiration, but on fighting a very different group of men.

What the exact result of this move would be, I didn't know. But its unexpectedness was enough to sap my confidence. It had caught me completely by surprise. Even more to the point all my actions had so far been aimed at a date more than a week away. I was unsure of precisely how close the President was to breaking point. Yet if I did not act soon, I might not be able to act at all.

By the time I returned home on Thursday night I was in a mood of gloom and doom. I felt it was no longer I who was manipulating things, but things that were manipulating me. Possibly it was the disquieting sense of being a victim, but my nerve weakened. Yet having come so far and risked so much, I began to loathe myself for shrinking from the final step. I knew that no matter how long I might live, the memory of shying away from the brink, a brink I had myself contrived to reach, would torment me. I was perversely torturing myself already as my mind, reeling and confused, remorselessly dredged up fragments and images that had shaped my own childhood notions of moral and physical courage. Horatius at the bridge, Nathan Hale on the gallows, the Old Guard at Waterloo, Pickett's charge at Gettysburg, Billy Mitchell's fight for the bomber, Roosevelt's comeback from polio—all these and scores of others crowded in on me. I remembered a few lines from well back in childhood:

He either fears his fate too much,
Or his deserts are small,
That puts it not to the touch,
To win or lose it all.

And the memory made me feel ashamed and cowardly.

But what could I do? My plans were not complete. And at this critical juncture they had been upset by an unexpected check.

I paced about angrily, and as if in a defiant gesture to the unseen world, I went out and bought a bottle of Bollinger. Late in the night I sat on the floor, sipping mournfully at the champagne, the strains of Elgar's Cello Concerto chiming with my mood, as I sifted through the stacks of mail, the telegrams, even several lots of flowers, sent by some of the many people to whom I was now something of a hero—a crusader for truth. I touched them and found a peculiar reassurance in the physical contact.

Then, slowly, hazily, but distinctly I started to find my confidence returning. Below any level of conscious thought an idea was stirring, trying to be realized. At first I tried to reach it quickly, to no avail. Only when I relaxed would it come, drifting up slowly from wherever it is that ideas are born. And when it arrived, it was like Athena sprung from the brow of Zeus: full-blown and ready to fight.

It was a simple idea. But it gave me back the confidence I needed. What it amounted to was that if a cool, responsible, clever man like Hutchison could be driven to act, and act swiftly, decisively and publicly, there was no reason to think that lesser men would be more restrained. Unwittingly, he had given back all he had taken away, and more. I finished my champagne in the spirit in which it's usually quaffed. At least, I told myself, even if you fail, you'll know that you tried.

The next morning, Friday, I found a pretext for getting a reporter from the New York *Times* to take a short walk with me up and down the drive. I whispered a few short sentences to him. And it may have been my fancy, but it seemed that even that hardened figure was unnerved. My last words to him were: "No questions. Just do as I say. If you do, you'll be in on the biggest story of your life. If you don't, you won't even be able to read about it come Monday."

Chapter Seventeen

It was the voices: They made it hard to think straight. Sounds of cheer. Maybe they really were thankful, joyous, loving, forgiving. Something said I ought to feel guilty. I tried to. I couldn't do it. There was only a sense of flow; of inevitability. What was going to happen . . . was going to happen anyway. If I was anything, I was . . . only inevitable. No guilt there. It was all logical; it followed from past events. I wasn't responsible for that. Of course, the details might have been different. The way it was done wouldn't be exactly the same in any two cases. But the central fact was the same: The Constitution was dead. And I hadn't been the one who killed it. I was merely stepping over the body.

"Glor-or-uh-uh-uh-or-uh-uh-uh-uh-or-uh-uh-uh-uh-oria, in ex-chel-sis day-oh!" It was the day. "Glor-or-uh-uh-uh-or-uh-uh-uh-uh-or-uh-uh-uh-uh-oria, in ex-chel-sis day-oh!" Sunday. My wife would be in church now somewhere, drawn not by religion but by an esthete's appreciation of the beautiful old ceremonies. She never missed this one. "Si-lent night. . . ." Christmas Day. It was one minute past midnight.

The people outside in the streets going to or from their different services: making happy, excited sounds, Merry Christmasing each other and wondering if we'll have any snow this year. I listened to them. I was lying on the bed, still, awake, waiting.

No hope of sleep—hope only for rest, rest for the body. No rest for the mind.

My wife . . . where? In the cathedral probably, unless she'd found a place where the music was better. Alone. Each alone for the first time at Christmas since . . . how long was it? Eighteen years. So alone. "All alone, by the telephone. . . ." Stupid song. Stupid sentimentality. But somewhere there were tears. I could feel them. But they wouldn't come. I blinked hard and screwed up my eyes. My nose felt damp. My Adam's apple bobbed up and down. Nothing. Not a thing.

This is silly; contemptible; feeling sorry for yourself. Now think straight. Concentrate. Yes. This . . . is . . . the . . . day. Yes. Soon—I looked at my watch, glowing bravely in the darkness—soon would be the hour. And what I'd made. . . . What *I'd* made? Had I in truth made anything? Or was something else making me? *Using* me? *The pendulum swooped down, close to my head, and I held on. Up, up, it curved taking me higher and higher. I did it; I did it, all on my own; nobody else could have done that. I. . . . It stopped. It hesitated. It stooped like a hawk, then went sweeping back down in another arc. I went down with it, and on the other side I rose again. I? I was only a tool, an instrument, no more important than a sponge. I was nothing. It stopped, stooped again, dropped down again, went climbing up the other side again. . . .*

And then I saw Dalgleish. He was saying that it was all a question of time. I looked around. There was my wife sitting in the seat behind me, laughing and crying but somehow busily taking notes. Hutchison was erasing something written on the blackboard. There were hundreds of people there, the President, Carter, Van Riebouw, Homan, almost the whole White House staff. But where, I wondered, were Farb and Specci? I looked everywhere, but I couldn't see them. Then I realized that Dalgleish was telling me to sit down and pay attention. Reluctantly I did so, still wondering where Farb and Specci were and what they were doing.

Dalgleish was going on and on about Greek temples and Swiss watches. I started muttering that he ought to get to the point. Someone whispered that he was talking about the Constitution.

I caught snatches of it, something about a tendency to think that history ends with us. He called it the "illusion of permanence," and they all laughed. Then he went on about secret uses of power and could it be reconciled with democratic government. Once you start somewhere, how can you contain it? How—and he put on his best sage's face when he asked this one—can you be sure that it has been contained? That even the reassurances aren't even more lies? And they all went somber and started shaking their heads.

The first signs of real danger, he went on, involved Presidents being allowed to wage war pretty much as they wished. Soon generals were doing the same. And when Presidents also started circumventing the courts and Congress, it wasn't long before mere assistants and aides followed suit. Then it was simply a question of time until the assistants or the generals, or both, grasped, like the legions of Imperial Rome, the "Secret of Empire." Namely, that power was there for the taking, and to hell with the traditional forms. Heads bowed as they all wrote that in their notebooks. And one thing these generals and assistants had that the legions didn't have to help them, he said, was the screen of executive privilege. Behind that you could do almost anything you had the will to do. I suppose that's progress, Dalgleish said dryly. There were a few derisive laughs in return. Anyway, by that time the Constitution was dead, wasn't it?

Wasn't it? Wasn't it? I kept trying to get his attention by waving my arm. I wanted to answer the question. It was a lot more complicated than that. . . .

I jumped up. My arm was raised. I jackknifed it to look at my watch. Nothing but a fuzzy glow. Come on, focus, focus! After three. I stumbled heavily from the bed, nearly falling onto the floor. A cold sweat breaking out on my forehead and down my spine helped bring me awake. I'd almost slept through it. Almost slept through this day—my day. And I was too shaken and groggy to appreciate the irony of it.

I quickly showered and dressed. I made myself some coffee, but I couldn't swallow it. I gagged on a mouthful and spat it back into the cup; was I that nervous? For fifteen minutes I forced myself to calm down. I looked unhurriedly through a couple of art books, taking in the still lifes and landscapes, eventually forgetting myself somewhat. The second lot of coffee was now ready. This time I got a cup down. A few minutes before 4 A.M. I picked up the telephone and dialed Homan's number. When it had rung three times, I hung up. After a wait of nearly a minute I dialed again. This time I waited only for his telephone to start ringing before I hung up again.

This was the day. Now was the time. I heard a drunk noisily stumble by outside. ". . . born this hap-pee mor-ning."

I drove quickly, wondering if they'd try to stop me before I got there. It didn't seem likely, but you never knew. They might get jumpy and. . . . No. They wouldn't. But I kept driving fast not because the streets were clear and I was in a hurry, but because I couldn't shake off a vague idea that the police might stop me. If they escorted me the rest of the way, that would make it even less likely that the others would try to pick me up. Not if they had the police to deal with, too.

As I came down Pennsylvania Avenue, the whole city seemed to be sleeping, dreaming. Almost all the Christmas lights were off, but I caught a glimpse of the big Christmas tree still blazing on the Ellipse. My eyes took in the bunting, the plastic Santas and reindeer flashing by overhead, the avalanche of styrofoam snow. The nation's capital looked for all the world like a great big gaudy, snugly wrapped-up Christmas present.

It was a little after 4 A.M. when I came bustling into the Executive Mansion through the East Entrance, to the astonishment of the White House policeman on duty. Was there anything wrong?

"Get me the chief, would you?" I ordered him.

"You mean my chief?"

"Yes. Your chief."

"Should I tell the Secret Service detail?"

"Tell them nothing," I snapped. "Now hurry up. This is an emergency. Tell him to get here as fast as he can. I'll be on the roof."

And with that I pressed past him and headed for Homan's office. He wasn't there. I headed for my own. He wasn't there either. "Come on, come on," I muttered to myself. It shouldn't take him any longer to get here than it had taken me. I told the switchboard to stand by and told them the kind of line I wanted. I didn't yet tell them the number.

Homan came charging in. I did a double take. For years I'd seen him in nothing but his dress greens. But here he was, in his combat fatigues, his stars not shiny chrome now but black cotton.

"Got here as fast as I could," he grunted. He started unbuckling his belt and pulled down his trousers.

"What the hell . . ." I began.

Then I saw that taped to the inside of his thigh was a .45 automatic pistol. He ripped the tape off his leg—I winced: he didn't—then hurriedly tore it off the pistol. He pulled up his pants and tucked the weapon inside his belt.

"There. I didn't think the guard at the gate would frisk me—not even in this outfit." He was probably the first person ever to smuggle a gun into the White House. As if reading my thoughts he said, "In for a dime, in for a dollar."

I started to remonstrate with him; he could have ruined everything.

"That was a crazy thing. . . ."

"Look, if push comes to shove, I want to go down with something in my hands to fight with. Now, what's happening?"

I picked up the phone and gave the girl the number. If only one call went through in the whole of the United States today, I was betting that it would be this one. If they hadn't moved yet, then it had to be because they were waiting for this. I waited until I heard a voice say, "Hello?" He sounded wide awake already.

I passed the phone to Homan. "Merry Christmas, General. . . . Early bird. . . . Early bird"—from the way he repeated it I gathered that Taggart had sounded incredulous. "Coming soon." That meant Taggart had asked for confirmation.

In a few minutes now—I looked at my watch, nearly half past four—Taggart's paratroopers would be rousted from their beds. First light was almost two and a half hours away. Long before then they'd be in their aircraft. And somewhere nearby, maybe just a few hundred yards away, other men were already going into action.

"Now what?" asked Homan.

"We wait. Come on." From my desk I pulled two pairs of infrared binoculars. "Let's go up to the roof."

We made our way to the attic. In its time it has been used for all kinds of things—a playground for TR's children, secretaries' offices, a spare bedroom. We stepped out into the cold night air, shivering at first from the shock.

"So we wait?" asked Homan. "Here?"

I was adjusting the focus on my binoculars. "Yes."

"But don't you think we ought to tell the President?"

"Yes. But let him sleep a bit longer. There's nothing he can do yet."

The police chief came lurching through the screen door, trying to sound absolutely calm, as though this sort of thing happened every night.

"Merry Christmas," he boomed.

I almost dropped my binoculars. "And a Happy New Year" was the best I could manage in reply.

"Is there something you wanted to see me about?" he wondered. Idle curiosity.

"Within the next hour or two there's going to be an attempt on the government."

Now the words were out. We stood there, each with his own thoughts, responding in his own way.

"That's a pretty big claim," the chief decided.

"It's not a claim—it's a fact."

"Well, now," he said, as if confronting a philosophical proposition, "I've heard what you've had to say on television, sir, and there might be something to it. . . ."

My patience snapped. "Look, this is no bullshit. Do you think General Homan and myself would be up here right now if we weren't certain. . . ."

"Begging your pardon, sir, but have you been drinking?"

"No, we haven't," I shouted. "And you'll have all the proof you want in the next couple of hours."

"And what is it you want with me?" He was starting to sound surly.

"Let me tell you what you're going to see first. Then I'll tell you what you'll have to do. Is that fair enough?"

"Fair enough," he conceded.

"Very well. By the time the sun comes up this morning you will see an army of occupation come rolling in here." I gestured with my arms. "They will proceed to seal off this whole area. They will then try to take the President prisoner."

It was too dark to see, but I knew that the police chief had now lost his airy composure. I could also feel Homan's eyes boring through the darkness, trying to scan my face.

"Impossible!" spluttered the chief.

"But true."

"You mean there really *is* a plot?"

"You'll soon see it with your own eyes. You can judge for yourself."

"Well, what can we do against an army?" he pleaded.

"General Homan and I have already sent for assistance. You'll have to help us hold the fort."

"Of course, of course." He was almost bobbing up and down in nervous excitement. "But shouldn't we tell the—"

"They're in it too."

"The Secret Service?" It was the voice of a man who could not believe what his ears were passing on to him.

"Not all of them. Most of them are probably loyal. But Chief Steele is certainly implicated, and we can't take any chances."

"Well," he said numbly, "do you want us to try to disarm them?"

"Not yet. They don't want a shootout in the White House any more than we do. But if things get really tight, I'm counting on you and your men. Don't let any of them go off their shifts until this thing is over. And make sure that all of Steele's men are covered. All right?"

He went back downstairs to do as I'd asked, a different man from the one who'd wished us a Merry Christmas a few minutes before. Homan said to me, "This is going to be a pretty hairy show." I nodded and scanned the darkness with my binoculars.

Every step had now been taken. I had only to wait. I remembered how Von Moltke had worked for years preparing the plans for the invasion of France. When the day came in August, 1914, he had gone home on time for dinner for the first time in twenty years. For once there was nothing left for him to do.

A chill breeze off the Potomac snapped my reverie momentarily. *What,* it made me ask, *if instead of everything happening, nothing happens? The sun comes up—and there's nothing there? What then, little man?* I shivered.

But then, I thought, *so what?* It was all self-delusion, don't you see? I thought I smelled a rat: I tried to bait a trap. No rat; no trap. I would have lost. But what could anyone ever be able to prove? Nothing very much, if I kept my mouth shut. And I'd at least know that I'd tried—I'd gone all the way. There was nothing unfair in devising a plan so that I could minimize my losses and still go all out to win. If they showed up, I'd won everything; if they didn't, what had I lost? A job I was going to lose soon anyway. Face. Reputation. And what was that but other people's opinion?

But they'd show up. They must. Anyway, I'd soon know if they were going to. I looked at my watch. Almost five.

"I think I ought to wake the President now," I said. "You wait here. I'll have someone let you know when he's ready—probably in about ten minutes."

"Okay." He was still looking through his infrareds. "But there's not much time left. Bill's probably about loaded up by now."

I turned to go, thinking he'd finished, when he said, "What happens if he can't get through?"

"I don't know," I replied.

"What happens if he gets through, but the planes aren't allowed to take off."

"I don't know," I repeated. "We'll have to face them down somehow. Try to bluff our way out."

"Great," he said tonelessly.

I put a hand on his arm. "But I've got another string to my bow. You'll see." And I went back downstairs.

I could break him now in one of two ways. Either tell him everything, pull out the one prop left for him to lean on and watch him collapse. Or tell him that he was about to become the first President in the country's history to be removed by a coup d'état. I smiled to myself when I thought of that phrase, and I thought too of Luttwak's observation: "The countercoup will be very difficult to distinguish from the coup d'état." If I could, I would make it impossible.

Sure enough, there was another young warrant officer sitting there, straight of back, alert of eye, hands clasping the briefcase. There was also a Secret Service agent. He looked up, surprised, but he didn't say anything. I knocked on the door and went in.

A small night-light burned by the bed. He was nothing but a lump, huddled in the darkness. I shook his shoulder.

"Mr. President," I hissed. "Mr. President." I turned on the light.

"What?" He flung an arm across his eyes. "What is it?" He sounded like a man speaking from the bottom of a well.

"Wake up, Mr. President. There's an emergency. Come on, wake up!" I shook him roughly. And like a man shouting "Fire" in a crowded theater, I said, "There's a coup."

"What?" he said numbly, not comprehending at all. "A what?" Idiot.

"A coup." I nearly shouted it in his ear. "You know, the Army—in the streets—trying to seize the government." I let it sink in. "They're coming to get you.

Now he was trembling and shaking, his puffy, lined white face looking like a death mask. "Soldiers?" was all he could say.

"Yes, Mr. President—soldiers. An armed revolt. A coup. And they're coming to get you."

In this hour of peril and haste all he could think to ask was, "Will they shoot us?"

I had now decided. I would *play* it straight. If he didn't crack under that, I still had the truth in reserve. As if teaching a child the alphabet, I began to spell it out:

"At this very moment. Mr. President, there are soldiers getting into tanks and planes and troop carriers. In an hour, perhaps less, they will be rolling into the city. General Homan and I have taken some preparatory steps to get some soldiers of our own here. The White House police have been alerted. And I've tipped off a reporter from the New York *Times*. If he's done as I told him, he's right now calling up every newspaper editor he knows and telling them there's a coup in the works. If there's enough publicity, we might be able to scare them off."

The assassination attempt had aged him twenty years. Even as I spoke, I saw him gain another decade. The white flesh turned to gray, and the tears flowed down his face.

"No," he moaned. He started to burrow into the bed. "Noooooh."

Exasperated, I said, "You've blown it. The Constitution's collapsed. The Army's in revolt, and we probably *will* be shot. I thought you ought to at least know."

"Oh, please," he whispered. "Not me. Don't let it be me. I tried, you know. I tried. *You* tell them."

"It wasn't good enough. You failed. Do you realize that?"

"Oh, please," he pleaded.

I picked up the telephone by the side of the bed. "Get me this number," I began. I turned back to the desperate man in the bed. "I'm getting the doctor here for you."

A couple of minutes later I had someone go up to tell Homan to come down. I waited for him in the corridor and whispered to him when he arrived.

"Listen, I told him what's happened. But he's come unglued."

"Then what in the hell are we going to do?" he whispered, agitated.

"I'll take you in there so you can see for yourself. But I've already sent for the doctor."

As we approached the door, the Secret Service man stood up, eyeing Homan's belt.

"I'm sorry, General, but I can't let you take that weapon in there."

Slowly, Homan took the automatic out of his belt, and in one fluid, deliberate gesture pointed it at the agent.

"Don't try to stop me." He kept on walking. I hastened to reassure the agent.

"It's all right. I'm with him."

The agent said, "I'm not responsible for what happens if he goes in there with a loaded gun."

"No, you're not. I am." And I hurried after Homan.

Inside the bedroom the President was half in, half out of bed, self-pity incarnate. As soon as we walked in, he wailed, "They're going to shoot us, Jack. They're going to shoot us."

"Nobody's going to shoot anybody, Mr. President." Homan tried to reassure him. But he looked pretty incongruous, standing in the Presidential bedroom at five o'clock in the morning of Christmas Day in combat fatigues with a drawn pistol trying to tell the President he needn't worry. Homan himself looked in need of reassurance as he took in the President, who was now reduced to spasmodic jerking and violent weeping.

"Mr. President," he said, "I want you to make a phone call."

This is it. I held my breath. If he somehow pulls himself together, calls Taggart and talks to him rationally, then there'll be parachutes over the Monument—and nothing else.

But the President wasn't coherent. The shock on top of the strain had quite broken him. My calculations were correct. Homan turned to me. "Well?"

"We'll have to try it ourselves."

"Taggart won't budge. You know that."

"Then it's up to you to convince him." I picked up the telephone.

We managed, without difficulty, to get through to Taggart, even though he was in an aircraft on a runway near Fort Campbell.

"Bill," said Homan, "something's happened . . . no . . . look, it can't be done that way . . . you'll have to trust me . . . hello . . . what is this?" He looked at the receiver. "They've cut us off. And Taggart won't move." He replaced the receiver. "We've lost."

But we hadn't. We'd won. I couldn't tell him that. If Taggart had taken off, *then* we'd have lost. All he had to do was load his men into planes. Someone would be watching. How could

I tell Homan what it meant? The jammed line, the stalled planes, the collapsed President—they were not defeat but victory.

A few minutes after six Homan said, "They're coming."

I raised my binoculars. "Where?"

He pointed straight ahead. "Rochambeau Bridge."

I looked, focusing on the Jefferson Memorial, then lowering. At first there was nothing. Then I saw it—the blunt, sloping front end of an M-117 Armored Personnel Carrier. Behind it I could just make out the dim, foreshortened column, in three-quarter view. The leading APC eased its way across the bridge, looking as if it were towing the others behind it. But though we could see it, we couldn't yet hear it. I stared, hypnotized for a moment.

"Goddamn those trees," muttered Homan. I turned and saw him now looking off to the right. "I think . . . yep . . . they're on the Arlington Bridge, too."

I raised my glasses. I thought I could make out movement, but I wasn't sure.

"Anyway," said Homan, gloomily, "you know they'll be coming that way sometime."

I went back to looking down past the Jefferson Memorial. Sure enough. The line of vehicles was debouching off the bridge, and for the first time I saw the tank—a Main Battle Tank—squatting smack in the middle of the Mason Bridge. I looked over to the right again. You could hear the clanking, creaking, groaning sounds of armored vehicles clearly now, coming from the direction of the Roosevelt and Arlington bridges.

"What do you think?" I asked Homan.

He seemed to shrug helplessly. "If they've got the manpower—and they probably haven't, this being Christmas—they could try to cut every bridge from Bannockburn clear around to Bladensburg, and all the main highways on this side of the river from the Beltway over to the Baltimore Parkway. But I'd guess they'll have to settle for a line from the Roosevelt Bridge across to Lafayette Square"—he gestured by tilting his head back—"then down around the Capitol to the Sousa Bridge. They're going to be stretched pretty thin."

I tried to picture it, to imagine what I couldn't see. Then

he remarked, "Say, have you noticed something funny?"

"No," I grunted, fascinated by the sight unfolding before my eyes. I could now clearly see the vehicles, their unit pennants flapping and fluttering to an accompaniment of metallic clanking. I could make out trucks, loaded with soldiers, and jeeps mounting machine guns and recoilless rifles. I could hear the clanking and rumbling, the creaking and squeaking growing louder by the minute. I could see a tide of guns, vehicles, soldiers pouring across the Rochambeau Bridge as calmly and unhurriedly as if they had rehearsed it for a month.

"Haven't you noticed?" Homan reminded me. "Everything's gone quiet, up there." He jerked a thumb skyward. And sure enough, it had been some time since the noise of a plane had been heard. What, I wondered, had they done? Seized the FAA and told them to divert all aircraft away from the District, including private planes?

"You're right," I agreed. "Okay, I think it's time to try the last card we've got." I pointed in the direction of the flagpole in the middle of the roof. "Would you get somebody to run up the flag. But have it put upside down, and get a spotlight on it. Then see if you can find a bullhorn."

I could feel him looking at me. "What in the hell good is that? Some sort of symbolic . . . ."

"That's only part of it. I took the precaution of letting a reporter in on this. Right now, he and some of his friends should be holed up in hotels in this area—let's hope with a portable TV camera."

"You're kidding."

"Far from it, Jack. Now get a move on. If we catch 'em by surprise, we might still be able to bluff our way out of this." I waved my binoculars in an arc that took in the Potomac, its bridges and what was now on them. "Most of those soldiers probably have no idea what they're being used for. If we appeal to them, with the whole country watching, it might work."

"I wouldn't bet on it," he grumbled. But he pushed past me to get someone who'd run up the flag and turn on the lights.

When he went, I was able for the first time to savor the taste of victory—alone. I hugged it to myself in the darkness. What a scene was taking shape out there—the final act and I the author of it all. There were soldiers in full combat equipment up and down Pennsylvania Avenue, on the steps of the Capitol, on all the bridges, at the big intersections like Washington Circle, along the Mall. As far as the eye would be able to see by the dawn's early light there would be guns and uniforms. It would be a mystery.

Yet they—Farb, Morrissey, Specci, the Army Chief of Staff, Steele, Reedy—they had figured it out. It was all so complicated, yet oh so simple, once they'd grasped the point of it. The gamma pad they were "lucky" enough to get hold of; the secret meeting with a combat division commander; the chance sarcastic remark to Specci that was supposed to throw him off the track; the obvious attempts to throw suspicion on the FBI, the Secret Service, the Army and the Cabinet, so that the President would feel he had no one else to turn to; the insistence on televised hearings, which would both create an instant celebrity and spread fear everywhere—all pointed to one thing, once you grasped the truth about the President's condition. He was desperately ill. When he went, so would I. But I obviously had no intention of going. And that fact made sense of all the others. Together they spelled coup d'état—an attempted coup timed to coincide with the President's imminent collapse.

With two groups reaching this conclusion on their own and at about the same time, each took the other's conclusion for independent corroboration of its own.

They then had three choices. They could do nothing and hope for the best. That was the choice with the highest risk. If they were wrong, it would be not only calamitous, but irreversible.

Second, they could try to force Van Riebouw to assume the Vice Presidency. Then he and a majority of the Cabinet could invoke the Twenty-fifth Amendment which gave them the power to declare the President incapable—over his objections, if necessary—and then make Van Riebouw Acting President. But this could be pointed to as final proof of a plot against the President and the Presidency. I could then split the country so deeply we might be on the brink of civil war. Van Riebouw simply didn't have the guts for anything so hair-raising.

The third choice was to move against the impending coup—whenever it was launched. They knew of Taggart; there might be others. After all, that suspicious Sunday drive could easily indicate an expectation of armed civilians arriving in private planes. All they had to do was wait for Taggart to move; then they could spring their trap.

How could they have ever known there was no coup—only the shadow of one? Taggart was only a trigger. And the head this pistol was pointed at was theirs, not mine. Even Taggart didn't know it. He thought I wanted paratroopers here. For that he demanded a verbal order, thinking he'd covered himself. Poor Taggart.

By now the sound of the intended countercoup was growing, taking on a variety of textures and intriguing noises. I thought I could hear shouted commands being swallowed up in it. I took another look through my glasses. There they were: a ring of vehicles and soldiers stretched along the arc of South Executive Drive, no more than five hundred feet away.

What a sight it was! A city that had been burned by an invading army, had heard the sound of rebel gunfire—but never anything like this. Here was the waking nightmare come true, and the whole country fast asleep. The Man on Horseback, the most powerful symbol, next to the Cross, known to our medieval ancestors had arrived at last, nervous, in a personnel carrier. Yet he was about to be toppled. The soldiers had nerve enough for this, a secret anticoup, but not for more—at least, not yet. But their anticoup needed a *real* coup. Otherwise, it was a blow that wasted its force on a void: Those behind it would be thrown off balance by insubstantiality. I took one final look at the ring of steel beyond the ring of painted iron spikes. They were now ripe for the taking.

There was a flash behind me. I turned around and saw the flag go fluttering up. For an instant I held my breath; then it unfurled. Good for Homan! It was flying unmistakably upside down. No one could miss it or its meaning.

I went downstairs. The President was comatose, tranquilized. The doctor, who had apparently thrown on whatever oddments of clothing were handy, looked up.

"How is he?"

He shook his head. "We'll have to get him back to the hospital."

"Is he going to . . . die?"

He straightened up. "I sincerely hope not, but he's got to have rest and quiet."

I turned back to the door. He said, "There's something going on, isn't there?"

"Yes, but don't worry about it. You just take care of the President."

Homan came charging down the corridor, carrying a bullhorn. "D'you see the flag?"

"I saw it. Let's hope and pray other people saw it, too. Come on."

We almost raced downstairs. On the way I looked at my watch. Almost seven. Soon it would be light.

We clattered noisily across the lobby and out through the front entrance with its enormous lantern blazing above our heads and emerged into the feeble gray world of predawn. The first thing we saw was the APC, sprouting antennas like a metal hedgehog; obviously some sort of command-and-control vehicle. Though it was hard to pick them out from the crowd of soldiers, I could see several generals and colonels. Then I saw the others—Farb, Morrissey, Specci, Steele, Reedy. I did a doubletake: Specci was in his black robes.

I noticed, too, that there were several weapons trained on us. But I was certain they wouldn't shoot—not unless we shot first. They might try to rush us, though. Out of the corner of my eye I noted appreciatively that Homan was keeping one hand resting lightly on the butt of his pistol, as if to say, *Don't try to grab us if you don't want bloodshed*. But the people across the street were really counting on us falling effortlessly into their hands. They expected us to be overawed by their massive show of strength, demoralized by how thoroughly and daringly they'd checked us. Our defiance was, at this moment, supposed to be turning to dust under the crushing double weight of guilt and failure. Once we grasped how we had been routed, we would no doubt surrender.

Homan passed me the bullhorn.

"What do you want? What are you doing here?" I was slightly surprised at the distorted, echoing sound of my amplified voice.

I saw Farb gesture, and someone placed a microphone in his hand. He had a question of his own: "Where is the President?"

"At this moment," I bellowed, "he is lying critically ill—*thanks to your treason.*" There was an audible buzzing among the troops.

"We insist on seeing the President," demanded Farb.

"Two of you—unarmed—may enter the White House."

They hurriedly conferred. Then Farb and Morrissey started walking across Pennsylvania Avenue. I'd somehow assumed that only one of them would come, plus a general. But no, they wanted to make a show of strict scrupulosity. When they had almost reached me, I turned without a word and led the way to the front entrance. In silence we crossed the lobby. The entire mansion was in the grip of an expectant hush. We went down the west corridor, up the stairs and back along the central corridor above to the President's bedroom. I waved the Secret Service agent away, opened the door myself and stood back.

The President was huddled in his dressing gown and a blanket, with the doctor and a male nurse hovering over him. He looked ghastly and preternaturally still. Before any of us could speak the doctor barked, "Would someone please explain why I can't get the White House helicopter up here to move the President to the hospital?"

It stopped them dead in their tracks.

"Yes," I asked, "are you trying to finish him off?"

They didn't answer. Instead, Farb said to Morrissey, "Get on that phone, John."

Farb and I stared at each other while Morrissey whispered urgently into the telephone. "I gather, Mr. Secretary, you and your friends are going to take advantage of the President's illness and seize the government. You're our new 'leader,' I suppose." It was half statement, half question.

"Don't be absurd." He was shocked by the stupidity of such

a remark. Then the first glimmer of comprehension started to break in on him, and the color went out of his face. "You . . . of all people . . . you should know better!" he exploded.

Morrissey hung up, and I started walking toward the door. Over my shoulder I replied, "You've nearly killed the President, you've brought the Army out on your own authority, and you've done it all in secret. There's only one logical explanation for that."

They hurried after me, Morrissey now red in the face with rage. "How do you explain going to Mexico? How do you—" he began.

Still walking briskly, I shouted back, "This isn't a debate or a court. I don't have to explain anything to you. There are just two important facts here: You have an army outside the White House—and all I have is a single brave and loyal officer. The whole world can judge for itself what those facts mean."

I almost ran down the stairs, with them bustling after me, angry and confused. What about this? What about that? I ignored them.

Once outside I picked up the bullhorn again, while they went down the driveway in animated conference. It was fairly light now, ushering in a cold, gray winter's day. Light enough, I hoped, for television.

"Soldiers of the Army of the United States," I bellowed, slowly enunciating each word. "You know who I am. I am the man who said there was a plot against the government. Your presence here this morning is conclusive proof that I spoke the truth." I paused. "At this moment, the entire nation is watching and listening—waiting to see what you will do."

There were stirrings in the group straight in front of me. Farb and Specci looked over toward the APC. A young officer put his head inside the vehicle for a moment, withdrew and nodded affirmatively. I could have burst into song.

The response across the road was very different. They were plunged into utter confusion. The very last thing they imagined I would ever want at this hour was the full glare of publicity. The tables had been turned. The world was watching them.

They now had two choices: They could either hurriedly summon the courage to seize the power and sort things out later, or they could lay down their arms. I was not going to give them much time to think about it.

"You have been betrayed by your generals into an act of treason. Each one of you at this moment is dangerously close to becoming a Benedict Arnold. Whatever you have been told about this operation has been lies. Because of what you have done, the President is now close to death. He has had a breakdown—he has been stabbed in the back. These men"—I pointed straight ahead—"refused to let the President be moved to a hospital.

"You have broken your oaths to defend the Constitution. You have almost killed your Commander in Chief. Before it is too late, I appeal to you, as men who love your country . . . ." I broke off, the tears streaming down my face.

In a matter of seconds I had wiped the tears away and composed myself. I walked slowly down the driveway, my heart thumping, my throat dry, feeling that I had seen it all before. But where? Then I remembered: Gary Cooper in *High Noon.*

At the edge of the sidewalk I stopped and pointed across the street to a major from the Third Infantry. I shouted to him, "Major, would you please take these gentlemen—these civilians—into your custody?" I gestured at Farb and the rest.

The major's face went white, and I saw him swallow hard. The soldiers around him looked increasingly worried and tense, evidently fearing they might be somehow dragged even further into this confused and dangerous dilemma simply by standing near him. The major and I looked at each other, both of us sweating it out. Then I realized. Of course! I motioned to Homan to join me. When he came down the drive, I said, "Jack, will you tell him?"

Without a word Homan strode out into the middle of the road and looked the major in the eye. The officer saluted. Homan returned the salute, taking his hand from his belt for the first time in this showdown.

"Major." He looked at the man's name tag. "Major Collins, you will place these civilians in the Fort Myer stockade, pending further orders from me."

Farb, Morrissey and Specci began to protest, as did the lieutenant general with them. Homan pointed: "And the general, too."

Just then there was the chop-chop-chop sound of a helicopter. It slanted overhead and down toward the South Lawn.

I walked back up the drive, feeling more sorry than ever that Homan would have to be broken. But I had no choice. He was not a stupid man. Before long he'd be wondering how I could tip off the press more than a day in advance, but not tell him until almost the last minute. He'd remember a lot of other little things as well. Given enough time, he was quite capable of working backward and figuring most of it out. Well, I could take care of him later.

I put a call through to the press secretary and told him to issue a statement: I would be the "temporary custodian" of the President's powers until he had recovered; Senator Van Riebouw could not be made Acting President until certain matters tying him to the attempted coup had been clarified. I then told the press secretary to cancel the tape of the President's Christmas address. I would be addressing the nation myself. He accepted it all without demur.

I went upstairs. The young warrant officer was still sitting there, impassive, sphinxlike, guardian of the tomb.

"You know what's been going on?" I asked him.

"I think I get the general idea, sir," he coolly replied.

"Would you come with me, please?" I turned and started to go. He didn't move. I stopped.

"Look, the essential facts are these: The President's in a coma, there's been an attempt to seize the government, the line of succession's been broken—and the whole world knows it. Right now, almost anything might be happening in Moscow or Peking. Or maybe some two-bit country is figuring that this is a chance in a million for them."

I scrutinized his face. He looked calm as ever, but he was clearly weighing what I'd said.

"Now, would you come with me, please?"

I turned and walked down the corridor slowly. Nothing. No sound. Then I heard movement and soft footfalls behind me. He was coming! I was home free.